Elle

Edwin Newbery

Elle

Chimera

CHAPTER ONE
ELLE

He caught me by surprise. Usually when George lashed out, I saw it coming and rode with it. Not this time though; he punched me squarely on the side of my head. I immediately felt dizzy, then out of the fog Lucy came running to me, crying. "Has Daddy hurt you again Mummy?" As she reached me, George aimed a kick at her bottom. Whatever he intended, it sent her staggering across the room to land in a heap against the sofa.

That was the moment that I finally knew it was all over for us. I could put up with his controlling behaviour, and occasional violence; he was, after all, Lucy's father and our provider. No one is perfect, I reasoned.

Not this, though. The vision of my beloved Lucy kicked across the floor finally opened my eyes to what I should have already known from my experience since arriving in England. Maybe it was because the blow to my head reinforced the message; but in that instant, despite my confused state, I had a flash back of my experience married to George, and the trauma that preceded it. The reason I was married at all to a man I did not love and who did not love me. Despite the fog in my head, I saw our future clearly stretching out before us. If I stayed in the house with George any longer… I knew for both Lucy and for me it was time to leave. I always planned to do so, but running away with Lucy was a different matter to escaping by myself, as I had originally intended when I married George.

Even in my muddled state, I saw the future for Lucy. She would look like me as she grew into a sensual teen, then a woman. George was going to treat her just as he did me. Strangely, Lucy seemed to be unaffected by this sudden rough treatment. Was it because she had seen how her father treated me and expected the same? If so, how sad. Either way, I saw my duty clearly, it had to end then, one way or another. It was all over.

For the first time I also saw how I was complicit in our situation. I didn't grow up in Poland to be a weak and feeble woman, treated this way by any man. I used to be strong and independent. I kicked my stepfather in the balls when he tried it on. Why had I let it happen to me, and then to us here? We had to go and lose ourselves where he couldn't find us. We would suffer the consequences. If we were caught by the authorities, I would be sent home without Lucy, who was born here. That's what they all told me, and that's what I was always so afraid of. Being sent back to the gang's clutches and recycled somewhere else. I must then, somehow, finally break us free from the nightmare that started for me in that promised hotel job, that turned out to be a godforsaken brothel.

George had gone to London—what for I had no idea—but this was our best chance. I packed as much as I could into two wheeled suitcases and slammed the door behind us. We walked the few hundred yards to the village cash point. It was then that my befuddled world shut down completely. I was obviously concussed; I simply lost all power to understand the problem or make decisions. Why was my card for the joint account, the only bank account I was allowed, refused, for no funds? I was unable to work out what was wrong. My head spun. There had been more than a thousand pounds in there yesterday. George, controlling as ever, must have transferred it out when he left home. What could I do now?

I grabbed Lucy and struggled back up the road towards home. I instinctively knew, despite the ever-increasing state of helplessness, that I had to unpack before George came home and found out that I had gone. But it was no use. I could not continue any longer. I collapsed beside the road. I sat on the suitcase clutching Lucy and cried in despair.

I saw a car stop in the road beside us, but it didn't register in my semi-conscious state. I saw the pair of feet in front of me, but they did not register either. I heard the man's voice, but this also didn't wake me from my trance. I watched, as if in a dream, as a man led Lucy to his car parked in the road. I saw him buckle her up in the back seat, and still nothing, not even the possibility that she was being kidnapped got through to me. The man came back to me and pulled me to my feet; he held me closely to stop me falling again. "Come and get in my car, you can't sit here crying," he said. "I'll take you both somewhere safe while you recover and tell me what the trouble is, so that I can help you. I understand from your daughter that you have left home." He half led, half carried me to his car and strapped me in. I heard the boot open and shut then we drove away.

Our good Samaritan helped me into a warm house and sat me in a comfortable kitchen chair. Still in a daze, I watched him take Lucy to the seating area in the kitchen and put on a film for her to watch. I could see she was happy—she clearly liked the man—but none of it made any sense to me. It was as if I was taking part in a film myself. Were we being kidnapped? It was a very nice kidnapping, if that was so. I expected he would take me somewhere and abuse me. I don't think I actually cared; he seemed a nice man. It was not a new experience for me to be raped. Without Lucy, I would have gone back to George, admitted that I loved his friend, and let him finish me off.

The kind man brought me a cup of coffee and a brandy. "Try sipping that," he said, "it might help. I see you have a big bruise on your face. I'm going to take a photo of that. We can deal with it later, but for now, pull yourself together if you can. If you can't, I will have no choice but to call for an ambulance. I'm not a medic and can't risk your health by unnecessary delay."

That slowly sank in and I began to assess my situation. He spoke again. "When you're feeling better, you have two options. Firstly, if you trust me, and only if you are quite sure, then you will stay here and let me help you. I'm sure that I can help sort out your problems and get you up and running again. I have a room with twin beds where you can both stay. If not, I can't let you go out of this house on your own. I can't see any other option but to call the police, who will take you to a place of safety and no doubt arrest your abusive husband."

He came and stood me up again, holding me tight, so that I could feel my heart beating as my breasts were pressing against his chest. He spoke to me gently. "You look a little better now. How do you feel? Walk about and see if you are recovered enough not to need medical attention."

I walked up to Lucy and back again, and he automatically took me into another embrace. "Good, well done, my little love," he said, with obvious relief. I put my head on his shoulder to stop it spinning and get some sense into it, and thought hard. It felt so good. I had not been cuddled like this before. Yes, he was totally safe, that I knew instinctively I could see deep into his soul through those loving eyes. That was now, in fact, the problem. He looked back into my eyes with such emotion and sympathy, he was trembling with his uncontrollable feelings. I had seen and felt all that before, in fact that was where all my recent troubles took a turn for the worst. George saw it too and knew for sure that, as he suspected, his friend was in love with me. He guessed that I loved him back, though I had never dared to show it. He beat me that night as he had done before when in a bad mood, but now more often.

Now this man, whose name I still didn't know, was in love with the damsel he found in acute distress and was determined to know me better. He surely wanted to love me gently I had no doubt of that, no rough sex from this man. Believe me, I'm a good judge of men, this one would not hurt a fly; love me to distraction maybe. My mind wandered; it would be no hardship to pay this man for safety and comfort with my body. I had been forced to do that often enough before. What was not to like. I have not had loving sex in the brothel or in my marriage to George. I would do it for Lucy and yes, why not admit it, for me, too.

Nearly fully recovered I pulled my head back, looked him in the eyes and asked, "What do you want from me in return?"

He looked shocked. "What do you mean? I can assure you I ask for nothing but the pleasure of helping such a beautiful woman and her daughter in distress. I want to solve your problems and see you smile." I felt a bit guilty, but knew from long experience what any man in his place would hope for from me. "I am James Jefferies, by the way. I see what you're thinking and will make you a promise. I will not make any attempt to seduce you; even if you want me to. That will be for one month, then we can review the situation. Trust me, I'm a man of my word."

I felt even more guilty and did trust him. I seemed to know enough about him just by looking into his eyes. "Please, James, I don't want the police involved, I don't want anybody to find us. I'll explain later. Yes, my husband hurt me, not for the first time, but it won't help Lucy to jail her father. I won't go back, whatever happens. I'll try to minimise her contact until she's old enough to look after herself. So yes please, may we stay? Will you try to protect us from my husband and the authorities just for a week or two so that I can sort myself out?"

His face broke out into a broad smile. "Yes, I will, and please allow me to take care of you, all of you my love, starting with that nasty bruise to your pretty face. I'm sure it's not you the police will take in; it will be your husband."

CHAPTER TWO
JAMES

I was driving to the local shop for a few staples to last me over the weekend, when I thought I saw an angel sitting on a suitcase beside the road. I slowed as I approached so that I was able to focus on the scene before me and absorb it to my memory, where it will haunt me for as long as I live. There, sitting incongruously on a suitcase, truly was an angel, one of the most beautiful women I have ever seen, head bowed, crying, with a five or six-year-old girl clinging to her. I stopped and went back to investigate. She was obviously impervious to everything around her as she looked up, clearly not seeing me. She appeared to be in some sort of confused state as I stood and talked to her. Her daughter told me they had left home and could not get any money to go away.

The girl called herself Lucy and agreed to sit in the car while I fetched her mother. She also agreed to come back to my house to help her mummy. She seemed very mature and sensible. I stood the angel girl up and led her to the car; she was quite unresponsive. I was worried about her distressed and confused mental state. Nonetheless, I thought it better to take her to safety at home, to give her a chance to recover before I took desperate measures and called the authorities, either an ambulance or the police. Whatever had happened, I couldn't leave them beside the road.

I settled them in the kitchen and put on *The Lion King* for the child Lucy to watch, while I tried to speak to her mother and assess her exact problem and medical state. I gave up trying to get through to her and instead made coffee and fetched a brandy, which I suggested she sip to help clear her head. She had thankfully stopped crying, which was a step in the right direction. But now her pretty tear-stained face was driving me insane. A little round face with big dark eyes looking through curly black hair, the dearest little snub nose you ever dreamt of, her mouth and lips quivering as she sobbed, thankfully now quietly. I knew what was happening. I had been in love twice before, both suddenly on first sight as then, and both hurt me for months like an illness.

The angel was recovering; the brandy helped. Thankfully, the danger was over, no need for an ambulance. I introduced myself as James. She was Elle. I asked her if she felt better, and she said she did, thanking me. I explained why I had brought her to my home and told her that, if she trusted me and only if she did, would she like to stay. If not, I would call the police to take them to safety. As Elle looked around and saw her daughter, she appeared to rapidly recover. She started to look at me with a strange, knowing but resigned expression that I could not identify, as if she recognised me as a long-lost friend. She was emphatic in her instruction not to involve the police.

Eventually she asked me what I wanted from her in return for staying. This, not surprisingly, cut me to the quick. Surely she didn't think this was all about me taking advantage of her. There was not a man alive worth his manhood that would not want to bed Elle, but that was actually the last thought in my head at that time. I made her a strong guarantee of her safety, which seemed to satisfy her, although she was still acting strangely under the circumstances.

My god, I was in deep, deep trouble. I stood the angel up and embraced her tightly, looking into her eyes and feeling her breasts pressing against my chest. I could feel her heartbeat. She put her head on my shoulder and snuggled up to my neck. She was breathing fast, and my heart was beating even faster than hers. We had only known each other for less than an hour and I was a quivering wreck. I thought that I was too old for this sort of thing. I wanted a quiet life, to spend the money I had made in selling my business. Many women was what I dreamt of, not just one woman, however special she might be. At least that *was* what I wanted, before I came across this enchanting girl beside the road today.

Shit. What were my three daughters going to say, when they come home from university? Like Elle, apparently, they would never believe I did not have ulterior motives for installing a sex goddess and her daughter in my spare room. Why wouldn't they believe it? Well, because they knew me too well. My history with women was common knowledge. I had acquired quite a reputation. I was fully aware that I was known to be a gullible, oversexed fool, easy prey to a sexy woman.

Within days, this baby and her dear little daughter would have me exactly where they wanted me. I would refuse them nothing. Already I just loved them too much to be sensible. I was incapable of saying no to a pretty girl and everyone knew it. If they had not already spotted that, Elle and Lucy soon would.

At least my kids would see the funny side, when they heard the story of the girl sitting on the suitcase weeping as I drove by. They would egg Elle on to wind me up, assuming she was not already doing as much as she could, and then they would watch the fun. Three wild girls for daughters, and now these two. I was truly lost, my retirement plans out of the window. There was no hope for me. Frankly, I wasn't sure that I cared. This girl was way more special than any I had loved in the past. She was in a class of her own.

CHAPTER THREE

I fetched a bowl of warm water with a towel and antiseptic and bathed Elle's adorable little face, kissing the bruise and most of the rest of her still tear-stained face. As I did so, I spread the cream gently. "Do you have more bruises that I can attend to, my angel?"

She grinned back at me. "James, do you really expect me to strip so that you can look for bruises?"

I laughed. "Yes, something like that. I live in hope. So, is that a no then?"

The ice was truly broken. We were not children; we both knew what the stakes of the game were for us. I had everything Elle and Lucy would want and need to survive and move on. She was the one thing that I wanted at that moment. I think she knew that. There was something about her that told me she was not the helpless female she had so far appeared to be. The advantage was, in theory, delicately balanced, except that I am a fool with women. She was tough I guessed, battle hardened by the treatment meted out by a brute of a husband. In practise it was no contest. Elle would have the advantage, and that was before my girls weighed in on her side just for the fun of seeing their supposed alpha male father in a rare moment of confusion and disadvantage. Girl power, they would all cry. I thought Elle, with my girls, would have the advantage.

"Before I take you up to your room, girls, have a look in the fridge and cupboards and tell me what you would like for lunch. We can shop again later for supper."

Elle chose the cold meat and salad.

"One last thing, Elle. Come to me, please. I want to have a closer look, to make sure you have recovered." I embraced the object of my sudden passion. "I'm afraid that I am a bossy sort of man, used to being in command and getting things done. Please don't hesitate to tell me off if it annoys you. I want you both to be happy here. I suggest that in order to make sure your lovely little girl, who is already my friend, does not suffer more than necessary, you should concentrate on giving her all your attention. I would like to look after you in the same hands-on way. Will you be my baby, Elle, and let me look after you? How does that sound? Will you let me spoil you while you recover?"

"Yes, James, you can spoil me like a baby, or even a grown woman if you want to. I would like all of that, but how hands-on do you want to be?"

"Maybe not literally hands-on straight away, not yet anyway, although for some reason I would love to bathe you if you would ever let me. Just seeing that you have everything you need, and a cuddle now and then, is what I have in mind. You obviously need someone to worry about you."

"Then yes please, and cuddle me whenever you want to. I find it very comforting. You're a kind man, but take it slowly, then who knows, you might get to bathe me if that is what you really want. It could be fun. A little love will help me to recover. I won't get over today in a hurry. I'll tell you all about it later, when Lucy goes to bed. I agree, she is, as always, my first concern and duty. I think that I've always known that this day would come, but never saw it as it has happened. I hope Lucy is not too affected by her father's bad temper, but I for one will never be the same again. It's our good fortune that you came along, and not some pervert or my husband. So, within your new rules, do what you want with me. I trust you to love me and not to abuse me."

"Yes, I will love you and not abuse you. That's what falling in love means. We both know what the other one wants. It's obvious to you that I love you, therefore you most likely love me back, to be so perceptive and trusting. I'll go slowly and stick to my promise, whatever transpires between us. It will be a matter of honour and trust to ensure that we have a future. Now, if you fetch Lucy, I'll take your suitcases upstairs."

ELLE

James led us upstairs to a large room overlooking the countryside where there were two beds, easy chairs, and a television. Leading off was a bathroom. We will be comfortable and safe here, I thought, and I thanked James very much with a kiss. He left to get lunch while we unpacked.

I sat Lucy on my knee and started to explain as best I could what had happened to us. It turned out to be easier than I expected. She was an intelligent girl and had worked out most of it for herself.

"Daddy lost his temper and hit me, then kicked you, darling. I cannot live with a man that can do that to us. I'm so sorry because he is your daddy. You'll be able to visit him later, but for now we must hide away to be safe. Do you understand, my love?"

"Yes Mummy, and I know he's hit you before because I heard you crying and saw you with a black eye."

"My darling, I am so sorry, so very sad. James stopped to help us and has asked us to stay while we sort ourselves out. He's a kind man and we must be good and polite."

"Yes, Mummy, I like James. He talked to me like a grown-up, asking if I would get in the car, not telling me to. He was kind to you. I could see how he carried you and kissed you. He likes you, doesn't he, Mummy? I think he likes me too."

"You are a clever girl, Lucy. Do you mind that he loves us both so much?"

"I heard him say that you need loving and so do I. Will he be able to love us both?"

"Yes, darling, I think James can do a lot of loving if we let him."

"I will let him, Mummy, I want to be loved by him. He even put on The Lion King for me."

I could not help smiling at my daughter, so wise for her age, but yet still so innocent. I must watch their relationship to make sure it is all safe for my trusting Lucy.

We went hand-in-hand to the kitchen where James had prepared a meal for us. "Come here, girls," he called. "I'm not the world's greatest cook. I'm afraid you will both have to help out in the kitchen."

He took Lucy's hand and then lifted her on to a stool so that her face was level with his. "This is my special little girl. She was so sensible beside the road and she did everything right and was a great comfort to her mummy. She is very clever and unbelievably beautiful. Already I love her very much." James gave her a long hug, running his fingers through her hair, then he kissed her on the forehead.

I could see that she was overwhelmed with pride and pleasure. No one had ever treated her like this before. James stood back and told her, "You don't need to worry about your mummy any more. I will take over and look after her for you. She is an incredibly special mummy. I will spoil her and love her until she is a happy mummy again."

At that moment I loved James so much I resolved that I would give him his treat at the next opportunity.

When we had finished, James suggested that Lucy explore the house to see what she could find. He then made two cups of coffee and we sat down opposite each other at the table. "Do you realise, Elle, that I know nothing about you or you me, other than the simple fact that I fell in love with you on that roadside."

"Yes, James, I thought of that, except that we seem to know all the important things through this shared love. I know that you are soft and gentle and will never hurt me or Lucy. You are kind and generous, you have a way with us that is unbelievably comforting and decent, so very loving. It's exactly what we both need."

"And you, you are perhaps the most beautiful woman I have ever seen. You are also soft, gentle, and feminine and everything a woman should be. In addition to that, you are also ridiculously sexy. I'm sure you know that, but what you do to me is impossible to put into words. The image of you weeping on the roadside will stay in the front of my memory as long as I live. I would have died for you right there and then. Furthermore, your little daughter is a real chip off the block. She will be everything that you are one day. I do hope I can be around to see that."

"I have a feeling that you might be, James."

I stood up again and was back in his comforting embrace. "I love you, Elle, please tell me I'm not wasting my time hoping that there might be a future for us."

"No, James, you're not wasting your time, but neither can I make any promises. There's so much you don't know about us. One thing I will promise, I will not lead you up the garden path. I will try to give as much as I take, to be honest at all times. I just don't know what the future holds for me, it's all too sudden." I started to cry again; it was all too much of a rollercoaster.

James pulled me closer and for the first time kissed me full on the lips. The surprise and instant pleasure rush stopped my tears instantly. "Yes," he said, with a satisfied expression, "that's the way to do it."

I couldn't help it, I just laughed. What a difference a day makes, and a real lover. My thoughts turned to the problem of explaining our history and how this might affect James' love. I was truly afraid it would all end in tears for me.

"Right, enough romancing, let's get serious. With your permission, I will manage all interaction with your husband. My lawyers will act for you. Please, neither of you have direct contact. The object will be to reach an amicable parting of the ways and future rights for him with Lucy. Please leave it to the experts, rows never help. Allegations of domestic abuse will be formalised into sworn statements. These will be shown to his lawyers as a backup. This should be enough to keep everything straightforward. If you have a mobile phone, get it now and switch it off. They can identify your location. You don't have a phone? Well, we will get you one. Do you agree to this? If so, I'll get things moving later on. Stand up, baby, and come to me."

James once again held me in a tight embrace while I melted against him and put my head on his chest. "Now, my darling, it may be less than a day, but I intend to treat you as my own girl and, starting now, guide you back to full health., You've had a shock and a close shave. Please obey me, so that I can look after you properly. For a start, you need to eat plenty of healthy food. You feel a little fragile, then plenty of sleep or I might get cross with you and you don't want that."

"Why, oh master, what do you do to bad girls?"

"That, my love, is for me to know and for you to find out one day. To be serious, tell me what happened today to prompt your leaving home."

"Well, my husband, George, aimed a punch at my head. I usually see them coming and roll with them. Not this one, you saw the result. I believe I was concussed. That wasn't it, though, that was nearly normal behaviour. What did it was the kick he gave Lucy, sending her across the room. That crossed a line. Starting on Lucy at her age, where would that lead to? I packed up and left. Then my bank card didn't work as he had stripped out about a thousand pounds before I got there, leaving me penniless. He must have thought I wouldn't leave without money. Without you, I expect I would have gone home for another beating, so thank you for saving me that. The rest you know. I was walking back home when I went dizzy and fell down. That was when you came along."

"My baby girl, thank god I did, because now you are mine to take care of. I will hold you close and mend the damage. I love you, Elle, so much it hurts, so please be kind to me."

"I will, darling, you are so special I really mean it when I say you can do what you want with me."

"Elle, don't ever say that again. Don't mistake my feelings for you as just lust. It's love for you as a person, not just for your body. You're stunning, but I don't want to have you used as a sex object by anyone, especially by me. When we finally cement our love, it will be a special occasion, believe me. In the meantime, everything else is allowed and we will have fun."

CHAPTER FOUR

James and the girls spent the rest of the day being a family unit and getting to know each other. There were no more history lessons. That was left for another day. They went to bed with kisses all round.

James was up by seven o'clock preparing breakfast. He made tea and coffee, and toast, and had cereal ready. Eventually Lucy appeared by herself. James asked where Elle was.

"Mummy is crying and can't come down yet," Lucy answered.

James flew up the stairs two at a time and into the spare bedroom. The sight that he beheld was truly pathetic. Elle was lying in the foetal position, a picture of misery; she was sobbing her heart out. James ran to the bed and scooped her up into his arms. "Whatever is the matter, my little love?" Her replies were inaudible, so James held her tight and whispered sweet nothings in her ear. Eventually the tears ran out and James repeated the question.

"What is to become of us? We have no money, no home and no relatives or friends. George has made sure of that."

James slipped his hand inside Elle's nightdress and gently formed it around one of her breasts. He kissed her on the lips as he gently played with the nipple. After a time, a smile appeared on Elle's face. James withdrew his hand and pulled her back into a cuddle. "You have me. I have a home, I have money and I have many friends. Do you not trust me to take care of you both, my baby?"

"How can I expect that for two strangers you don't know, James?" Elle wailed.

"Listen to me, Elle, you both belong to me now. I found you, I'm going to keep you and I won't put up with you doubting my sincerity. In future, you will sleep in my bed where I can look after you properly. I'll put a stop to all this doubt, is that clear?"

"Yes, James." Elle gave a knowing smile. "What do you propose to do to achieve that, smack my bottom like a naughty schoolgirl?"

"Maybe that's not a bad idea, because actually I would love to, so watch out. Now get dressed, and in future be a little more obedient. Be in no doubt, I will take charge of you and sort you out, Elle."

When Elle had come downstairs James looked seriously at her and Lucy. "Now, girls, for the time being, it is most important that you are not seen. Don't go outside or stand near the windows. Do you understand that, Lucy? Daddy will be very cross that you have run away, so you must not let him catch you. When the lawyers have started proceedings, it will be easier. We can get an injunction if necessary. When we go out shopping, we will go to Lymestone, as it's not local. I think it might be fun to go away for a few days, what do you two think, girls?"

"Yes please," said Lucy, "where to?"

"Lucy hasn't travelled very far from here, so how about Devon?"

"Good idea," said James. "I'll make the arrangements. This is your home now, girls, so go and explore and see if you want to make any alterations. Get ready, then later we'll go out to lunch."

When Elle and Lucy were ready to go, they met James in the kitchen. "Good, here we are then. Wait in the hall until I open the car door, for you to come quickly and get inside."

"Where are we going James?"

"A magical mystery tour to the golf club, all aboard."

They kept their heads down during the journey, then parked and walked into the clubhouse, which was full of people drinking and talking, most of them having played that morning.

James went up to two county-type women and kissed them both. "Hello, Joan, may I introduce a special friend of mine? This is Elle. Excuse me, ladies, while I take Lucy to the putting green."

Joan and Elle eyed each other up. "Why special?" asked Joan.

"I don't think he meant that," Elle replied. "We're just staying as we became temporarily homeless and James has kindly put us up."

Joan looked again at Elle. "Nice try, but I think it is more than that. James is in love with you, isn't he?" Elle blushed and didn't know what to reply. "Sorry, darling, I didn't mean to upset you with my prying, he is a lovely man and will never let you down."

"Come on, Joan," said Stella, "come clean, let Elle have the truth."

"Yes, well, Elle, I should know because I am James's ex-wife. Don't look so shocked, we're still all friends. I can recommend him both as a husband and as a man, also as a lover, but then you must know that already."

"Actually, no, we only met yesterday."

"Hang on, let me get this straight. You only met yesterday, you're staying with him, and he's in love with you, but you have not been to bed with him?"

"Yes, that about sums it up, except to add that we met beside the road while I was sitting on a suitcase crying my eyes out."

Joan and Stella looked at each other and burst out laughing.

That was when James came back. "James, can you confirm that you met beside the road and took Elle home, but not to your bed, despite being in love with her, and yes, she was sitting on a suitcase crying?"

"That sounds about right, Joan, just a normal romance, you know me."

"Yes, James, I do, so there is a lot more to it than that, so come on, tell all."

James looked at Elle who shrugged her shoulders, so he explained it all to his ex-wife.

"How utterly fascinating. I am so sorry for your treatment and distress, my darling, but you are the lucky one to have been rescued by James. He is perfect for you and I think it is mutual. What a great romance, Stella. May we be friends? Old and new wife-to-be, for that is where this is headed, isn't it."

"Yes, I would like that, please, and give me the low down. Is he dangerous? He threatened to spank my bottom."

"Your bottom and the rest of you is in great danger, but then I assume you want that, you are one sexy woman, if I may say so. Oh, what fun! James, get champagne. Wait till my girls hear about this, they will have hysterics, goodbye bachelor free James, hello sexy new woman to wind him round her fingers."

James re-appeared with Lucy in his arms. Joan said, "Well, what have we here?"

James replied, "The prettiest, most intelligent little girl you ever did meet, and a chip off the Elle block. Say hello to Lucy, Joan."

Joan went and gave her a kiss. "You are the pretty one, adorable and the lucky one like your mother. James loves little girls like you. Stella, it gets better and better. James has actually turned the clock back fifteen years. The girls will just love this when they stop laughing. Especially they will love you, Lucy, you are about to get super spoiled."

"Joan, stop making fun of me. I suppose you will be on the phone now and I can expect a rush of over excited female tornadoes to make my life hell."

"Yes, James, but surely you knew that would happen when you picked this goddess up from the roadside."

"Very funny, Joan you're enjoying this as much as the girls will, aren't you?"

"Well, darling, it is typical of you, that's why we all love you, and so will Elle. I am very happy that a lovely vulnerable girl and her daughter have been rescued by you. There is no one better and it will keep you out of mischief. You can rely on me to help as much as possible.

"Oh my god!" James cried in mock distress. "I am truly lost, my rampaging oat sowing, drunken orgy of a bachelor life, on permanent hold. On the other hand, I have got the most beautiful, sexy little baby angel to play with. I'll survive."

They found a table in the window and ordered lunch with Champagne. Joan took Elle to one side and told her that she was to call her at once if there was any problem that James needed help with. "I am, in fact, a solicitor; may I represent you in your divorce and any other problems?"

"Thank you, but I have no money to pay you."

"Don't be silly, darling, that's what James is for. He is particularly good at that; he still helps me out now and again. He would be insulted if you ever mention money, he's old fashioned that way. He will expect to take care of all your needs and more besides. This is not a game with him, Elle. Get used to him taking charge of you and fixing your problems and giving you everything he thinks you need. Lucy too. Don't stop him—that was part of my problem, I wanted to be independent financially. If you want to work, do charity organising or something similar."

They parted, agreeing to meet and discuss the legal issues and to give Joan instructions.

Once back in the warm kitchen and general living room, Elle put the kettle on and made a pot of tea. James was sitting on the sofa in front of a children's television programme with Lucy. Elle looked at them and for the first time knew for certain that she would say yes if he asked her to marry him. She began to feel happy, as she had not done for years. Joan's reassurance that her ex-husband was the genuine article had made all the difference. Up to now, she could not be certain that it was not all an act. Her faith in men was understandably low.

She took mugs of tea and a glass of milk and joined them on the sofa. "May I ask you a question, James?"

"Yes, my love, let's go and sit at the table. Excuse us, Lucy, we'll be right back. Now, what is it, Elle?"

"Well, you and Joan seem to get on so well, why did you not remarry?"

"Good question and not one that I can easily answer, except that she is happy with her current husband, a judge. He is a kind man and not demanding, also they have the law in common. You might also sum it up by the simple fact that we all get on better as friends than we did when we were married. Joan is a career woman; she really likes to be her own boss in all situations. I am an old-fashioned husband. I like my wife to be active and talented, but shall I say, domesticated, with an interest in the bedroom. I want a wife to love and one that wants to love me and her children and make a home for us all, rather than earn a living that we do not really need. I do my share around the house, but the wife is in charge. Joan never wanted that, she thought servants were for domestic duty, not wives. That's it really, she was not in any way a submissive woman. I believe you are, my angel. I tested you several times and you always react without trying to correct anything I suggest. You are happy to let me lead you as long as I don't step over any red lines you must have set after your experiences with your abusive husband. Are you shocked by this revelation, Elle?"

"I'm not shocked. Surprised, perhaps, that you even needed to test me. All I have done so far is cry and cling on to you. Of course, I am submissive, that is why I have never managed to leave George before as

I should have and faced the future. Joan would have left home first punch, having no doubt smacked him one back. I can't change, so what I need now is a man that I can trust so that I can give myself to him without getting hurt. Are you that man, James? Your wife says you are."

"My poor little angel, of course you don't trust any man. How could you, and nothing I say will make any difference. Joan's testimony must help, though. I always knew you needed to be convinced, which is why I made you the no sex promise. If I keep that, you will know for sure in a month's time what sort of man I am. I love you so much, Elle. I cannot bear the thought that we might be parted, so as soon as you can, please say you will stay here with me forever and let me love you properly. I have everything you and Lucy need, my two adorable girls. Please let me help you. I love you both so much and want to make you both happy."

"James, I am fairly sure now, but there is something inside me saying, hold on, now you are free at last—do not sign up immediately. I think time is what I need to recover and look at things without stress and emotion. Your month is a good idea. Let's wait and I will make up my mind by then. I don't want to sound ungrateful, James. As things stand, I can think of nothing better than you and this house. There are serious issues. Ones that I cannot ask for help with, that I have to resolve before I can move on. I do love you back, as you know full well, and Lucy loves you like she never had the chance to love her father. I just hope nothing changes during the month to stop me moving on."

"Well said, darling. I quite understand and would not want you to rush to decide. After what you have been through it would be silly to jump at the first man you meet, beside the road, I might add. Someone in a Rolls might just pass your way."

"Watch out, I might just smack you. That would be different and, now I think of it, something that I would not have dared do to George, that says something in itself." The lovers hugged and kissed each other as Lucy looked on with a happy smile on her face.

Later, after supper, James picked up Lucy and asked her if she minded sleeping on her own so that Mummy could sleep in his bed, so that he could stop her crying during the night. He said that he would leave the lights on in the house and that she could come and join them if she wanted to. Lucy was quite happy with that. She didn't at all mind being in the room on her own, and Mummy needed a cuddle in the night to stop her crying. James thought, not for the first time, how understanding and sensible this little girl was, more so than her mother, it seemed. With his experience of daughters growing up he was excited to imagine how this one might turn out. Not as wild and a lot more serious than his own three away at university, he was sure of that; well, two of them to be fair, his eldest was more sensible than her sisters.

They all went up to bed. Elle spent time with Lucy, bathing and chatting with her, before going to James's bedroom for the first time. They sat on the bed, both unsure what to do next. James suggested Elle used the bathroom and get into bed with her knickers on and a nightdress. A relieved Elle did just that and waited for James to do the same. He took her in his arms and told her that for now and the next week at least she would be topless and no more. He said that he was out to prove to her that he could control himself and respect her as a person, not the sex goddess she obviously was.

Elle smiled to herself; not a sex goddess but an expert nonetheless, and wondered if it would be fun to really test James with some of her little bedroom tricks. She decided that that was unfair when he was making such an effort for her and meant so well. She would play along and make it as easy as possible for him. She slipped off her nightdress and cuddled up to her new lover.

James shuddered as Elle took off her nightdress and embraced him with her breasts pressed against his chest. He took off his pyjama top and pulled her back. The sensation when her hard nipples on her firm breasts pressed against him was almost more than he could control. She kissed him and he almost had an ejaculation right then. She knew as well. He could tell by the way she moved against him. She obviously could not help testing him and he was no match for her skills in the bed. That was immediately clear to him.

"No way am I going to keep this up for a month," he worried.

She whispered, "No one said you cannot cum if you need to, even over me if you want to. I like that."

So, the pattern was set. He was going to have fun, but was not able to give her the same because of his own rules. Elle said, "Let's not be silly. Kneel over me and I will do it for you, that must be allowed."

James gratefully straddled and kissed his angel. She gently and expertly gave him the first orgasm of their lover's union.

"James, don't you think there is something just a little unfair here? By your rules, I am here with my knickers on and you have just wanked all over me with a super climax. I am not a bloody nun, you know."

James could not help himself. He burst out laughing and Elle joined in. "Go to sleep, you brazen hussy. You did all that yourself. You're teasing me. Go on, admit it."

Elle giggled and said, "We'll talk about it in the morning."

During the night James became aware that Elle was restless, tossing and turning, then she cried out, "No, no, no," and tried to get up.

James caught her and took her in his arms. He held her face against his and whispered, "It's me, James. You're safe here. I'll look after you. Elle, wake up, my love." She was fighting back but gradually subsided, sobbing her heart out. Elle woke up, realised where she was and forced herself into James' arms, clinging on around his neck. Silent and breathing heavily, they both lay still for a long time.

"Thank you, darling," she said eventually. "Thank you for being here and for comforting me."

"Elle, does that happen often? Will you tell me what you are afraid of?"

"For now, James, yes it does, and no—I am not ready to talk about it. Hopefully, it will stop with you here to catch me. I might talk to Joan about my issue. I can't handle it on my own. But it's a big decision and has implications. You might think differently about us. More I will not say, because you might do something drastic."

Elle was crying again, and James felt so helpless. All he could do was cuddle his troubled angel and try to kiss her better. "Oh, James, I can't do this, I'm going to have to tell you about my problems, my secret, then I'm afraid that you won't want me any more. Arrange for Joan to meet us and I will confess my problem to you both."

James, worried and confused, asked Joan to come as soon as possible. Then he took Lucy down to breakfast while Elle recovered and dressed.

Joan arrived in time for the mid-morning break. James made coffee and settled Lucy with another film, then they sat around the kitchen table.

Elle said, "I am not what you think I am. I'm a girl from Poland. I was working in a hotel there when I was offered a job in an English branch of the same group. One man made the arrangements and accompanied us across on the train. At the station in London, we got into the bus provided and were driven to the hotel, but no, as you have probably guessed, it was not a hotel, it was a brothel. I was a teenage virgin at the time with no experience of men.

"I was raped and put to work. There was no escape. It's a long story that I can tell you more about another time. We girls stuck together and made the best of it. We were friends and it was not all bad. Some men were fun. That continued for me until George, who was part of the gang, offered to take me home and marry me. That was better than the brothel and Lucy arrived and made my life worthwhile again. That's my story, except I could not run away because I have no passport and am illegal. I would be sent home and then recycled to Germany or somewhere like that. We girls thought it better to stick to what we know. We were secretly saving tips in the hope of escaping." Elle broke down again and sobbed, breaking James' heart.

Joan and James exchanged horrified looks, and both went to comfort Elle. James carried her to the sofa and held her on his lap, rocking and whispering as he held her as tight as he could.

Joan sat and stared at Elle with such concern as she tried to gather together all the implications of Elle's illegal status. The marriage was surely a fraud, for a start. She went over to the sofa. "Elle, darling, thank you for telling us your story. We love you all the more now we know how you have been treated. None of it is your fault and they must be made to pay for their crimes. Go and sit with Lucy while we talk it over and see what can be done.

"James, what a tragedy. The only possible good news is that Elle might not be married at all, so a way out may be to marry her and make her legal."

"Yes, I thought of that, you will investigate the possibilities. What happens if we arrest George and bust this gang?"

"I will chat to the authorities without giving anything away and see what can be done. A deal for giving evidence is possible. Whatever,

James, you look after Elle. Be very loving and find her a good shrink as soon as possible. I will go and get to work."

James sat back on the sofa and took Elle into his arms again. "Elle, my darling. Listen to me carefully. None of what you have told me makes any difference to the way I feel about you or my love for you, except to make it stronger. I am so very sorry for your suffering. A young girl treated this way. I want to see them pay a heavy price for what they did to you and others. Joan has gone to investigate your position and what can be done. We will not let you down, my love. I will never let you go, so take comfort from that, and wait to see what we can do. One thing, my angel. I am going to take it for granted that you will stay with me and let me protect you and make you safe. You are still my baby, Elle. I love you more than ever. You will marry me when we sort this out, won't you, Elle?"

"Thank you, James, of course I will marry you if you still want me. Before, I was afraid that you would find out my dirty secret and let me go. I am sorry I am not the innocent girl you thought I was."

"Elle, nothing has changed. You are the same girl that I fell in love with. I knew nothing about you then. What I now know that you have suffered makes me love you all the more. It is my countrymen that abused you. I will make up for that as much as I can."

James sent a text to Joan telling her not to tell anyone about Elle's problem, especially the girls. 'We do not want Lucy to ever find out, also about her criminal Father,' he wrote.

After putting Lucy to bed, Elle found James in his bedroom. "Come here, my love, the rules will change now. The no full sex rule must remain. It is still my oath of trust for you. Now I think, after hearing your story, you must need that reassurance about me more than ever. There is no other rule. We will not have a repeat of last night. Come into the bathroom with me, baby. I am going to bathe you like a baby, Elle. For some reason I cannot explain, it is what I have wanted to do almost since I met you. You just be my good baby girl and do as I tell you. I will run a nice hot bath; come here now. I'm going to undress you very slowly."

Sitting on a stool with Elle facing him, James took off her clothes, one by one, until only her bra and knickers were left. He reached around and expertly released her bra, letting it fall to the ground. James eased

Elle's knickers down, put them on the chair, and stood back. There before him was, indeed, the goddess he had been expecting. He was overwhelmed with emotion as he lovingly turned Elle around and studied her from all angles. James then embraced his naked angel who was watching his expression of wonder with a wry smile on her face. She was used to this reaction, but not from a real lover, only punters paying extra for the best girl. George never seemed to appreciate her beauty, only that others wanted her, and he could keep it all to himself, so he took her home. "You are simply stunning," James said, as he helped her into the bath.

Elle lay back and relaxed, allowing James to swill the water over her while he explored her every nook and cranny with gentle hands.

"Is that nice, darling? Let me concentrate on your breasts. They are so perfectly shaped with those great nipples."

Elle closed her eyes and felt content as he lifted and massaged each breast in turn. *This is what I need she*, thought. *A man who is gentle and likes my body as a thing of beauty, not an object to take maximum selfish pleasure from, raped and abused for their pleasure and to humiliate me for added amusement.* She really had no experience of men giving her pleasure, only of them taking it. James helped her out of the bath and carefully dried her before slipping on a towelling dressing gown. Elle could see the love and concern on James' face and wished he had not insisted on a month of no sex. She wanted to treat him to the one thing she knew far more about than he did.

My lover is every woman's dream come true—that is, every submissive woman. He is handsome, strong, and capable, but also loving and gentle. A typical alpha male, with a look in his eye that is irresistible to girls like me. I just know he is a naughty boy and I also know that he will make his lover's life exciting. That is, as long as she wants plenty of varied sex. He will take control and make me feel safe and loved. He does want to fight a little, not to have it too easy. He wants a naughty girl with spirit. That is me. I will run him ragged at times, but when he finally masters me, we both win. I had no idea that I could love any man as I do James or trust any man as I do James. I have no means of defending myself from men that mean to abuse me, other than to kick them in the balls and run away. But you cannot do that to a man like George. I would finish up in hospital, and where would Lucy go if I lost a fight with someone like George? My beautiful lover, James, is what a man is supposed to be. A defender and protector of women. I will take great care of him and try to be everything he wants me to be.

"I'll have a quick shower, then join you in bed," James told her.

She waited to see him undress. Just as she expected, he was in good shape. Well-muscled and no fat. Just the sort of man she and her friends hoped for. No trouble. A satisfying hour, and a good tip. Elle went to bed and waited.

James slipped in beside her and took her naked body in his arms. "Elle, my darling, it is very hard for me to imagine what you have been through. All that I can ask is that you do not keep any of it bottled up inside. Let me share it all with you. It is always going to be part of us as a couple. The more I know, the more your burden is shared and halved. My role is to take as much of it from you as possible so that you can enjoy a normal married life with a family. Is there any reason why we should not have more children?"

Elle instantly burst into tears again. She was always so near to the edge. "James, is that really possible? Would you want to start all over again?"

"Yes, I would. Lucy is now my pride and joy. She is just perfect. Two more like her would make my life complete."

Elle hugged James. "Yes, please, James. That will make my life as near normal as it is ever going to be. George refused to give me any more babies." Tears poured on to James' chest.

"Sleep now, baby. No fun tonight. Sex must take a back seat while we get things sorted out. It will be a distraction. I will just hold you and love you for yourself for now." The night passed without incident. Lying close to her protector, Elle felt safe. The burden had, as James said, lifted a little, in that he shared it with her, so she didn't feel isolated in her own secret sordid past. Maybe one day she would believe that none of it was her fault, but not just yet.

CHAPTER FIVE

Joan arrived in time for coffee. "Hi, James, hello Elle, how are you today?"

"I am better, thank you Joan. James is being very kind to me. I'm not sure that I deserve it, but it is so reassuring to know someone believes my story and is supporting me."

"Your story is true all right, Elle. I have gathered many details since I started looking into it. To start with, what was your name, Elle?, We never asked."

"My name was Elle Debrowshi."

"Is it now? That's interesting, because it still is your name, because you never married. Do you know Anna Kowalski?"

"No, I have never heard of her."

"Well, you should have, because she married George Wheeler seven years ago. Was that about the time you married him? Well, never mind for now, we can go into it later. You were fooled. There was no proper marriage for you. Anna most likely was a friend of one of the gang and made a UK citizen by the marriage. It was her passport and details. For some reason she was not there herself. She looks like you, but I knew it was not your passport picture. You thought he was marrying you. No, they secured your obedience and made a friend UK legal on that day. It's good news, Elle, you're free."

Before she could cry again, James took her in an embrace and kissed her.

"We're still working on the rest, but they are still operating, and I intend to see them, not only closed down, but put away for a long time. But we have to manage it without making your name public. You might need to help if any of your friends are still there and prepared to give evidence. For now, darling, please accept that none of this is your fault and let James love you as he wants to."

"I will, thank you. It is what Lucy and I need. Thank you both. I feel so much better."

"I am in touch with your embassy to find out how we get you a new passport, without giving them the details at this stage. Incidentally, they lied to you about being deported. I was not thinking properly yesterday. There is, of course, free movement for Polish EU citizens. You were never illegal. You are not now, as long as we get you properly registered and get your details up to date."

Elle looked astonished, then extremely upset indeed. It turned out to be the moment that Elle went from victim, to avenger. She became very energised with a burning desire to get even with her tormentors who, in addition to the abuse, made fools of all the girls. "James, Joan, forget my friends. I want to stand up in court and tell my story and get those bastards put in jail. I will spit in their faces as the verdict is read out. My poor Lucy is the innocent party in all this. She will understand and forgive any bad publicity as she grows up. She would fight back for me, as I intend to do for myself and the other girls. Let me meet the police. I will name the men and the women that organised the brothel. I care nothing about what happens to me. I warn you both, I might try to stick a knife into any one of them, but especially that cruel bastard George. I don't want him still on this planet as the father of my Lucy."

Joan looked at James, alarmed. They could both see that it had all changed. There would be no more tears. Elle had no room for any more self-pity. Hard cold revenge now motivated her. They would have to watch out, as she warned. She might easily do something really stupid.

"Wait now, Elle," said Joan, "Don't go and spoil everything. We must plan this carefully if we are not to drive them underground."

Joan left to get on with the investigation. James fetched the car and said to both his girls, "Hop in. We're going shopping."

They drove to the nearest out-of-town shopping centre, which was an hour away and quite safe, James thought.

"Right—coffee and a milk shake, girls? Lucy, come here," James said, and asked, "What is it that you want most that you have not got, my little love? Mummy, help out here. What does Lucy want or need?"

"No darling, that is too expensive."

"What was that Lucy?" She didn't answer. "Elle, speak up please."

"Lucy has seen some children with junior computers."

James told Lucy, "You will have one, darling, if that is what you want."

They went to the big store selling computers and televisions. James summoned an assistant to show them their range of children's computers. Lucy pointed out the one she had seen at school. James spoke to the assistant and they settled on the top of the range model that had the most features.

"There, my little girl, you have been so good. You are so special and deserve to have the best that I can give you. You will have what your friends have from now on." Lucy bubbled with excitement and pleasure. Now James said to the assistant. "Please, show us the latest iPads." James chose the newest model. "And your leather covers, please. Now, Elle which of these do you like?"

"You must chose for yourself, James."

"No, Elle, it's for you."

Elle was shocked, but eventually chose a pretty pink case.

"There," said James, "now you are both set up with computers that are essential today. Now, Elle, my big baby girl. Follow me, it's your turn to be spoiled."

James took them into an upmarket jeweller. "May we see some necklaces, please?" he asked. "Something like that." He pointed to one costing five hundred pounds.

Elle put a hand over her mouth. She said, " No, no, not that much, please, James."

The sales assistant ignored her and went to town, hopefully laying out his wares all above that price.

"What about this one?" said James. "It is simple and understated. It will set off your beautiful neck well, just a clean emerald."

Elle was completely overawed. No one had ever bought her a present, certainly not like this before. Now this one was eight hundred pounds. She was speechless.

James turned to Lucy. "What do you think, little one?"

"I like that one. It's pretty, like Mummy."

"Good, we will have it please." Elle was shocked and still unable to react. James smiled to himself with deep satisfaction. Spoiling his two girls was going to be real fun. He paid, took Elle in his arms, and kissed her excited face.

I cannot get my head around what has just happened. James has spent eight hundred pounds on a necklace for me. I have never seen that sort of money, let alone had it spent on me and on jewellery. I am in shock and don't know what to say. How do I thank him for that? I must find ways to make him happ,y apart from in the bedroom. I will ask Joan what he would like from me. It can't be all one-way in our relationship, but how do you thank a man that spends that sort of money on you, except in bed?

As they made their way back to the car, Lucy was still bubbling with joy and excitement and Elle was still silent. At home, James put the necklace around Elle's neck. It looked stunning, he thought, with her black hair, dark eyes, and pretty face. It truly set off her extraordinary beauty.

Elle looked in the mirror and agreed it was exactly right for her colouring. "Oh, James, I love you so much, please give up your month rule, it is all I have to give you in return for everything you're doing for Lucy and me."

"Elle, how many times do I have to tell you. The rule will never be lifted if you feel you should pay me back in sex. I've tried to explain it to you. Important as that is to me, it is not what I want most from you. I want your love. Sex is something for us to share. Your reaction in the shop and at home to my gift was what I want. That was my reward. You were both simply gorgeous. I loved you to bits and you looked so bewildered but happy, that is what I really want. Baby, to see you both happy after all that you have suffered, it is so satisfying for me to give you things that you have not had before. After the month has passed, then it will be time to take the next step in our life before we marry. It will not be this month, it will not be in this house, it will be special. I want all the rest of you and your love before we finally cement our relationship with sex. You of all people might understand that, Elle, because our relationship must be different to any that you have had with men in the past. It is based purely on our love for each other. Believe me, my love for you exceeds my lust for your body. I have to prove that to you before we move on. You have to believe that I am not like all the other men that have abused you, so I have to protect you and show you that not all men are bad. Then we can have a normal lovers' relationship."

CHAPTER SIX

Joan phoned to say she was coming round for a conference. Then they were going to be interviewed by the police. "Here is what I have so far," Joan said, as they settled down around the table. "The embassy are aware of the trafficking of women and would like to help stop it. They believe that the hotel in Poland must know, or at least someone there must know what is going on, otherwise where do they think their employees disappeared to. They will fast track a passport for you with Lucy on it, without questions, provided the forms are filled out and they can check your identity. You travelled here on a temporary document. You will need to go and collect your new one in person and be questioned.

"The authorities take your evidence very seriously. Trafficked women in slave conditions, both nail bar type and sex workers, is a big issue. Several forces are working on it. They have someone inside your old establishment already. I suspect it is one of the girls because they can easily meet a potential customer who is, in fact, an undercover detective recording what goes on. They will take your evidence as well to build up their case before they strike. So, let's go, Elle. James will look after Lucy."

They drove to the regional headquarters of the police. Joan introduced Elle to the superintendent, who she obviously knew. There was also a middle-aged policewoman. They settled into the interview room and sat opposite each other.

"Turn on the recorder, please. Now, Mrs Debrowski, I understand that you came here from Poland. Please tell your story, starting with how you came to leave Poland and, for the Polish authorities, name who at the hotel was involved in organising it."

Elle carefully told her tale in meticulous detail, including all the names of the staff, and ending with her arrival at the brothel.

"Turn off the recorder, please." The superintendent looked at Elle with admiration. "That was amazing, you must have a photographic memory. I can hardly ever recall hearing such clear and precise evidence. Have a break. I'll get coffee, then we will continue."

The interview continued. "Turn on the recorder, please. Now, Mrs Debrowski, you have been taken to somewhere that is clearly not the hotel you expected. Tell us what happened next."

For nearly an hour, Elle described, in graphic detail, all that went on in the brothel, her marriage to George, his violence and her leaving home. It all had a visible effect on the hardened officers. The policewoman was emotional, as was Joan. The superintendent was looking at her with compassion and making gulping noises. There was silence when she finished.

"Turn off the recorder. My God, you poor girl, I am so sorry that you have been treated like this, but have no fear, with the benefit of your evidence the CPS will prosecute them all and hopefully the court will put them away for many years. You have so many facts and little details that it can only be true and provable. My guess is that they will be advised to plead guilty, saving you the need to give evidence in court."

Joan gave her a hug and said, "Well done, darling. Again, I agree. It is so detailed, it cannot be anything but true, but let's get more information on each perpetrator."

"Turn on the recorder, please."

Elle gave names and descriptions of all those involved.

"Now, Mrs Debrowski, describe the woman, Janet, that you say was in charge of the girls."

"She was especially cruel. She allocated the girls to the customers. Since she didn't like me, because I was the most popular with the regulars and she was jealous, she used to give me all the bad men and the violent ones. One man, Simon Franks, a schoolteacher I believe, was especially cruel. He would have to hurt me before he could get a hard on. When I was crying enough for him, he would give it to me as roughly as he could. I would like you to charge him with rape.

"I grew up in Poland, near to the death camps. Janet would have been at home there in the war. She would have been a good camp superintendent. She has no trace of humanity. Another cruel one guilty of rape was a local man, Ian Robins. He enjoyed anal rape. You can identify him because he has a tiny penis and only one shrivelled ball, *no doubt the reason why he was so mean*."

This brought a stifled laugh from Joan, followed by them all joining in. "Elle, darling, you are priceless. James is so lucky to have you, with your sense of humour. How can you take this so well? I would be in a mental home if it were me."

"Yes, but I do not want them to plead guilty. I want to stand up and tell the world what they have done to us."

"That, Elle, is exactly why their lawyers will make them plead guilty. You, in person, would get them another five years at least."

"Turn the recorder off," the superintendent instructed. "Enough for one day. You are truly magnificent, Elle. So brave. May I say, off the record, that we are all very much on your side. We will get them with all this evidence, have no fear of that."

On the way home, Elle asked Joan not to repeat the details to James. "He is emotional enough already."

Later that evening, James and Elle sat down in James' study with a bottle of wine. "How do you feel now, darling, now that the police are involved?"

"Actually, James, I am a new person. Before I felt that I was a failed wife with a shady past. Now, thanks to you, the police, but mainly to Joan, I feel like the wronged girl that I know I am. I am now fighting back and looking forward to having my revenge. I daydream of seeing their faces as they are sentenced. I don't feel sorry for myself any more."

"Wonderful, Elle. You are one amazing girl. Many people would have been driven mad after what you have gone through. Drink up. I want to take you to bed."

James went through the same routine in the bathroom. He stripped his expectant lover slowly, then this time he took her into the shower. They lovingly soaped each other all over and stood under the waterfall, James holding his Elle tight and kissing her. The water flowed all around them as they stood together locked in an embrace, legs intertwined, her breasts pressed against his chest. They dried together and went to bed.

James spread a towel on the bed and told Elle to lie face down. James spread baby oil over his angel's back and began a slow massage. *She cannot be more than five foot two,* he thought, *with a petite build.* But it was her waist that made her the goddess. It was exceptionally slim, making the curves to her bottom and breasts exaggerated. He worked down to her bottom, the place he wanted to go to more than any other. Any woman lying face down, even not especially in jeans, had the power to drive him mad. This cute little bottom was perfect. He kissed it and rubbed his face against its cheeks. He so desperately wanted to pull himself up her body and break his rule here and now. He was, in fact, rock hard and leaking. Fortunately, she could not see his distress. She would have tipped him over; he had no doubt of that. "Turn over please, Elle, that's better." He thought, *I can handle this side more easily. How did I ever get myself into this mess? I'm a womaniser, not a saint. It is what I do, and women love me for it.*

Elle relaxed as James massaged her back. *This is bliss*, she thought. *My lover being gentle and trying to please me. Now my bottom. That's his thing. I know that from the way he looks at it when I walk past him, and the way his hands always slip there. Many men are the same. I like that better than breast men. There is more they can do to my bottom, more fun for both of us. James is in trouble. I can tell he wants to take me now from behind. Will he do it or not? For his sake I hope not. For mine, yes please. Good man,. He's giving up the massage that side and wants me to turn over. Much safer for him to hide my bottom.*

My breasts, please. Yes, that's nice, James, lift gently and massage the tip. That's amazing, sucking gently and licking the end. That is good, James. Run your hands round the inside of my thighs and lift my legs. Now you have full view of what you want but cannot have. What are you going to do about it? Work your fingers up and down inside my lips and circle my clitoris. That is wonderful. You are good, James, but if you will not slide your fingers inside me how are you going to make me come? Oh my God, no one has ever done that to me before. Licking the inside of my lips and sucking my clitoris. That will do it for sure. Thank you, I'm coming, James. Bite me, James, or pinch my nipple. Do something now. Yes, yes, pinch again, I'm coming. Wow, that was so special, what a surprising lover my James is. We're going to have fun. Wait till next month when I can show him what I can do for him when I really try.

James thought, *My Elle, the angel, looks very special this way up. I have never seen any woman quite this sexy. Her shapely legs somehow set her body off to perfection. It's the way they form a particular shape as they separate, leaving a space to put my hand over the mound of black pubic hair and thank God for that. I really hate women that shave. Like an old-fashioned prostitute, they did it for basic hygiene. Why do some young women feel the need to be hygienic? What is wrong with a nice fuzzy minge, as we used to call it as boys. Muff diving is fun. You just bury your face in it. That's what I'm going to do. Bury my face and taste my baby. That's good. Lick up and down, slowly, with spit to lubricate as, under my stupid rule, I cannot dip my finger in to get normal lubrication. Up and down, round and round, find the clitoris, work it up with my finger and thumb, lick, suck, finger, thank goodness it's working. I thought that, after all the abuse she has taken, my baby might not react normally. My sexy little girl is close, she can't keep still, and her breathing is coming faster. Now I think it's time. Pinch between my finger and thumb. Yes, and again. Here we have a modest orgasm. Good girl, everything is fine. I can build on this.*

"Hello, baby cuddle up. Let me hold you. We're even now. One orgasm each."

"James, where did you learn to do that to a woman?"

"Do what, my love, make you cum?"

"No, James, suck me. No one has ever done that to me before."

"Really? I have always done that, my love. Maybe the first time was when I was sixteen and taken in hand by a twenty-year-old friend of my sister. I learnt a lot from her. I take it that you liked what I did."

"Yes, James. I can do with lots of that."

"Good girl, so you shall have lots of it. It's what I love to do, and much more besides. Now go to sleep. I will keep you safe while you dream of our future together.

CHAPTER SEVEN

Joan came for coffee again the next day. She embraced Elle. "It's all coming together, my dear, reading between the lines. No one will tell me, but I think they are near to having a daylight swoop on all the people that they have identified as guilty of an offence. They have to coordinate with the Polish police and other UK forces, then it's all go. Elle, your evidence was vital. I'm so proud of you. It is a strange situation. You will marry my ex-husband; you are not too much older than our daughters and I look upon you as a mother might. This is one strange situation we are in, is it not?"

"I can see what you mean, Joan. It would be unkind to suggest that I think of you as my mother, but I do look up to you for help and advice. James is older than me, but I am very experienced in the ways of men. Despite everything I have been through, or maybe because of my experience with so many men, warts and all, I appreciate their needs, which are not the same as ours. I love their weaknesses. Some nice married men are so driven by lust that they need a brothel. I should not say this, but James was a classic example last night. He does not know how to handle me with my history. He is careful not to act like a typical client. He has to hide his true desires. I love him so much for taking this much care with me. I have never had a man wanting to please me and not himself before. I love it and I know how hard it is for him to be so restrained. He will get his reward when we relax a little. Pleasing men is fun for me. The nice ones can be so sweet when they are satisfied."

"Elle, you are amazing. I must talk to you more and learn all your secrets. I'm useless with men; I just do not want to be an object of male lust. Shall we write a tell- all book?"

"Good idea—an instruction manual for new wives.

"Right, you can start with the avalanche of female exuberance that is about to descend on you. They know nothing of your past and that is the way we will keep it. They will love you and Lucy, you because you clearly have girl power to do what you have done to their father, the arch enemy of girl power, and lifelong womaniser; They cannot believe he has given it all up for one woman, but they will when they see you, and they will tease him mercilessly for his weakness. Lucy they will just adore. She will be totally spoiled. Such fun. I might just invite myself to watch—teach the old fool a lesson. Elle, believe me, we all love you, darling. Keep your strength up, I warn you now, anything can happen in this situation, especially when the press gets involved."

The front door slammed. There was a rush of feet across the hall. The door shot open and three girls burst into the room making a beeline for their father. They pulled him out of his chair and danced around him shouting, "Oh, Daddy, what have you done, oh Daddy, what have you done?" They pushed him back into his chair and fired questions at him. Eventually they gave him a hug and kiss each and moved to where Lucy was sitting, looking on in amazement.

"Now what have we here, girls? Oh my, aren't you the cutest little girl? May I pick you up, Lucy?" Leona said. "Don't be scared. We're only having fun. May I run around the room with you?" Lucy looked into her friendly face and nodded. The three girls danced around the room swapping Lucy between them, teaching her to sing, "Oh Daddy, what have you done."

Eventually they sat down beside Elle who, by this time, was sitting on James' protective lap. James introduced them all. "Elle, this is my eldest Leona, next is Lola then my baby Lisa. Now my super-baby, Lucy."

"Did you get stuck on the Ls then, James?"

"Looks like it, doesn't it, darling?"

"Well," Leona said, "I can see why you bagged this one, Dad. She is about the most beautiful woman I have ever seen, but what does she see in you? She could pull a film star with that body."

"Girls, please do not be disrespectful to Elle; she is not used to your loose talk."

"That's okay, James. Joan warned me what to expect. May I tell them exactly what you are so good at, James—my hero and super stud. There is nothing like a man with experience, girls, trust me. Your father obviously has had plenty of that, and it shows."

"Touché! Tell us later in private, Elle. You can give us all lessons. We need a sugar daddy to share and pay our living expenses."

"Come on," James called, "we're all going out to supper. Call your mother, one of you, we'll go to Charley's. They are a family restaurant."

They were enjoying a family gathering that consisted of James, one ex, one future wife, three daughters and a daughter-to-be. "This is typical of you, James," said his ex. "You and six women."

Elle felt emotional as she watched her beloved Lucy happily sitting among the three girls, being spoilt, her life transformed by a chance roadside meeting. She knew that things were going to get difficult because she didn't intend to hold back in denouncing their enemy to as wide a public as possible. She trusted these friends would stand beside them and give comfort and support.

James tapped his glass. He walked up to Elle and presented her with a small box. "Elle, my darling, will you marry me?"

Elle looked at him open-mouthed while everyone held their breath. It was all too much for her in her heightened emotional state. She burst into tears and cried.

James was mortified. He led her back to his chair and cuddled her. "Darling, dry your eyes. I am so sorry; I should have had more sense. You are very stressed just now."

Elle hugged him and said through her tears, "Yes, James, yes please, I want to marry you."

Joan was smiling, his daughters went mad trying to be first to congratulate the happy pair. Lucy held on to Leona who carried her to her mother and handed her over.

Elle held her daughter close and said, "Darling, I am going to marry James. He will look after us and we will be safe, do you understand that, my love?"

"Yes, Mummy, will he be my new daddy?"

James leaned down and kissed Lucy, then Elle. "You are both safe now, my girls. You don't need to worry any longer. You have me and this mad family to love you."

Later, at bedtime, Elle said to James, "You have proved to me your love. All you have done for us. Now we're engaged, and I have that beautiful emerald. I don't want any more proof, my love. Please give up the rule. It is now counterproductive. Hand jobs are not good enough to show our love for each other.”

“Yes, baby, it is now counterproductive, as you say. It’s over.” They went to bed with the same bathroom routine.

James took Elle into his arms. They stretched out, fully embracing each other, legs intertwined. He spent time kissing every part of Elle’s face; she kissed him back. Gradually James worked himself down Elle’s body, spending time getting her nipples fully hard. He kissed and massaged the inside of her thighs as he pushed her knees up. He gently parted her pubic mound with his nose as he followed it up with his tongue. As gently as he could, he licked his way up and down. He turned his attention to her clitoris, working it gently. James slipped a finger into her warm, wet, pleasure trove that, up until now, had been out of bounds. He worked away lovingly with finger and thumb until he felt the reaction he wanted. James instinctively knew when to move up, kissing his way until they were face to face. He reached her blushing face filled with love and expectation.

“It’s time, my love,” he whispered, and he eased himself inside her, determined to be a lover as different as possible from any previous partners. He took her in his arms, whispering in her ear, as he started a steady loving motion. Elle automatically pushed herself up to meet him. Together, they set up a mutual motion of pure satisfying, loving sex, but slow and gentle. To Elle this was bliss. A new experience and so different. Her lover was holding back, just to please her, to be gentle with her, ignoring his own needs. Elle would not be able to put into words how special this was for her.

Eventually she clung on to his neck and whispered, “It’s time for you now, James. Give me all you’ve got, Let yourself go and have fun.”

It didn’t take long. James came in a rush. Elle had a mild orgasmic experience, which she expertly exaggerated. Not entirely faked, as she had done many times before when she felt her lover had shown enough respect for her as a woman. They fell back on the bed, out of breath. They snuggled up together, kissed each other good night, and went to sleep.

She woke in the morning to see James watching her. “You are enchanting when you are asleep, my little angel.”

I have not known James awfully long, but I already feel so safe and comfortable. I love him with all my heart. I will devote my life to making him happy. To be the woman he wants me to be. I felt the warmth and love in the bedroom.

"James, put your pyjamas on. I'm going to fetch Lucy. I want her to share this moment with us."

Lucy was awake playing with her computer which Elle was sure she didn't yet know how to work, and was not actually plugged in. "Come with me, Lucy, darling. I want you to feel what true happiness is like."

In her short life Lucy has never witnessed love between a man and a woman. Not felt the love in the bedroom in the morning, never even had much love herself from her cold father.

"Come with me, darling. We are so fortunate, my little one. We have a man that genuinely loves us, he loves me and made me safe all night, and I want you to feel that as well."

She lifted her into bed beside James who was sitting up waiting. Elle climbed up beside them and sat against the pillows. James pulled them into his embrace and held them both.

"There, Lucy, my love," said Elle. "This is what it feels like to be happy with the man you love, as I love James, and as he loves us both."

James held Lucy's happy face in his hands and kissed her, then he did the same to Elle. It was all so warm and cosy. Lucy giggled as the new man in their lives tickled her and managed to slip a hand over her to tickle her mother, where it made her shiver.

"Right, girls," said James. "Enough now. Time to get up. Lucy, do you know where Cornwall is?" She looked confused, so he asked, "Have you ever been to the seaside?"

Elle realised that she never had and, in fact, had no idea what he was talking about. It was sad but true. Lucy was deprived, and so was she.

"Well, my two special girls. I have booked a hotel, so that is where we are going. Tomorrow we're going to the beach for a paddle.

James asked Elle if she could drive. This also took her by surprise. She had always seen the other mothers drive up to school, but never for a moment thought she would be able to do the same. She admitted that she couldn't. James said to her simply, "You will, my dear. There is a driving school not far from here where you can learn and pass your test. Then you shall have a car of your own."

Elle hugged Lucy and tried to come to terms with the idea that she might be free to drive her about wherever she wanted to without a man demanding a full report of her activities, then accusing her of lying and belting her. It was almost too much for her as clutched in her arms the one thing that she had from her life in England before James that had made it worth living, her Lucy.

That night in bed, James just wanted to hold her in his arms and play with her using his fingers and mouth, but mostly whispering love treats in her ears. It was sheer bliss as he caressed the cheeks of her bottom, confiding all the things he wanted to do with such a cute little bum. She couldn't help giggling as his thoughts got more and more outrageous and physically impossible. Elle know for sure one thing he wanted to do, and she was going to wait for the right moment, then do something really naughty and see what happened.

I cannot wait to have him take me over his knee. I can feel his hand now and then his fingers, sting and stimulate. I am as keen as he is. For some reason men often want to put me over their knee. But will I ever get used to a man not going straight for his own satisfaction, getting up and leaving me on the bed?

CHAPTER EIGHT
ELLE

Today we are going on our first ever real holiday. Lucy is beside herself with excitement. Some might think it impossible but neither of us have ever seen the sea. George took us for days out but never on holiday. It is truly an adventure for us both. Yesterday we went to the out-of-town supermarket and bought all the things James thought we would need for the beach and the hotel. We are to have a junior suite so we will be close together.

JAMES

In all my life, two marriages and bringing up three girls, I have never experienced the sensation of pleasure and satisfaction that I am now getting. My two girls are beside themselves with unbridled joy and excitement. Neither of them, sadly, have been loved by any man. Both have been deprived, and the one that has won my heart so completely, has been constantly abused, so neither has been on holiday before. They have no real concept of going to the seaside, poor babies. Just watching them load up my Range Rover, dancing around hugging each other, is giving me goose bumps and shivers. I love Elle so much; I want to take her in my arms and cuddle her. This is satisfaction way better than mere sex. God, how I love my two girls at this moment. They are true innocents. Hard to believe, with Elle's experience, but innocent she is of real-life experiences.

We headed west, making for the M5. Once on it, I shouted, "Who would like an ice cream?" they both shouted back, "I would," so I stopped at the first service station and we went into the café for a treat, where I joined in. We then cruised all the way down to the south coast and along the coast road until I found somewhere to stop overlooking the sea.

"There you are, girls, the big sea." They looked at it in silence, watching a fishing boat motoring out to sea. Further out, two tankers were passing by in opposite directions. All this fascinated the girls. We motored on until we reached our hotel sitting in the centre of a horseshoe bay with a sandy beach which, when the tide goes out, stretches away for at least five hundred metres to the sea. It is perfect for the girls' first visit to the seaside. The garden of the five-star hotel stretched down to the beach.

We checked in and were escorted up to our suite by the porter. We left the unpacking until later and went to explore. We went straight down to the beach where Lucy threw herself on to the sand and rolled about squealing. We walked around the bay, paddling in the water. Even for me, it was fun and very satisfying. Elle looking gorgeous in a skimpy sun dress, hugged and kissed me. I could see the love shining in her beautiful dark eyes and I was a happy man and very contented. What could be more satisfying for me than to experience the pleasure that I was giving to these two adorable girls, mother, and daughter, now mine to treasure and take care of? They deserve all the happiness that I can provide for them, a token compensation for the suffering that has been meted out to Elle and, therefore, second-hand to Lucy, by my fellow countrymen and women.

We made our way back to our room to change. I persuaded Lucy to wear a pretty little dress that we had bought for the holiday. I love my little girls to wear dresses, but I am happy for my big girl to wear her customary tight jeans. Nothing sets her shapely figure off better than jeans and a shirt or tight jumper. Having thought that, I must admit she would look even better in an old-fashioned mini skirt, but girls do not seem to wear them any more.

Tonight, we are going to have supper together as early as possible so that Lucy can join us. Tomorrow we will see if there is a babysitter we can hire for the evening while Elle and I have a gourmet dinner. We will not leave Lucy alone or with a baby alarm. She has never been separated from her mother, and I do not intend to ask them to do so now. But a suitable sitter should be fine for a couple of hours. Later, when we are living a normal married life, things will fall naturally into place.

ELLE

It is still surprising to me that any man can be so considerate, can take so much pleasure in making Lucy and me happy. It is just beyond my experience, even before England. Back home in Poland, men just do not worry about girls' interests as James does. Little things that get us excited, like calling "Who wants an ice cream?" A simple thing becomes fun. Big things, like taking us on holiday to the seaside and going for a paddle. Men do not really want to do things like that in my experience, but James seems to love it. Yes, any man is going to suck up to me for what he can get when we go to bed, but James does it as much for Lucy as for me, or so it seems. It takes so much strain off me to have him worry about my little girl. I have spent all our waking hours over the last few years making sure Lucy was not too adversely affected by our loveless existence. Now she is living in a world full of love, and I am living in a dream land where, to see our happiness, is all our lover seems to want from us. We are so lucky. My handsome James is so special, so strong and masculine.

The early evening meal was fun. We sat in the window overlooking the sea. We were a proper family. Lucy is so well behaved. She eats everything she is given, and chats away, happy as can be. James loves to talk to her. He can say the most ridiculous things, just to see her get confused and thinking. I am teaching her to call him a silly man when he does this, it is all so much fun. We must sort out school when we get back. James wants to send her to a nice little private school not too far away. Why not, if James wants to send her there. I want the best for her. They have a smart green uniform. I will be so proud when I see her dressed in that. My daughter at a private school. Who would believe that a month ago?

JAMES

We are going to walk to the other end of the bay where there are shops. It is fun to walk knee deep in the sea with little waves washing over our legs. It's a long time since I paddled in the sea. It is such fun with two excited girls. I am lucky not to have retired and gone native in the nightclubs. There is so much more living that I can now do as a family man again. I spy more ice creams.

ELLE

James is just like a little boy again. I swear he is more excited than we are. He has spotted ice creams and he obviously wants one as much as Lucy. I sometimes think that I am the adult and they are both children. "No James, thank you; I am eating too much and putting on weight. You would not like that, now would you?"

No, I must be careful. My body is truly the one special gift, together with my love, that I have to give in return for all that James is doing for Lucy and me. I must keep in shape. Fat is not an option. We sat in the seaside café enjoying the scene while drinking coffee. I bought Lucy a bucket and spade which she played with as we strolled back to the hotel along the sand. After showering the sand off we went on to the terrace for lunch.

A teenage girl came to our table and introduced herself as Elisabeth and did we still want a babysitter? I said we did for tonight, for three or four hours. She then said that she would like to sit for us. James asked her how much she charged. She was not sure, so he offered her fifty pounds, which she jumped at. It was agreed that she would come to our room at six o'clock and get to know Lucy before we went down to dinner. We spent a relaxing afternoon sitting in the sun in the garden while Lucy made sandcastles nearby on the beach, helped every now and then by James. It was just a perfect day for us all.

We dressed early for dinner while Elisabeth read a book to Lucy. It turns out that Elisabeth is also staying at the hotel and has sisters of her own. The receptionist asked if any of them would like to babysit another guest.

JAMES

Elle looks truly astonishing. Beautiful does not do her justice, in a simple black dress that I helped choose for her for the occasion, with its tight-fitting waist and bodice and simple three-quarter length skirt. Fitting nicely into the modestly cut neckline is her emerald necklace, and on her finger is my ring. I am stunned by how my angel looks, dressed as she is now. Naked she is the perfect sex goddess; dressed for dinner she has film-star class and beauty, but with no artificial aids or make up. Elle's hair, framing her pretty face, hangs in natural black ringlets down her back. In everyday jeans she turns heads. I cannot imagine what fellow guests will make of this. Elisabeth is staring at Elle.

Finally, she says, "Wow, you look great in that dress." Elle thanks her and I smile with pride, then take her in an embrace and tell her how proud I am to be escorting her to dinner looking like a film star and how much I love her. I put on my best blazer and a cravat to try and match Elle.

I asked Elle if she would like to have Champagne. She would love to, after having first tried it at the golf club. She explained that, in fact, she does not normally drink at all. We sat side-by-side on a sofa and gave our order to the head waiter Together we chose all fish as we are beside the sea. The waiter was very attentive towards Elle. Clearly, she was going to be well looked after wherever we go.

"Elle, tell me about your family. We still know so little about each other. So much has happened. We seem to have been too occupied to talk about ourselves."

"Actually, James, I do not know much about my own background. I was fostered, as my mother died when I was a baby and my father was unknown. My grandparents were not around but my adoptive mother told me she thought that they might be gypsy people. My new parents were good people, and loving. I had a happy upbringing and was always near the top at school. All was well until I got to my teens. At sixteen I was mature and looked much as I do today. It was about that time that I began to notice men staring at me, as they have done ever since, just like tonight. That was not unusual. Again, and like you James, they often focussed on my bottom as I walked past. One of those men was my stepfather. He didn't behave too badly but I was uncomfortable. I was streetwise and knew that he was lusting after me but ignored it until one day he went too far. He got me on the bed and tried to put his hand in my knickers. I belted him in the balls and escaped. Other than make a fuss, I had little choice. I gathered up a few things and ran away, much as I had done for a second time when you found me."

"You poor girl. But that would explain your beauty, a gypsy look."

"It also explains why I do not trust men. My experience with all men from the time I reached puberty has taught me that they only want one thing from me. Don't get excited, James, you are the exception. You, my love, have proved to me that you are different. I made up my mind years ago that by the time Lucy, who has my looks, gets to puberty I will be in a man-free environment. Now I am going to marry you instead. I love you, James, with all my being. I knew you were different and quite safe as soon as I came to in your house, just looking into your eyes. Then the promise you made me. More importantly the way you treated Lucy, like a person and with real love and affection, I know that you will look after my Lucy and keep her safe. Then, as if I needed more proof, your ex-wife promised me you were quite safe; she clearly still loves you. But, James, the final clincher for me was the invasion of your daughters. They swarmed around you, teasing. Clearly all three love you to pieces. That, James, is what I want for my Lucy when she reaches their age, to know safe love from her father. I expect that when I meet more of your friends, I will see there are more women that are looking at you with love and longing."

"I am no saint, Elle, my darling, and there are a few women that possibly do not dislike me as much as some of their husbands do. But one thing that I can promise is that I will always take great care with Lucy. I have a method for bringing up my girls as they grow. I develop their talents and interests, which may not be the same thing. Then as they focus on one subject, I push them to concentrate and learn the work ethic to gain maximum progress. Towards the end of school, I work with them as their friend. My Leona takes after her mother and is studying law. She will join Joan later this year. The other two are more like you and are both at medical school, starting the long haul to qualify. I love them all. They will make their mark. But your Lucy, she is super intelligent—wise beyond her years and emotionally stable. She will out-perform them all with the right support, which I shall give with your permission."

"James, please do it. It will make up for everything if Lucy can be educated and be what I never had the chance to be."

"Elle, it is never too late. When this is all settled, I will take you to the university and see a friend of mine. He can talk to you and see if there is a way for you to get more education. You do not have to use it you know."

We were shown to our table in the window by the head waiter and another colleague. A prime seat in the window with Elle having two of them usher her in and fawn over her while I seated myself. Something that I will just have to get used to. Actually, I love the attention Elle gets when I think of the state she was in just a few weeks ago. As I look at my wife-to-be with a glass of Champagne, deciding how to tackle a lobster starter—neither of which she has ever had before meeting me—I am filled with love to overflowing with the desire to give her so much more to make her happy little face smile. I want to get up and cuddle her. Sitting in the window overlooking the sea at night, in that simple dress with the emerald setting off stunning beauty, she is close to the apparition I saw beside the road. I have an overwhelming urge to take her up to bed. We both have Dover sole, then I have cheese. Elle refuses pudding. We go back and have coffee in the lounge, as we relax and enjoy the view out to sea at night. I cannot help it. I take her pretty little face in my hands, look into those big, almost black eyes and kiss her. The woman on the sofa opposite us smiles her approval.

ELLE

This is a new and amazing experience. A gourmet dinner in a five-star hotel. Two waiters escort me to the table and fuss me into a chair, giving me my napkin. I see James seating himself and love him for the way he puts up with all the attention I get as he looks after himself. This lobster is delicious, but I have no idea how I am supposed to eat it properly. My heart goes out to James. I do love him so, but he is so distracted. I wish he would just enjoy this dinner and leave me until later. He is bubbling over with hormones. He would rather be taking me upstairs and undressing me. It is special to be so wanted by my lover that he would rather take me to bed than enjoy this amazing food. Now at last we are seated in the lounge again for coffee. He does kiss me, and I love it, as does the woman on the other sofa. "Yes, James, it is time. Let's go up to the room now."

"Get ready, Elle."

I think this might be the night James, full of drink and seafood, forgets to treat me with kid gloves. Bring it on, and about time. I do love sex. After this dinner, what better than a rampant lover. Look out, girl.

Elisabeth is pleased to see us. James pays her and she tells us how she loved playing with Lucy, who is fast asleep in the annex, which is fortunate under the circumstances. We will let her know if we need her again, but we only have one more full day. I show Elisabeth out, and check up on Lucy who is fast asleep. By the time I reach the bedroom James is naked. He gets my dress off and I strip for him.

"Face up, or doggy?" I ask.

"Doggy please," he says excitedly.

Almost before I am ready, he is in me. "My, he is so wound up. He grabs my breast and my hair and slaps his thighs into my bottom. It does not take long. Wham, bang, and it is over; this is so familiar to me. I have no chance to get going and catch up. James falls on the bed, exhausted. Well, at least that has blown away the elephant in the bedroom. Hopefully, sex will be normal from now on—some loving and gentle, some like this. I can train him to slow down and keep it going. This will be fun for me, to teach James to fuck me properly and enjoy it more himself.

JAMES

God, what have I done to my baby? I am a callous brute. "Elle, my love, I am so sorry I got carried away."

"Yes, James, you did. Was it fun?"

"Honestly, darling, yes, it was what I needed. It has been building for days—in fact for weeks."

"I know exactly how you were my love and thank you for trying so hard for so long. I really appreciate it. You now have to accept that your innocent baby knows more about this side of our life than even you, a very naughty boy, does. You try anything you like from now on, and I will help you, while being submissive, which is what I want to be for you. By the way, I would rather feel your firm hand on my cute little bottom than your bony legs."

We both cuddled up together, kissing and giggling.

I wake up early and go to Lucy. She is asleep, but I get her up anyway and sit her on my knee. "I want you to know how happy I am, darling."

"Why, mummy, has James loved you again?"

"Yes, my love he has. He is such a good man. Always listen to him, my love. He wants to help you. Try to do as he asks."

"Do you mean like my sums, mummy?"

"What sums, darling?"

"James leaves a page of sums on my desk, then takes it away when I am not there. He puts it back with a sweet on each one I get right. Each time there are one or two I cannot do. It makes me so cross."

I am shocked and deeply moved at the way James has reached out to my Lucy and is already working on her education. Their relationship is unreal for a small girl and a middle-aged man to be so close so quickly. With anyone else, I would worry. Not James. He is safe. I know it for sure, but, if it continues for the next ten years, she will know exactly the type of man to look for as a husband.

I go back and jump on top of James to wake him up.

"My god, woman, what are you up to now? Cannot you leave a poor man to sleep in peace?"

"I wanted to tell you how much I love you. Last night you sorted me out very nicely. I know you do not think so, but I want to assure you that you did exactly the right thing. Sex has to be real in the moment of need. You needed to stop holding back and do what you finally did. A real man cannot always just please a woman. There are times when a man must answer nature, then he can make up to the one who should love him and understand his predicament, as I am unfortunately so well qualified to do my love. Frankly, James, I have watched your frustration building and I would have been a bit hurt if, after that dinner, you had not wanted me so badly that it boiled over as it did with last night's result. We girls have to know that, and make it easy for you, as long as you do it with loving intent and not too often. I will have my turn, you will see; I will also help you to make it last longer. You will get a better finish, and I will be able to meet you and come as well.

"But it is not just me, James. I hear you are working on Lucy's sums."

"Yes, Elle. Your daughter is a clever little girl and incredibly determined. She hates it that I do not let her get them all right. You watch. Sooner or later her frustration will get the better of her, and she will have a real go at me for teasing her. Elle, I adore your Lucy. Don't treat her as your baby any longer. She is exceptionally forward. You need to keep up and push her on. Make her your friend and ask her opinion."

"Thank you, James. Why are you so good with girls?"

"I love you all, I suppose. Women can be so much fun, so complicated and so utterly adorable, like you. A girl like Lucy, for example. I see her as a miniature you and automatically treat her as such. I do not see a child to be talked down to. To me it is interesting when she does or says things that no boy would do or say. Males are much simpler. As you just pointed out, sometimes a man is driven to do simple things, good or bad.

"Now, mummy , fetch Lucy. We must plan the day. Girls come here. Sit next to me, close together."

I look at my girls with their faces close together, they are just perfect, the prettiest woman you ever saw and a miniature version. They are just so special in every way, it is a mystery to me that anyone could be cruel to them. The pleasure they give me is priceless. I lean over and smooth their cheeks and kiss them.

"Now, who would like to go for a boat ride, maybe to see dolphins?" I have to explain what they were, so that is settled then. We have breakfast then drive to a local harbour that does trips around the bay and the dolphin or whale watching ones that I want to take them on.

ELLE

Lucy and I are in second heaven. James is so considerate. our lives are getting more exciting every day. who would have believed six weeks ago that my Lucy and me would be going out to sea in a boat full of people to find dolphins? It is sunny and not too rough. I have never been in a boat before and am a little scared, James is holding an excited Lucy, so she is not at all worried. We go out to sea and then turn along the coast; looking back to the cliffs from sea is something you would not imagine, with birds flying about, it is simply different. Someone shouts over there,

I cannot see anything, but then he shouts they are coming, then I spot them, maybe ten grey shapes skim at high speed towards us just under the surface of the water. They come alongside and swim with us, they are playing around the boat and appear to be laughing at us, swimming alongside then with a flick of a tail one would shoot ahead, cross over and come up the other side, diving back under and coming round again. you could lean down and touch them. It is such fun, Lucy is beside herself, jumping up and down, James is in his element holding her tight; she trusts him completely, as do I, it is so utterly perfect. The dolphins follow us for ten minutes or more then as quickly as they came, they disappear. We all clap and shout. I hug James and Lucy, is this all too good to be true, I love the sea.

We drive back to the cliff top café and have lunch, then James drops us off to walk back to the hotel along the beach, Lucy and me, mother, and daughter, happily walking hand in hand alone on a sandy beach. I am beginning to understand and believe that James does not have any ulterior motives, I can see that he is in fact getting great pleasure playing with us, he genuinely enjoys seeing us happy. It was not a concept that I understood or accepted, and I have worried ever since we met that it would all fall apart when he started to demand that I do things for him that I have been forced to experience with some men and have resolved that I will never do again for anyone. But now I know how disloyal and ungrateful I have been, is it that I was afraid to believe. But now I truly do as I watch him laugh and play with Lucy.

Back in the room I cling on around James's neck and hug and kiss him, forcing him on to the bed. He pulls me into a tight cuddle, and asks what this is all about. I am kissing him as I thank him for what he has done for us. He is so sweet, he holds my face in his big hands and kisses me back. We lie like this until Lucy comes in and jumps on top of us, breaking the spell. We decide not to have a babysitter; that would split us up. As a compromise we will eat early and let Lucy stay up.

JAMES

The head waiter escorts us to the lounge as before, and this time he makes a fuss of Lucy, who looks so pretty in her dress and socks and shoes, then he shows Elle to a seat. I make my own way, resigned to being a second-class diner forever more. I find this all so satisfying. Elle and Lucy cannot disguise their excitement and the pleasure of being in a luxury hotel dining room together, these two are simply inseparable due to their sad history, Lucy has no idea what is to come, she has never been in a hotel before. As we are led to the dining room, a young waitress rushes up and grabs Lucy and tucks her in to her seat. The waiter appears to bow and scrape in front of Elle as they progress towards the table, I attempting to hide my amusement stroll along behind, either because of the girls themselves or the behaviour of the waiters the other diners stop eating and watch. One woman catches my arm and askes who is she. I explain just my girlfriend and that the staff are all quite mad. We laugh. I must bring my phone next time and film the effect my girls have on hotel staff it really seems to make their day as it does mine.

ELLE

James and I decide to have fish again, a sole meunière starter and a seafood platter to follow. Lucy, bless her, says she will have the same. I add chips to the order just in case and ask for a children's starter. The sole is lovely, simple with a tasty sauce. Lucy ate it all. The seafood was a surprise to me and to Lucy; we had no idea it was shellfish, in their shells and cold. When I got used to the idea, I enjoyed it. James could see Lucy was intimidated by the sight, he would not let her try and be put off forever, he ordered fish fingers for her to go with the chips. Having had three of his own, James knows so much more about bringing up girls than I, her mother.

Back in the lounge with our coffee, I could see we made a perfect family unit and it made me immensely proud, but I am gradually getting used to the idea. I get the waiter to take a picture on James's phone. I long for our wedding when this will all become enshrined in law, hopefully for us to live happily ever after. James picks up a tired Lucy and carries her upstairs to our room and her bed. We order room service for coffee and brandy, then sit chatting about all the things that have happened over the last few weeks. We eventually slip into bed cuddle up and go to sleep.

What bliss waking up beside James who is still asleep, I quietly get up and go and get into bed with Lucy. I hold her in my arms and ask her what she thinks of our holiday by the seaside. She surprises me by not producing a catalogue of the delights, ice cream and others and her love for James. Instead, after thinking, she describes the feeling of walking over the sand barefoot and paddling in the sea, the sea coming past the boat in waves which made it go up and down over them. But most of all, in great detail, the dolphins just under the surface, their noses, and eyes. I looked at her serious little face and for the first time I realise what it is that James was telling me; even at this age she is not my baby any more, she is her own person, a serious minded one. I take his advice and discuss the points she has made that are important to her. I think there is a lesson for me here, I must make sure I am not just James's little baby, I must be his equal or he will be soon be bored with me and send me to wait for him in the bedroom while he talks to Lucy.

Our last day, so I go back to the room after breakfast to pack while James and Lucy go to the beach for a last paddle. James pays while the porter brings down the bags, and we pack the car and leave. We play I spy on the way home, something we all enjoy, and Lucy takes it very seriously. At home when we are all sorted, we go into the kitchen and sit at the table for tea. To my astonishment and delight we have a further example of Lucy's rapid development and social skills under the influence of our new situation and new life. She looks at James and thanks him very much for taking her on holiday. He looks equally nonplussed but delighted. He picks her up and stands her on her chair, holding her tight as he gives her a kiss. He whispers something in her ear and Lucy smiles at him indulgently as he puts her back in her chair. I continue to look from one to the other in wonder. Which of us is his true girlfriend, and how lucky we are to have a man that loves us both.

CHAPTER NINE

Joan phones and arranges to visit for tea and a chat. We settle down in James' study with our tea and cakes. Joan asks us if we saw the papers while we were away, and we say no, only for her to produce a file of newspaper cuttings.

"Well, it was all over the news," she points out. "Ten girls taken into care and fifteen arrests, five still in custody, from five brothels based over the south of the country."

I jump up with joy. "Is George among them?"

"Yes, Elle, he is."

It is like a cloud has been lifted, I am so happy. He is surely on his way to prison and we will be free to move about without fear of bumping into him.

"Next, your passport is ready, Elle, I will take you up to collect it any time, then you two will be free to marry."

We tell Joan all about our holiday and she smiles at James when she sees my excitement. Then I tell her all about the relationship that has grown between James and Lucy and her sudden burst of development with the stimulation.

Joan regards her ex. "I think you could call our James the girl whisperer, Elle. He had endless patience with our three and they all blossomed. What do you say, James?"

"I say that I loved our three and their education, but I have to tell you both that Lucy is ahead of any of them at this age. She is not only highly intelligent, but more than that, she is so mature and serious minded for one so young, she is more like a bright teenager, we are going to need help to advise on her schooling.

"I will fill her room with educational toys and brain aids and books, and we will see what she takes an interest in. So far she seems to study nature quite seriously, the dolphins and butterflies. A Mensa test will surely be next. By the way, Joan, her mother is also bright, although she does not know it. I will have a go at her education as well. Maybe they can go to university together, or perhaps start their own company, mother and daughter, Lucy the boss."

I look at him with surprise; he is serious, I think, I would love to study physiology, I tell him.

"It's Lucy's birthday next week, can we have a party?" I ask him.

"Good, yes please, I love parties. Joan, how many young children do we know these days, and the girls must be there, they will love it."

Time for bed, we are in relaxed mood tonight, so I intend to treat James to my best massage experience. We shower together, soaping each other all over, a long soak under the waterfall, and we help each other to dry and go to bed. I spread several towels over the bed, place the baby oil in warm water and lie on top of my lover, kissing and caressing his face. I run my hands through his hair, rub noses and tell him to turn over. I tip warm oil up and down his back, give his bottom a sudden good spanking just to be first to do it. We both laugh at my cheek and fortunately he is now too relaxed to retaliate, so I escape for now, but I will have to watch out. I give his back a firm but sensual massage, ironing out a few knots that are there. As I work down and between his legs, I slip under far enough to hold his balls gently and briefly. I work down to his feet and all the way back up to his neck, then turn my lover back over again.

Once I have oiled him all over his front, I do the same to myself. I climb on top of him, face to face, and slide up and down, rubbing my breasts against him all the way from his face to his cock, I give him a nice long breast massage; with my nipples now hard it feels good to both of us. Next I swing around to face his feet and do the same again only this time I push the pubic mound that he loves so much into his face and pause for him to lick me. I suck his cock on the down movement, pausing again. I slide up and down, enjoying myself as I have as much fun as he does. It is A body to body experience for both of us. I am small enough to slide about covering his whole body. Eventually, I sit astride him and lower myself down over his hard erection, face to face, and ride him like a jockey on a horse. I watch his expression closely; at the right time I speed up to a canter and ride him into a pretty decent orgasm. As I lay down on top again, he holds me and whispers his love and thanks. We do not move for some time, just enjoying the shared intimacy. This is true girl power, the ability to satisfy the man that I love in all his various moods, from receiving the brief but necessary explosive sex of the other night to giving tonight's long, sensual, play massage. James has promised to always take care of me and Lucy; in my way I will take care of him with love and whatever he needs. I will also become the best housekeeper that I can be when we marry, not the reluctant one that I was for George.

I wake early, still holding James, I gently massage his cock back into life then roll over and open my legs to be rewarded with the loving that I have often wanted but never experienced before, a lover still in my bed in the morning wanting to give gentle affectionate sex as a loving encore after the main event the night before. We embrace, kiss and move together slowly, all the way to a gentle escape of breath, bliss for me. James utterly understands my needs and when to be gentle. Time to get up shower and get breakfast for my family.

Joan arrives after breakfast and asks me if I will come with her to the hospital to interpret for the authorities and one of the young rescued women. Poor girl, she is so very young, as I remember that I was. Somehow I never felt as vulnerable as she looks, my upbringing and stepfather perhaps made the difference, but I learned to take it in my stride, even blank out the trauma of the early days, perhaps enjoy some of the fun times with the other girls and a few of the men. I sit by her chair and talk to her; it seems she has a few bruises and is in an emotional state, but otherwise appears to be in good health. I ask the social worker why she is here; it seems more for protection and her mental health; she is free to leave but has nowhere to go. The council will presumably have to look after her.

We are taken to a side room where two young policewomen are waiting to question her. We record her statement; it seems she has only been in the country for a week and no doubt because she is so vulnerable has not yet been subject to the sort of treatment that I and most others received to make us come to heel and work. Nonetheless, she has been raped, which she describes in detail, naming names, I do not like to ask if she was a virgin but presume not, as she does not say so, which she surely would if she had been, as I was. I ask what will happen to her, for like me she comes from a broken home and has no one to go back to, a pattern no doubt that to some extent explains why this traffic continues. As I suspected, she will go to a shelter. I ask Joan if it is possible for me to take her home and look after her until something can be arranged, She says she will ask the council then phone James. Joan goes away to phone then comes back. Bless James, of course, one more woman is fine by him. I explain it to Ava, and she jumps at the offer.

So here we are all round the kitchen table with a girl that speaks little English. I can see James wants to treat her as he did me, but I warn him to keep his distance for now. She is in no state for male attention, however well meaning. Lucy is interested in talking to her in Polish and they bond easily. Ava trusts Joan, and is grateful to me as her friend, so all is set to normalise her situation as far as we can. I take her up to a spare room next to Lucy's and explain all about myself, where I came from and how I was tricked just as she was, and how James rescued me. This makes her much happier and she visibly relaxes. She is just a nineteen-year-old girl who suffered abuse in a strange country and now needs time and loving care to repair the damage, I know James will ensure she has this and the rest of us will deliver it.

Today already Ava is a different girl, she is teaching Lucy to use her computer, something James and I are both a little ignorant about. She is clearly well educated and speaks well in her native language. Lucy may well be the best one to teach her English as they struggle to communicate over the computer. James is sitting back and watching them with obvious interest. As I speak to her, I always translate at the same time.

Clever, kind James, he has been out and bought a basket full of continental brand treats and presented them to Ava. Lucy takes it in her stride. She has no idea what is behind it all, it is another girl like the sisters she found so much fun, this time speaking a foreign language which she can learn.

James wants to know if I think Ava would like to be employed by us, to help me in the house and be a companion to Lucy; he clearly wants to extend this brainstorming they are doing as they learn the computer. It works so well because Ava uses the computer to translate into both languages and display the instructions on the screen. For Lucy, it is a new skill and a second language, my language; that must be good.

I take Ava to one side and explain what we would like and how much we value the influence she is having on Lucy. She jumps at the idea of earning some money and being able to have time to look at her options in England. She would like to make teaching her career. We agree a three-month deal, and she says she is interested in teaching, having worked with Lucy who is very clever girl, and she enjoys working with her on the computer and learning to speak Polish. She will also help with other subjects if Lucy wants to learn.

James is delighted, what a bonus for his education endeavour. He asks me to explain that she can make this her home and that we will be happy to support her if she can qualify for teacher training, or even perhaps the university. Ava looks at James, not sure how to react to such a generous offer. I know exactly how she feels, it took me a long time not to suspect that James has ulterior motives behind his generosity, Ava will just have to make up her own mind over time.

"Elle, will you ask Ava to look after Lucy for an hour as we go out to the bank. Time to get you fixed up with an account, my love."

We drive to the main branch of James's bank and are ushered into the manager's office; he is a friend of James, it seems.

"Hi, Fred, may I introduce Elle, you have heard all about her from Joan, I believe."

"Yes, I have, I am pleased to meet you, Elle, but I was not told she was a film star, James. Come and sit down, Elle, would you both like a coffee? Right, then I have what you asked for all sorted for you, James. First, Elle, I have a credit card on one of James's accounts. I believe this card is for all your domestic expenses. It gets paid off automatically at the end of every month therefore attracts no interest charge. I am sure James will explain its use, there is no limit so do not worry about that, it will not bounce. The pin etcetera is all there, again if in doubt ask James.

"This one is to be your own private account, Elle. It comes with debit and credit cards, this will be internet banking if you can manage to do that, you can, good. Only you will have access, it is guaranteed by James as you are not known to the bank, so no problem if it runs over the limit. Come over here, please, sit at this desk and sign the forms and fill out the details, answer the security questions. Then we can have a test run if you like, unless you are familiar with internet banking."

I fill out the forms with all the details and questions, inventing my password in my head which I must write down before I forget, and take them back to Fred.

"Right, Elle, we go on the website on his computer, personal banking, now you have to invent and keep secret a password, eight letters, you have already, good, I will look away."

Eventually, after much help and prompting, it is all set up and I gain access to my own bank account , only to discover that I already have a credit balance of five thousand pounds. I was so taken aback and yes, I am still in an emotional state, I burst into tears. I could not help it, the idea that I had that much money in my own private account to spend as I pleased, it took me completely by surprise. I have never had any money of my own before, only a joint account controlled and closely monitored by George. It was immediately obviously to me that James expected a such a reaction and had set me up, because both men were watching me expectantly as I gained access. James knew full well that I would react and that this this might happen. I could see Fred's face soften with pleasure as he watched my reaction. It was obvious that he wanted to hug me, but James got there first. As we left, I said, "That was mean, James, you knew that would happen, didn't you?"

"Yes, my love, I did and I am sorry to do it to you, but you looked so adorable and surprised. I wanted to show my friend, Fred, exactly what sort of a girl you are. Now he will tell all our friends that you are the genuine article not some gold digger, you really did not expect to have any money in your account, did you? And thank you, I also won a fiver on the bet."

I said, "Thank you, my love, for the account and for the money. Wait till I get you in bed."

"No, Elle, you will not pay me in bed. When will you stop saying that? I have told you before, your reaction was all the satisfaction I needed from you, you pay me in love, not sex, that is for us both of us to give each other. "

JAMES

How sad and cruel that just like Elle, Ava should be caught up in this trade in girls. If I could have done something I would have, but now it is too late, it is all closed down, but for how long. There has to be more publicity, men using the girls must be made aware of the possibility that they are not willing workers and be asked to shop the house, no awkward questions asked.

On the plus side, Ava is very much my sort of girl, quite like my own three. She is bright and apparently wants to study. It is a wonderful break for Lucy learning the computer in Polish, her mother's tongue, what could be better than that.

Now that Elle has the housekeeping credit card I am going to ask if she and Ava would like to take a taxi and go shopping for clothes and any other necessities that the women might require. They must feel free to shop as they want, In future, Elle needs to realise I am well off and she is able to go and get anything reasonable that she wants for herself, Lucy or Ava on that and anything at all on her own, which I will top up until we marry, then make better arrangements for her.

ELLE

James sent us shopping with my housekeeping card. We all three had fun buying things we need and a few extra treats. I found some sexy underwear to try on him, Ava has no suitable coat and has bought a rural type waxed jacket which suits her and will be most use.

Later James asks me to bring coffee and cakes to his study for a talk. I wonder what that is all about. We sit in his cosy room, just a man cave really, I am not too sure how much of an office James actually needs. He does not seem to work there and is not an office type person.

"Elle, my darling, there is something we have to discuss. It is not something I want to talk about, but it is not fair to you, as my fiancée not to discuss it. That is money. Only Joan knows the state of my finances and that is because she is my lawyer, not because she is my ex-wife. Any wife, as you will soon be, is entitled to know that her husband is not going to go bust and get the house repossessed, or that the bailiffs are not going to arrive and grab the TV. So, I will give you an overview of my affairs to reassure you for the future, without going into detail. Elle, this is all strictly for you alone and confidential. Please keep it to yourself and never speak of money to anyone else. I particularly like to keep my girls in the dark as to my actual wealth. We will not need to have this discussion again after I explain my position to you.

"My story is that I built up a successful engineering business over twenty years. During that time, I patented two devices that have now become standard equipment on most oil installations in the oceans around the world. Things were always tight for us as a family, so we didn't live in luxury. I was pursued by a number of companies and funds to sell out my patented products, but I resisted for several years until eventually I was persuaded to sell my whole company to a much larger rival who just kept upping the offer until I could not refuse it. I gave in and I sold out for a sum in excess of ten million pounds. I invested my money wisely and made more, quite a bit more actually. That's it, Elle, really, my secret, so you see you have no need to worry about money or be too grateful for the money in your account. It is actually rather mean, and I can assure you is only a down payment to get you started. Once we are married, I will set up a formal arrangement for you. I am already preparing trusts to provide for you and Lucy in the event of anything happening to me, so your future will be safe and assured you have no need to worry. We can help all the girls and do charity work if you want to. Lucy will always be treated exactly the same as my other three daughters, now and in my will."

I was shocked at this news, I had realised that James was not short of money, but this is hard to get my head round; he has much more than ten million pounds. When he adopts my Lucy, as he wants to, she will have a super wealthy father. I do not know what to say, this transforms everything. My lover is a multimillionaire, is that good. I am a simple sort of girl. I do not want that much, I do not want a life of luxury. What is wrong with me, if I am not careful I am going to cry again and I don't know why, does this make a difference? Am I good enough for such a rich man, that is what worries me.

JAMES

I can see my darling is shocked. I do hope nothing changes, but this must be hard for her to come to terms with. I take her in my arms, as she is looking emotional again.

"Elle, darling, nothing has changed. I am the same person, we are still in love, money is not important to me, as I believe it is not to you, but think of the good we can do with money. These girls, for example, we can save Ava and get her a career. Lucy can do whatever she wants, as can mine when they leave university. Like my girls, they will not know we are rich. They will work hard as we oil the wheels. If you want to, so can you, baby, you can do whatever you want to. I love you, Elle, you look and feel adorable. I want to take you upstairs and cuddle you properly. Please don't cry."

ELLE

My problem is I cannot see how I deserve all this; the love was enough but the money as well, I have done nothing to deserve it. I am poor girl that worked in the sex industry. James should have someone from his own country. His friends will never accept me when they find out the truth. It is not going to work. I cannot hold back my fear and dread of the future.

JAMES

Elle is inconsolable and I really do not understand quite why, does money make that much difference? My angel is so soft and vulnerable, so very feminine. There can be no better example of a young woman that has suffered as she has and come through it without turning bitter. My job is to help her recover and fulfil her ambitions, but first I must try to understand what is troubling her now. Maybe Joan can help me, why would me being wealthy upset her so?

ELLE

Joan has come for coffee to check up on Ava. We three sit and watch Ava and Lucy. It really is amusing, they are playing some game on the computer, talking six to the dozen, but in what language? It seems every other word is either Polish or English mixed up, they have invented their own computer language. James is fascinated I can see that. He drifts away to get a closer look.

Joan asks me how I am managing. James, it seems, has told her that I was upset by his money. I try to explain to her that James should have an English wife because I am not going to be acceptable to his friends, I am afraid it is all going to end in my being rejected. I cannot see how a man with that money can spend it on me, I am not worth it. Now Joan has made me emotional again, I cannot shake off the feeling that it will all end in tears.

JOAN

Oh dear, poor Elle, she has decided that she is not good enough for James. She feels his friends will reject her when they hear her history. How do I go about this? I call James. "Sit down, both of you. It's ridiculous that we should still be having this conversation. This has got to end here and now, James. Elle thinks she is not good enough for you and your friends. You need to work harder to convince her that she is, meet some of them and introduce her. I know all our friends want to support Elle, they are horrified by her treatment. Elle, you have got to stop feeling that you are not good enough and look at the simple facts. You two are perfectly matched. James is older than you, Elle, he has everything except a wife. You, Elle, are the perfect wife. All you need for yourself and Lucy is a husband that loves you and Lucy, with enough money to look after you both. James fits the bill perfectly. That, my dears, in my opinion, is a match made in heaven. When I say perfect, Elle, you know that well enough. Is there any woman that can make a better wife than you? You are also intelligent, sensible, and tolerant, not to mention your looks. I would say James is the lucky one here."

ELLE

We both look at Joan with surprise, I doubt this is what James expected, certainly I didn't. James starts to laugh, and we all join in. James picks me up and cuddles me. "Not good enough for me, is that what you think, my angel, I will soon put you right on that. Stay for lunch, Joan, and thank you, I had not realised that was the problem for Elle. This afternoon I have something to show you both."

"Good man," said Joan. "I think I can guess what that is, that should do it."

After lunch, James said, "Get your coats, all of you and get in the car. We are going out."

He drives us to the outskirts of the town and into a gateway leading up to a large house. James has a key and goes straight into the entrance hall. He takes me in his arms and asks me to do him a favour. I ask him what he wants. He says for me not to cry when he demonstrates how much he loves me. I agree and James says, "I love you so much, Elle, that I have asked Joan to arrange the purchase of Dunwood House in both our names. It will be finalised the day we marry, and you will own this house equally with me. Elle, that is how much I love you."

Well, how do I keep my promise after that bombshell? Ava looks at me and wants to know what is being said. Eventually I tell her, and she goes straight up to James and kisses him, saying in English, "That is thank you, for my friend."

Joan is smiling at me. She says, "Enough now, Elle, believe in yourself and prepare to be the wife and mother that will go with this house, and the man that truly loves you."

I resolve, not for the first time, to stop feeling sorry for myself and look forward to being a good wife to my beloved James.

James has gone to play golf with friends which gives me a chance to talk to Ava and Lucy, who has been watching the goings on here and in our new house. She is puzzled and wants to know what James means about me owning half the house. I explain that when I marry James we are going to live in the new house and that I will own it with James, equally, it will be our family home. I can see that Lucy is struggling with the whole concept of me owning half a house, so I leave her to think it through and speak to Ava. I speak to her in English and ask how much she has picked up. She was, of course, already learning before she was taken to hospital. She replies in Polish to explain that she understands everything that is said quite well but cannot speak enough to have a good conversation. What we will do, I tell her, is to have lesson every evening after supper. I explain to her we will have an hour and Lucy can learn Polish at the same time. "What do you think of James now, Ava? I saw you kiss him, that was good for you both. I do know exactly how you feel about men, but if you start with James you will gradually learn to trust again."

"Yes, Elle, I like James. He is very good with us all, especially Lucy. He loves you very much, you are a lucky Polish girl, Elle." I agree with her and warn her to watch out when his daughters visit; that is love on a grand scale.

Lucy has reached a conclusion. She believes that James is buying a new house because we do not fit into his old one any more. He is giving half to me because he is sad that I do not have a house or car, and he loves me. Well, I do not know what I expected, but Lucy has made me think, wake up and smell the coffee, more or less what Joan was trying to tell me. I have been selfish and self-indulgent. So unfair to James who is trying to make up for the years that we have suffered because he loves me and innocent Lucy can see that. If I cannot, I do him no favours by being pathetic. My job is to make James happy and as Joan hinted, I am eminently qualified to do just that, so that it is exactly what I shall do from now on. No more self, just give as much back as I can to the man that has saved us both.

James comes home and I rush up and welcome him. I hug and kiss him and gently stroke his cock with my knee. He looks at me with surprise and then bursts out laughing. I see the funny side and join in, maybe that was a bit over the top. James picks me up and carries me to the sofa. He asks me what brought that on.

"Our new house, James, when we live there it will be just perfect. I cannot get used to the idea that it is for me, everything has happened so quickly. I want to show you how much I love you. "

"Elle, please don't try, all I want is that you just behave normally. You are perfect, my angel, just as you are. You do not have to act, just be yourself, please."

I tell James that he can pay more attention to Ava, she is ready for some gentle loving care, but do not frighten her.

JAMES

Good, I can pay more attention to Ava. I so want to show her some love to repair some of the damage. Only a man can really do that, it is men that have abused her. I am going to join them at the computer and have an impromptu English lesson.

"Hi girls how are you today?"

"We are having fun," Lucy says.

Ava looks at me, trying to decide why I have come, I presume.

"Ava, how are you today?"

She looks at me while she thinks. "Fine, thank you, how are you?"

"I am very well, thank you."

We have this sort of conversation for half an hour. I pick up her hand and kiss it and say goodbye. She smiles at me. I think she realises I am going to pay her more attention and says, "Goodbye, James"

Later I notice that Ava is crying her eyes out. This is unusual, she never gets emotional. I go and stand her up and embrace her. She puts her head on my shoulder and sobs. I whisper comforting things which she will not understand, but she'll get the message. I send Lucy for her mother.

ELLE

Lucy comes running and tells me Ava is crying. I go to the kitchen and initially think that James is somehow hurting her, then I realise he is comforting her and keep back to watch. He is being very James at his best, Ava appears to be loving it. He holds her face and kisses her forehead; she kisses him back and stops crying. My heart leaps; it is a special moment in her recovery. I go up and ask her what the matter is.

She tells me, "I have just realised that today is my birthday, and no one knows, I have no family to care."

I look at James and tell her in Polish that someone obviously cares for her, and that so do Lucy and me. She thanks me and tells me I am lucky, can I find her a James.

We are all going out to dinner tonight to celebrate Ava's birthday. Joan is coming with her husband Simon, the judge. James and I have been out to buy a few gifts for Ava which we are giving her as we have tea and a birthday cake. It is all going very well, I have banned Polish, so Ava is speaking in English, not badly as it happens. Ava is now part of the family. James does not need to say it, but I know he is not going to let her go. He is going to ensure that she has some sort of education and future before she leaves his house. James is truly a pied piper for girls, three daughters, me, Lucy, surely to be adopted as a daughter of the future, now Ava a Polish version of his three; six women and James, who we all love in our own different ways.

This is special, we are in a posh country restaurant, James has got a private room at short notice so we are all sitting around a large round table. The judge is fun, Simon Tweed, telling all sorts of tales that, if true, he should not be repeating. The seating is interesting. Lucy has followed James and is sitting beside him, Ava has also gone to sit on his other side. I cannot explain his quiet appeal to them, two completely different females, but I love it. I will sit beside Ava in case she wants to translate anything. James is helping Lucy chose from the menu with great patience. I should perhaps be put out by her preferring to have James help her, but I am actually over the moon with happiness as I watch the two people that I love above all else, so close and trusting with each other.

James makes a short speech wishing Ava a happy birthday. Ava replies in English thanking us all, then adds more in Polish. I translate for her. She wants us all to know how grateful she is and how she would like to keep her job for longer to learn English and see what is possible for her in England. James stands up and assures her that she can stay as long as she likes, and she is not an employee but a friend. Ava understands and thanks James saying that she will earn her keep by helping me and doing what she can for Lucy. We all clap. James looks embarrassed but pleased with the result. When we finish eating, Simon presents Ava with a jewellery box from Joan and himself to say sorry for the way that she has been treated in our country. I translate to make sure she understands. The box contains an expensive gold bracelet. I can see that Ava is nearly in tears, I know I would already be crying, in fact I am quietly sobbing, it is all so perfect. I like the judge.

JAMES

My Polish gang are having fun helping Lucy to bed. They appear to be talking in Polish, does Lucy understand already? I would not put it past her, I would not put anything past that exceptional little girl. She is developing so fast now she has stimulation, we must get expert advice on her education needs.

ELLE

James is waiting for me in the bedroom, that is different, it is rather early. I will shower and join him naked. I want to feel him close to me. I am excited by everything that is happening to us all in his house. I must give James everything he wants from me, representing his Polish girls, including Lucy, his pride and joy.

"Elle, my love, come here. You smell so good, you are a gorgeous little baby. Cuddle up, I want to explain something to you. I really had no idea that you thought that you are not good enough for me. We are so close you surely must know how much you mean to me. You are my life now, I cannot now live without you, you must know that. When I saw you at the roadside, I loved you for the image that I was seeing. But later, when you came to and I looked into your eyes, it was in that instant that the magic happened, as it has to me before. It is a meeting of minds, almost a merging of our brains, a complete understanding and knowledge of everything about you as a person. It was a recognition of a deep mutual love and a promise of lifelong union. I know it was the same for you, baby. I felt your response, you knew we were one it at that moment, so what went wrong to cause you to have such doubts?"

"Yes, you are right, James, I knew you, just as you say, at that moment. I knew you would not hurt us, that you loved me and always would. I saw my future with you and felt safe."

"Well, then, baby, if you know that I cannot live without you by my side, is that not enough for you who could be worth more to me. Why the doubt now?"

"I am truly sorry my darling, it is not rational, put it down to my life experience. I was being pathetic. It will not happen again. We will build a family together in our new house. Now what do you want with me tonight, lover boy?"

"Elle, my love, I want to hold you close, baby, and go to sleep beside you. Your amazing cuddly little body, naked, is all I want, just to hold and dream."

James is still asleep; the joy of this early morning feeling and warm smell of two people sleeping together. Why am I naked while James has his pyjamas on? I cannot remember. I undo the cord of his trousers and find his cock and balls. I do not want to wake him, so I take him in hand very lightly. I lick gently around the tip; my lover is stirring. I wait then go again, I slowly work it up then suddenly, bang, he must have woken up and got his brain into gear and thought sexy thoughts because it has shot up to full size. I hold his balls as well and work harder. James is groaning and will soon have to cum. I speed up and work him hard by hand and mouth, then squeeze his balls, while I nip the end of his erection. Wow, that was rather more than I expected. He nearly throws me off the bed when he cums, covering me with his life juice as I go. I struggle back and up to his face; he laughs when he sees the state I am in.

"Serves you right, you wanton hussy. Cannot a man sleep in peace any more?"

I get off the bed to go and shower. My man gives my bottom a hard smack with his hand as I go.

"Watch it, girl," he shouts, "any more of this insubordination and you will be across my knee."

"Yes, sir, please." This is my sort of fun, a real man of my very own to wind up, happy days.

When I return my man is pretending to be asleep, stretched out on the bed. I climb up and sit on his face.

"You love my bum so much, so have some more, James," I whisper in his ear.

His response is to give it a bite. I squeal and grab him round his neck and try to smother him into submission with my breasts. It's no good, I am never going to win this fight. I get seriously manhandled and finish up face down over his knee with a firm hand stinging my bitten bottom. He holds me close, laughing at me and my feeble attempts to fight him. He tells me that in any case I do not fight fair; bottoms and breasts are not supposed to be weapons. I tell him that I would not get far if I didn't use all my assets, to which he points out that I will never win anyway, but keep trying it's fun. Well, yes, maybe for him, poor deluded, masculine darling. He is kissing me and goes exploring with his hands.

"Elle, I adore you. I love you so much. You are not only the most beautiful and sexy woman, but a bundle of fun as well. Let me hold you tight. I have never ever had this much fun in bed. Now tell me, you little minx, you knew exactly what to expect when you attacked me like that, go on admit it."

"Yes, well, I think you are pretty much a stereo typical alpha male, James. Look at all you have given to me and to Lucy; in return I will always give you as much fun as I can, it together with my love is all I have to give you back. We love each other, we are always going to have sex, in every way I can think of."

"So, admit it, that is what you expected would happen to you just now, you adorable little angel, and the inevitable result, go on, admit it. You did it for me to have my fun, you are so incredibly special, Elle, my baby."

"Maybe I did, my love. I felt sorry for you. I know how much you have wanted to spank my cute bottom and yes, I thought it time you had your fun, not that I didn't enjoy it just as much. It was fun, I love being manhandled."

"Thank you, baby girl, you are one in, a million I love you so much. Was it too hard for you, did it hurt?"

"Actually, James, you got it just right. Any less, it would not be worthwhile; much harder, I might begin to worry that you were trying to hurt me. That would be a real setback for me."

Little does he know that I do have a plan involving handcuffs while he is asleep, but would I dare risk the punishment? I just might, but I am not quite sure how mad he really would be. I might finally push him over the limit of his super tolerance. Better wait a month or two to be sure I know him in all situations. I do not want to provoke too much aggression, that really would be a setback for me, for sure.

Breakfast is English Continental, nothing cooked but cereal and pastries, cold meats, and fruit, both fresh and tinned. Everyone is chatting away happily. I address Lucy in Polish, asking her how she is today. She answers me in Polish, saying she is fine, thank you, we all look at her in astonishment. Ava looks smug. She knew perfectly well how good she is but was keeping their secret. James is finding it hard to conceal his excitement. His little prodigy is gaining confidence by the day. I shudder to think what would have happened if we were still with George, or escaped and not been rescued by James, but what next, how do we cope. I really must talk to Joan. James must have an official position in her life. It's if not fair for him to manage it and pay, just as a friend. I want him to replace George as her stepfather, at least as guardian. But I never want him to be challenged by George, now or in later life.

I shall be able to talk to Joan today. She is kindly taking me to the Polish embassy in London just in case there are any legal complications. We are going by train and will be back with any luck in the early afternoon as I have my first driving lesson after tea.

It is as well that Joan came with her report of the police case to support my story. They stamped our passport for me and Lucy in my own name, my maiden name. Next, the plan is that because Lucy is legal, we have asked for a separate one for her. Such a relief we are regular and legal in England. Joan advised me to wait until we are married, then address the adoption of Lucy by James. She believes it will depend on whether George will contest it. If so, it will be a fight in the family court, where we will show how he abused her and me, and how she needs the love and care James gives her due to her exceptional ability and requirements.

I find Lucy and show her our passport. She is as excited as I am. I think that she understands what it means for us to be established as free citizens in the European Union, as James had explained it to her. We both know it is the final link with the recent past broken. We now live with James and will eventually become British citizens, me by marriage and

Lucy, who was born in England with an English father. We will establish her right with a UK passport but in what name?

This raises another issue I had not thought about before. I will ask Joan to investigate her birth certificate and registration. Am I listed and if so what was my name given as. I will fight for sole custody, then, when I have it, I can bring in James as guardian. After that we will be a normal family, if any of us is truly normal with our experiences.

That is new, James has been extremely strict with me, and seriously cross. It is not something that I want to happen again. Today it is a hearing of the gang in court, when they will be committed to a trial at a later date. I said I was going to go and laugh at them. James said I will do no such thing, that I am not even going out at all. I tried to argue that it was my right to do so. We got quite heated and he treated me like a naughty child; it was surreal, my lover suddenly going all fatherly and all but sending me to my room. But really, when I think about it, how sweet and how lucky to have him able to stop me doing something stupid. He is not going risk letting me do anything so childish. He really cares that I might do so. He is right, of course, given the chance I would stick a knife in one or two of them. Maybe this is a good bedroom act I could play for him to show his masculinity. I could dress up and be a wayward schoolgirl who needs a strict master. Either way I must show him that I will behave now, so that he can stop worrying. As to the court, Joan will come and tell us all about it later.

CHAPTER TEN
JAMES

I am taking my gang to the university to meet a scientist friend and have lunch. He is gathering a few others to join us; they are going to see if we can devise a plan for each of my girls, for potential education, just as an option, should they want one. Ava is top of our list. I believe the university should offer her a free education to compensate for the abuse that she suffered in our district. They can test her before referring it to the powers on high. Lucy, who is also a top priority for me, will be tested by a friend that knows about primary education. We are meeting in the canteen. Several of my friends' other colleagues have come to join us for lunch to see what's going on.

After we settle down to eat, they start by setting Lucy some simple sums appropriate for her age. Well, that gets them talking for a start. They set Lucy the maths test and seriously underestimated her. She puts the answers down on paper without doing any working, or explaining how she did them. Now she is concentrating on some she cannot get right, well above their expectations. She does not give up until they explain the problems then take the paper away, even more impressed by her determination to find the answer to an impossible task.

One of the younger women is chatting to her to discover what education she has received at the state school or how she was able to do such sums. Another has interrupted just to ask her a question in Polish, as a test knowing, how recent her introduction to the language was, then continues to speak Polish, some of which Lucy understands but cannot speak. Now, prompted by her mother, they are all talking to Lucy about her holiday. Lucy is describing the feel of the boat in the sea and the dolphins in minute detail, not a single mention of ice cream or buckets and spades. They are seriously impressed, I can tell by the way they keep talking among themselves. They ask more questions then leave her to finish her lunch.

Now I see a kind looking lady is questioning Elle, no doubt about how much she has educated her daughter.

Over coffee it is Ava's turn. Elle helps with translation. They ask about her education and interests. One of them is familiar with the Polish school system. They are going to talk about it and write to me, but to sum up the session, they say to both Elle and Ava that if they wish they can study for a career. They are sure that in Ava's case, in the circumstances and on her merit, the university will offer her a place doing a full course starting at the beginning of the next year, quite possibly, in the circumstances, a full scholarship. They tell her that she must study English and read about history before she starts, in order to take full advantage.

Elle can study by other means that they will outline, I presume internet, night classes or open university.

As to Lucy, they are at some loss, not being experts in her age group. They are surprised by what they have found and are sure she is heading for special education, but not sure what that will be. Their advice is that she should go to the best local school we can find for now and let her develop some more naturally from home, aiming at the grammar school or serious boarding school later.

ELLE

It turns out that I am quite good a driving. I will have a concentrated set of lessons, with my test booked for three weeks' time.

Joan came to give us the news that we were waiting to hear, which was that they are all remanded in custody to appear at the crown court. I wonder if James will stop me going to the trial. I certainly intend to make an official statement, if only a victim one to catch the headlines and deliver a kick up their asses, leading, I hope, to extra time in prison. I want them to know it is me they have to thank for their long sentence. I am entitled to my revenge, after my suffering. Everything is coming together for me, because our wedding is planned for two weeks' time, then I will final be free of their influence.

After endless discussions, we all agreed that a no fuss wedding is to only way to go. If not legally, I thought that I was married and have a daughter as a result, and dear James will be on his third wife. Family and very close friends will be invited to a local venue for a simple service and some good food, then we as a family will move into our new house for the first time, for a honeymoon at home. We plan to go shopping to furnish the things it needs and then get decorators in to do up the whole house, so it is exactly as we want it. I am excited by the idea that I can create our family home from scratch. James is so kind and understanding to put up with the upheaval and discomfort that are entirely unnecessary to such a wealthy man. He could have ordered the whole house done up already but understands that as my first home I want to have a say. It makes me so happy to think of our own house, James Lucy, and me. The girls with Ava will have the old house to themselves, because James does not want to sell it, but let the family use it.

We are celebrating Lucy's birthday with a mainly family tea party at the weekend following the actual date, this so that the girls can join in. Despite Lucy now only being seven and on the small side like her mother, the party is not a children's type, in fact there are no other children there. Tea with lots of treats and presents that are educational, all by the request of the special little girl, one who has taken the trauma and excitement of her recent adventures in her stride. The adults without exception marvel at her composure and ability to examine and file away all the conflicting emotions, especially those of her mother and the change from George to James. None have any clear idea where it will all end, for surely she cannot continue this burst of growing up. James for one is trying to slow her down, rather than his usual strategy of trying to boost his daughters' progress.

James cannot resist the temptation to pick Lucy up and give her a cuddle before standing her on her chair. "Happy birthday, Lucy, darling," he declares.

She looks at him, gives him a kiss and smiles a somewhat 'I better indulge him smile'. "Thank you for my party and presents," she says to the table, sliding back down into her seat before James can pick her up again. Some of us smile at the two of them. I almost giggle with amusement. James will have to practice what he has been preaching and stop treating Lucy as a child. It is clear that if he wants to pick one of us up to play, it will soon have to be only me. Lucy is never going to be submissive for any man, however much she loves James he will just have to start talking to her standing on the floor.

All James's girls including Lucy and Ava are sitting around the table playing games on the computer, Joan and the judge have gone home, as have the various other special guests. James and I have decided to go to the pub and leave them to it. We leave Ava in charge of Lucy, with instructions not to be too late to bed.

This is quite special; it is the first time we have ever done something like this on our own. James knows some of the other people in the pub and they seem pleased to meet me. Everything gets more normal as time goes on, but I am aware that sometime soon it will all blow up with the scandal of the court case and my possible public denouncement of the criminals. What will they all think of me then, or more to the point will James even allow me to go public? I have not discussed this with him if he says no, I cannot defy him. After all he has done for me and Lucy, it would be total disrespect for a wonderful generous lover and man. My future must be more important than revenge for the past wrongs. James must want to see them denounced by me and all that entails with the publicity, or I cannot do it.

Much to my surprise, I am on the way to London with Joan and the three girls. James has instructed them to buy me a complete new wardrobe of clothes to get married in and to start my new life as a married woman with. He has told me to have everything that I want myself and not to stop them adding to the purchases, as long as I approve of what they have chosen for me. He gave me no chance to protest and now here I am, outnumbered three to one. Did a girl ever have a better lover and friends than I now have? They are chatting away, excited by the idea of spending James's money on my wardrobe with no limit.

I had no idea people lived like this, we have been in all the famous shops in Oxford street that you see on television, buying in many of them, instructing them to deliver to our house before moving on. We are now wandering around Harrods, making our way up to eat in the restaurant before going home, all of us truly exhausted. I am getting used to being spoilt but still, I will remember this day, James's and his family's kindness and generosity, as long as I live. It makes up for so much that I have suffered over the last few years.

JOAN

The girls and I love spoiling Elle. Everything is such a surprise to her, the look of pleasure when trying on a dress or suit to enhance her extraordinary beauty is worth every penny James is spending. None of us could do these designer clothes justice as she does, she looks like a model. The shop staff get excited and find more for her to try on. It would not surprise me if someone offered her a job on the catwalk. Elle will look stunning, easily the best dressed woman for many miles around at home; when she enters a room everyone will turn and look, James will be so proud of her, as I think we all are that know her history.

With Elle's permission, I explained it to our three girls before they heard it from someone else. I am not sure where they came from, but rumours have been circulating ever since the arrests, with Elle and Ava both named; in fact it was most likely the Ava connection that let people put two and two together. Or it is always possible that Elle was recognised by a visitor to that notorious establishment. Either way it will all come out at the trial if Elle goes through with her intention to give evidence in open court, so it is better to explain it to the family ourselves.

I have to say that they have taken it in their stride, if anything they are most impressed at what they imagine she must have done and that she has remained so normal. They long to ask her about the workings of a brothel.

We carried a few selected bags home with us for Elle to show James. Elle has just come into the room wearing a designer dress. She is standing there looking nervous, waiting for James to comment. But poor James cannot speak; he's staring open mouthed at his lover. She is unbelievably sexy, even to us that are used to her looks. She is dressed in a red silk, tight fitting pencil thin outfit with splits up each side and a simple top with no sleeves, not too revealing, but then not disguising her amazing figure either. With her pretty face and long black hair, the effect is truly sensational. Lucy and Ava are looking at her, not sure what to say. James is also for once completely lost for words.

He eventually takes Elle in his arms and kisses her. They stay motionless for some time, holding on tight to each other, James whispering in Elle's ear. A smile gradually spreads across her anxious face. Not yet sure of his reaction, Elle knows that this is a special moment, James's Elle dressed, no expense spared. Elle has always been reluctant to acknowledge her beauty, possibly because of the trouble it has always got her into, but now she is enjoying our admiration, but she needs to know that James approves. Maybe she will dress up and not down from now on. We all clap and the girls wolf whistle. Elle runs to the stairs to change back to her normal sexy self.

***

Joan and the girls lead James to the kitchen table to sit him down. Lola goes to make coffee. Joan looks at her one-time husband with sympathy. "James, my love, you had better shape up and keep in trim, your wife to be is getting more outrageously sexy every day. Like Lucy, she is developing as she loses her cares and stress. She had put on some weight and is radiating vitality and good health. You will have to try to match that to keep up. Serves you right, you old fool, this is how you were always going to end up with the womanising you loved to indulge in, now it is quite out of your control."

"What do you say, girls?"

"We say what fun, real live girl power, and some, who needs the Me Too movement when you have an Elle?"

"How long do you think he will survive, girls? Let's make a sweepstake."

James groans and drinks his coffee. He knows when he is beaten, but at least it took a truly exceptional woman to do it. Anyway, she is his woman after all, so what's the problem. Elle returns and sits next to James looking radiant, much to the girls' amusement.

"What has happened?" she asks sensing that James is being teased by his daughters.

"Nothing, my love, let's finalise the wedding plans, it is now less than two weeks away."

***

James has gone to stay with Fred, his best man. No doubt they enjoyed a final bachelor night out, for today he will marry Elle, the biggest love of his eventful life. James's harem of daughters, including Ava and Lucy, all his girls, are now busy getting Elle ready for her big day, a day that will finally put an end to the trauma that started when she arrived in the UK to begin a new job in the hotel industry. She will be dressed expensively, but in a sober outfit to play down her more exotic image, not wanting to stand out too much as the centre of attention. Ava and the three daughters are identically dressed in simple gold satin dresses. Lucy is wearing her holiday dress.

The judge had asked if he could have the privilege of giving Elle away as a token of the love, respect, and admiration that he and Joan feel for her. He, as a wise senior lawyer, was also conscious that the local press were well aware of the facts behind this marriage. They had been invited to send one representative and a photographer to attend the wedding, following a request from the editor. A photograph and report will make the next edition, stirring up the already active rumour mill with its tales of scandal. Then, in time, as the trial takes place, possibly the nationals will be able to use the photo. His obvious support will give Elle some of the respectability she will need when the full publicity hits the headlines, as it surely will.

By agreement, the judge will make a short statement praising the work done by James's girls in fighting back and bringing the culprits to trial. Significantly, the chief constable and his wife are guests, again when asked by Simon he was very willing to help right the wrong done to the girls by lending his support to bolster their image of innocence.

The official brief, legal ceremony took place at the registry office with only those directly involved and the immediate family present to witness the signing of the register. Then the wedding party travelled to the venue for the actual celebrations, a country house hotel where a second ceremony took place with a licenced wedding practitioner, this time with the full traditional service, ending with the declaration and the kiss. As this ceremony came to its happy conclusion, Elle held James tight as he kissed her. She would not let him go, she whispered her love, promising to devote herself to his happiness for as long as they both lived. James equally held his angel tight, and in return vowing his love and his promise to spoil her forever.

They eventually parted to the cheers and barracking of the assembled gathering. Elle gathered Lucy in her arms kissed her and passed her to James who did the same, and the three boisterous Jefferies girls fought to be the first to hug their father and congratulate their new stepmother. Ava joined in and James held her in a close embrace, and had the satisfaction of feeling her melt against him. She just needs her own lover and then things will come right for her, he thought.

Lucy understood fully what this meant for her and her mother. She watched them both hug and kiss after the second ceremony, realising that now she would be like all the other girls at school, she would have what they had and would be able to talk about her holidays and fun times with her parents. Her mother, who she loved so much for doing her best to make her happy in their old home, was being loved by her new father and will never be hurt by him as she was by her old father, that she was sure of. She gave them a smile and a wave and went to the table with her sisters. The bridesmaids were all spread around two tables of ten together with friends of theirs and some of the children of other guests.

The total number sitting down to eat was ninety, most invited at rather short notice due to setting the date as soon as it became legally possible to do so. James had no relatives close enough to attend at the short notice, but had so many good friends that most of the other guests were selected with difficulty from his local friends, the golf club set and the business world. He chose mainly married couples, especially younger ones that he wanted to get to know Elle and become their friends to socialise with in the future, as he settled back down to family life with a young daughter and who knows, maybe one day a baby.

The main table, which was in the middle of the room, had, in addition to the happy couple, Simon and Joan, Fred and his wife, the chief constable, John Stevens, and Mary, his wife, also Peter Soames and his wife, Anne, who are long standing and special friends of James's. Elle was sitting between Simon and James. John Stevens, like most men present was excited to be near to such a beautiful and notorious woman. Elle looked radiant and quite stunning.

James, now used to the attention she drew, was fascinated by the way all his guests watched her as they made their way to the table. He was sure that they all knew the story, but nothing read or heard prepared people for the real thing, Elle dressed up and looking as she did today. The publicity and the coming trial, added to the way she dressed and looked, would continue to ensure that she would not for a long time if ever be able to fade into anonymity.

Towards the end of the meal it became apparent to both Simon and James that Elle was in an emotional state and had stopped eating. She was obviously having difficulty in controlling herself, holding back tears. They tried to comfort her, which was the final straw. Elle started to sob gently. Simon gestured to James, who led his new wife away to the sitting room annex.

ELLE

It is no use. I cannot help it, I am going to cry if I am not careful. It is suddenly all too much to take in, it is simply impossible to act normally in these extraordinary circumstances. Here I am, sitting among the most senior and respected citizens of the county, dressed in clothes that most women can only dream of, and would have cost a year's salary for a hotel worker. I am now married to a loving, wealthy man who seems to want nothing more than make Lucy and me happy, a man who is determined to make my life as spoilt as he can. Yet am I not really just Polish Elle, with a notoriously shady past, who a few short weeks ago was sitting beside the road, crying in total despair. What has made me well up at this moment is not actually my situation, it is the sight of my beloved Lucy. She is calmly sitting at a separate table, the centre of attention of her new stepsisters and their friends, and she is chatting to a boy as happy as can be. My Lucy seems to take everything in her stride. It is clear to me that for her this is already accepted as her new normal. That, for me, is more special than anything else that has happened to the two of us, it is what has brought tears to my eyes as I watch her. She is safe and her future is guaranteed. She will never suffer in her life as I have in mine, she will now be in the care of a new step father a wealthy and loving, well respected man who will make sure she wants for nothing as she grows up and requires special education to develop her exceptional talents. She also has big sisters to help her. Look at her, tiny against her friends who are several times her age, yet she holds her own, chatting away. I am just too overwhelmed and happy for her not to cry. It was such a struggle to make her life acceptable in George's house, now I need worry no more. My darling James is coming to my rescue, bless him.

***

Whatever is the matter with my Elle, she looks as if she is crying, thinks James. "Come with me, Elle, darling, now, baby, whatever is the matter, tell me please."

"I am so sorry, James; I did not want to spoil the party, but I was suddenly overwhelmed by what has happened to me over the last few months. It seemed so surreal sitting between a judge and near the chief constable, expensively dressed at my wedding to you, a loving husband. How did this all happen to me? But what really set me off was watching Lucy, the centre of attention among a table of young people chatting away happily. Her future is now so bright she will never suffer as I have. It was just too much for me. I am not sad, James, it just suddenly hit me as a flashback, all that we have gone through in her short life. The thought that I might still have been in the gutter or back with George without your intervention, then when I saw Lucy happy and clearly not affected by her past life, it was all too much, I am just too happy not to cry."

"Oh, Elle, my baby angel, you deserve all you have now, so does Lucy, you are both special people that have been abused. We will all make it up for you if we can, including Simon and John, they know how special you are. Let me hold you while you recover, then we will go back, and you will both be where you belong from now on, among your new friends."

As James escorted Elle back, Simon and John stood up and looked at her anxiously. James explained that she was not unhappy, just overwhelmed by the wedding.

John asked if he could give her a hug, and James said she loves hugs, so John embraced Elle and kissed her, whispering for her to keep her chin up, that everyone was her friend and all are behind her with support if she needed it. "I know what you have been through, Elle, I have read your statements. You are an amazing woman, they will get what they deserve because of you."

Simon chided, "You have been wanting to do that all evening, you sly dog."

John grinned as Elle happily sat down. It was true he had been tingling all evening. He had never seen, let alone kissed, a more exciting woman than that lucky sod James's new wife. James winked at Simon. "She does love hugs and kisses and who better than the chief constable."

James went back to his seat a contented man. He saw John whispering support to his wife; it was clear to him now that everyone, at least the important people, were on his Elle's side. As the meal came to an end Elle's two companions were explaining the local politics and the regions history.

There was to be no music or entertainment; the reception was only intended to be an extended meal for James's friends to meet his new wife so she would be made welcome into the social life of the community. As everyone finished eating, the guests moved around and formed new groups. James and Elle stayed put and were joined by some of the many guests that were anxious to meet James's new wife.

Several of the women were anxious to meet Elle for personal reasons. They had all heard about the roadside meeting, mostly from Joan, and wanted to hear more, James dramatized it even more than the amazing facts warranted; his audience thought it unbelievably romantic. With Elle's looks and recent experiences, and James's reputation as a womaniser, their minds were in overdrive, imagining the bedroom scene when they got back to his house. Elle strongly suspected that more than one of the women was relating to the story with personal experience of James's romancing ability. The look on their faces and James obviously avoiding making eye contact told its own tale. She was amused and heartened that again like Joan, her very naughty boy's lovers parted friends. She added her two penny's worth of exaggeration to spice up the tale. By the time they were serving tea, Elle had been introduced to all the guests and to James's great relief, the women seemed friendly and sympathetic; he never had any doubt the men would be.

James called for silence, as he was going to make a short speech. On behalf of Elle and himself, he thanked everyone for coming. He wanted to tell them all how much he loved his new wife and Lucy, his very special new daughter. "We met in unusual circumstances," he said. "You all know the story by now so I do not need to repeat it, except to say that it was my lucky day when I came across the two people whose love has changed my life so completely. "We will be moving into a new house and hope to see you all there in the future. Now that I have abandoned my bachelor ways and settled back into the family mode again. I already have three wonderful, loving daughters who are as excited as I am with my marriage to Elle, although stepmother might be stretching it a bit, especially when they all gang up on me together. One thing I do know, my trio will guide and spoil rotten their new little stepsister Lucy, as she grows up. She is so adorable and talented they will need to watch out or she will out-do them if they do not knuckle down to their studies." James sat down to raucous barracking and applause.

The judge then stood to address the gathering. A local reporter and his photographer appeared by arrangement to record his words and take photographs, all of which would be shared with any other news outlet that was interested, then ultimately by the national press when the trial made the news. It was agreed by all that this was the best way to publish the truth and protect and enhance the girls' reputation. He explained for the record how James and Elle met beside the road as she was collapsed and concussed following an assault by her abusive so-called husband, following a sham marriage. Simon gave a brief and accurate description of the cruel deception perpetrated by the criminals against young foreign girls who thought that they were going to London to work in a hotel; instead they were sent to regional brothels where they thought there was no escape due to their supposed illegal status. He described in detail the part that Elle had played in bringing then all to court. How the police had praised her courage and exceptionally detailed evidence. He explained that she could have remained anonymous but has bravely decided to represent the other abused women by standing up in open court and denouncing them with her evidence and being questioned by their defence team. "She will be explaining in person to the jury the abuse they all suffered. Elle," he said, "was determined to ensure a conviction and influence the court to get the maximum sentence possible. Our Elle is a fighter and she will have her day in court," he declared.

He then got quite emotional as he described how brave she was, having arrived in this country a young girl with no experience of men, to have suffered as she did, but now to be so outgoing and normal. "My friend James is a lucky man to have Elle as his wife and her daughter, Lucy, is also quite exceptional, to talk to her you would never believe her actual age. Elle," he declared, "is a beautiful girl in every respect. She deserves the support and gratitude of all of us who did not know what was being done under our very noses, in our town to her and others. To these vulnerable foreign girls, on behalf of us all, I say how sorry I am, how sorry we all are. I will do what I can to help them, I urge you all to do the same."

As he sat down there were calls of hear, hear. Many were moved by the emotion that the judge clearly felt for James's new family.

John then stood up and called for quiet. "I know this is a happy event but in the circumstances, for Elle and her fellow sufferers, and for their future in our community, it is important to those of us in the know to support them in public, so I make no apologies for dwelling on the subject. I just want to reinforce what Simon has just said. I cannot comment on the impending court case, but I can confirm that Elle is a very brave young lady and deserves the support of us all. My friend, James, will ensure that her life will be quite different from now on. They make a fine couple and are well suited. I wish them well as they move into their new house. Raise your glasses, please. To Elle and James."

Lucy was not present during speeches; Ava had taken her into another room by prior arrangement before they started. The reporter asked for a photograph of Elle with James, the judge, the chief constable and their wives. They were all happy to oblige so one of the main objects had been achieved, publicity with Elle the hero, not the sex worker. James thanked them and requested that they be left in peace by the press until the trial at least. Elle was apprehensive and grateful as the two well respected men made their speeches, she thanked them for their support and kindness.

James and Elle made their way to the table where Ava, the girls, Joan and Lucy were sitting chatting to each other in a happy mood, all excited by the wedding for their different reasons.

Lucy clearly had the most to celebrate; not only was her mother married to a man that loved her every day and made her happy, she now had a father that loved her and helped her with her work and took them on holidays.

Ava was happy that her friend was married to a man she herself loved and knew was the sort of man she needed.

The girls just loved everything about the conquest of their father by the outrageously sexy Elle, and they loved little Lucy as well. Life at home would be more fun in future with Father back on the straight and narrow as a family man, when he is at his best.

Joan was also very satisfied that James was back as a family man. She took Elle to one side, put her arms around her and asked if she still did not think she was good enough for James's friends. "I can tell you, my darling, that many of the women here today have been pressing me to introduce you. They are dying to hear your story first hand. They want to have a hen party with you to discuss your experiences and tell all about the men that you have met."

Elle smiled at that and said that she did not ever intend to tell tales about men she had met, other than those charged with offences. But yes, she now realised that she was accepted and could hold her own in this company. "Thanks mainly to James and to you and Simon. I will always be grateful to you, Joan, more than anybody other than James you have given me support and love when I most needed it, it meant a lot to me and still does."

"You deserve it, Elle. You have been seriously wronged and we all need to help you. For me, you can now look after that reprobate husband of ours. He was in danger of going seriously off the rails with boredom. He is a good man and deserves you; there is no one better to cope with his needs, and no one better than James to look after you and your Lucy. It is a perfect marriage, so good luck to you both."

They returned to the table and Joan said, "Sit down, you married people. Lucy has something to say to you."

Lucy went to her mother and said, "We have all decided that you must stay in this hotel tonight, then tomorrow or the next day go on a honeymoon. What is a honeymoon, Mummy?" Everyone laughed at Lucy's verbal skills and yet still her innocence.

"It is a holiday for two people that have just married my love, but we have no night things here and no holiday booked."

Leona intervened. "No problem, we will go and pack for you. I am afraid it is not optional. We will make your life impossible if you do not do as we say."

Elle said, "Is that really possible, James?"

"Yes, my love, if Lucy says so and is happy to be looked after by the gang."

"Very well," said James, "we give in, just fetch things for two nights. Also please bring my laptop, then we can go to our room and see about booking a holiday. We will have to go home and pack for the holiday ourselves, agreed? Now if Joan and Simon would care to join us for dinner later, while we talk holidays and explore the internet, the rest of you go home and thank you all very much, we have had a wonderful wedding day."

Elle said, "Ava is in charge of Lucy but, girls, please all help. Lucy and I have never been separated before, it will be hard for us both. Joan I expect will keep in close contact, won't you, please, so any problems call her."

"Yes, girls, I am always available and will pop in to see you every day. Now I will come with you to pack for the happy honeymooners."

Elle hugged her daughter and thanked her for being so sensible. "Be good, darling, I will be thinking of you every day."

James said excuse me to Simon and took his new wife in his arms and hugged her. He kissed her and told her what a gorgeous little wife she was, and he wanted to cuddle and not let go.

Elle giggled with pleasure and kissed him back. "I want to be cuddled and never let go, husband, but wait till I get you in the bedroom".

Simon, who heard it all, grinned at them. "You lucky bugger, James," was all he could say.

Elle gave him a hug as well, thanking him for his support and kind words. They went to the reception desk and booked for two nights. Not surprisingly, the wedding suite was vacant, as they were the only newly married couple in the hotel.

They were having an early dinner to decide where they would like to go on honeymoon. Elle listened as the other three discussed the merits of different destinations that they had holidayed in. James asked her if she wanted a complete rest, a sightseeing type holiday or perhaps a resort type hotel with swimming pools and gourmet restaurants. Elle thought a complete rest would be ideal after the events of the last few weeks. James agreed; all he wanted was time with alone with her. Joan suggested that the Maldives would be ideal, and the others agreed, so the decision was made. Joan offered to look for a booking in the morning for them. They parted company and the newlyweds went up to their room.

James carried his bride into the honeymoon suite and laid her on the bed. He lay beside her and enveloped her in his arms. Neither moved nor spoke for some time. Eventually, Elle said, in a serious voice, "Today I think I finally became the woman you need to look after you and be your companion socially. Thanks to Simon's speech, everyone was so kind to me, particularly the women. I would expect that of the men. It made me finally realise that I can hold my own in their company and be a worthy wife for you. Up to now I never thought that I would be accepted. The past is now just that for me. I have come to terms with it and moved on, so James, we will face the world together, look after all the family and each other."

"Yes, Elle, my love. I too saw that, it was obvious to me as well that they all look on you as a wronged woman bravely fighting back, as indeed you are. Joan and I have been telling you that. Sitting next to John helped as well. We will join in with them all socially and you might learn to play golf or have other activities like yoga if you prefer."

"Now, you naughty boy, tell me the truth, how many of the women that came to see us after the meal have you have slept with?

"What do you mean, Elle, why do you say that?"

"Because, you bad boy, it was obvious to me that there was at least one, so no fibs, tell me what were they like in bed."

"No fooling you, is there, baby. Yes, it was two of them actually. Their husbands are away on business for long periods, so I might go to see them to make sure they are managing and do not need anything. They have both invited me to supper and clearly needed comforting and a little loving which I helpfully gave them. Lovely girls, both of them, yes, Elle, they were not in your class, but good in bed and it was nothing serious, only a short affair while their men were away."

"I will be watching you now, James, you bad boy, I will give you all the sex you can handle from now on."

"You will have no need to worry, baby, you are the only girl I have ever truly loved. You are adorable. I am in sex heaven now, so let us start as we mean to go on."

"Yes, please, James, my handsome husband and lover. Hold on James, calm down take it slowly. This is our first night as a married couple. Let's make it special for both of us, so no rushing. I can see how much you are wound up, so slow down, hold me tight darling and be still, let that monster cock go down again. We will learn to come together if you let me take charge just for tonight."

"Yes, baby, I know that I can be selfish, so you show me what you want me to do."

"You already know what to do, my super stud, you did to me the other night what no other man has ever done before. It is just that you must take time to bring me along with you. First let's undress and get rid of these expensive clothes, then a shower, massaging with soap suds in the warm water, then take your wife to bed and show her what you can do for her."

Eventually back in bed, Elle lay on her front as her lover slowly kissed and licked his way down her back to the bottom that gave him such a thrill. He gave a little massage to show that he understood his lover's needs. He then turned his angel over and buried his face between her shapely legs. They both had a thrill as James rubbed his face in her black pubic bush, with his nose and tongue exploring her lips, licking up and down, pushing his tongue in as far as he could reach. James worked his way up and down before settling on Elle's clitoris. He made circular motions with his finger and tongue until it was fully formed and his lover was breathing heavily. He worked his mouth back up to her breasts, where he sucked each nipple until they were hard. He gently replaced his finger with his cock, sliding it fully into his aroused lover. James took her face in his hands, and kissing her, whispered his love in her ear.

"Is that slow enough, my love?"

Elle nodded and was in a state of bliss. This was the sex she had longed for and never received from any of the men that had used her in the past.

But now her lover was speeding up and leaving her behind. Grabbing his cock with the powerful muscles she had developed over the years, she held him and then released, slowing him down. At the same time, she set up a rhythm, pushing her hips up and down, holding him in and releasing until her lover got the message and fell into step. Elle gradually increased the pace until she was near to her climax, then lay still urging her lover to let rip. This he did, thrusting in and out until he came with a violent climax, triggering Elle to shout and come herself again and again, a new thrill for her despite years of sex.

They lay together without speaking for a long time. Neither had ever experienced mutual sex like this before. James was thinking of all the lovers he had taken in his life and how not one of them had ever held his cock or controlled him as Elle had just done. Elle was thinking how sex as an act was nothing for her without love; it was James's arousal and whispers that gave her the mental boost and satisfaction while reaching the heights of the climax she had just experienced.

She rolled over on top and held him tight and kissed him. "That was way the best I have ever had, James, my love, thank you, I am so happy."

He replied, "I have had a lot of sex with too many lovers, but nothing close to what you did to me, baby girl." He held her in his arms, and they lay together face to face. Both knew that for all the difference in their basic nature, him an alpha male and her a submissive female, they were in fact equal in their marriage and in the union of their bodies.

They slept in each other's arms with their legs intertwined. Elle woke early and for the first time since puberty she felt free of all fear and completely safe. She ran her fingers through the hair of the man that had saved her, kissed him awake and told him exactly how she felt and that he was responsible. He replied that she was worth everything he could give her; she was special, and he would love her forever. They lay together for a while longer then rose and showered. They ordered breakfast in their room.

CHAPTER ELEVEN

In the Jefferies' old house, there was some chaos as none of the younger generation had much idea how to cook or even do basic chores around the house. The three sisters were fighting over what to give Lucy for breakfast. Ava looked on with amusement, and Lucy herself was watching them squabbling, fascinated. While they continued the dispute, Ava fetched some cereal and milk and she and Lucy had breakfast. The girls saw the funny side and managed to put some toast on and make tea. Ava asked Lucy if she was missing her mother, she seemed rather sad.

She replied, "This is the first time she has not been with me and I am sad."

"I am your special friend, Lucy. When I came here I was hurting. You, Lucy, made friends with me straight away and made me feel much better. I will always love you and look after you as my special friend. Come here, let me cuddle you. I will be close to you all the time your mother is away. We will do some lessons together, I will teach you how to write in Polish. You can teach me English."

Lucy cheered up as she loved Ava who was always so kind to her, treating her like an equal. She also realised that Ava had suffered before she came to live with them and that she needed love.

Leona asked, "Who is coming with me to the coffee shop? I am going to meet some of our friends. Ava, Lucy, would you like to come? It will be fun."

"Ye, please," said Lucy.

So that was settled. They all piled into Leona's battered car and went to the central coffee bar in the shopping centre, and were soon swamped by their friends, local young things out to have fun. The sisters were obviously extremely popular with the local boys. Ava and Lucy kept themselves apart, drinking a milkshake for Lucy and coffee for Ava, until a young man came and sat with them.

"Hello," he said. "I'm John, you are Ava and Lucy, right?"

Ava ignored him, and Lucy said, "Yes, that's right."

"May I talk to you?" John asked.

"Why?" Ava replied rudely.

John looked at her and said, "Because I want to know you better, Ava. Wait, I will be back."

John returned with three cupcakes. "There," he said, "now I come bearing gifts."

Ava looked at him and said, "You know nothing about us."

John looked straight back and said, "I know all about you, Ava. That is why I want to talk and be friends with you. I think you deserve some friendship, and Lucy, your mother has just married James Jefferies. You are both special girls and we locals want to help you make friends. Give me your hand, Ava." Not waiting, John took her hand, held it in both of his, then kissed it. "Trust me. Ava. I just want to be your friend, nothing more."

Ava was confused and did not know what to do. She was off all men, but John seemed so nice and was a friend of the girls. She felt that she was getting emotional and about to panic when John took her hand again.

"Ava, please don't cry."

Ava suddenly felt better. John holding her hand was a comfort and the look he gave her was one of pure compassion and even love. He was no rapist, and anyway, he was her own age, she could handle him. The men she hated were all middle aged, dirty and disgusting. Unlike Elle, Ava was not a virgin. She had known some good men and boys like John and had sex with many of them. She smiled. "Keep trying, John. I might eventually speak to you if you explain what you have heard about us, but not today, I am off men."

They bought food for lunch and went back home, taking some of their friends with them.

Later, Leona came and spoke to Ava. "John is wanting to visit and get to know you better, Ava. He is a serious young man that I have known since primary school. His sister was killed in a car crash two years ago. I think he sees something of her in you. Will you see him? He is quite safe, I can vouch for that."

"Yes, Leona, he does seem to be a nice boy. I will talk to him here to see what he wants from me. I am happy with you all here near me."

John came at teatime with an expensive selection of pastries and a bunch of flowers. "Hello, Ava, thank you for letting me come to see you." He sat next to Ava. "You want to know what I know about you, Lucy, and her mother. Well, my father is on the council and has worked with the police to close down the establishments and look after the girls. The details are well known locally. He told us about Elle and Lucy and some others. You were not mentioned, but when I saw you with the Jefferies, I guessed you were involved. You are Eastern European, still learning English, living with Elle, not hard to work out why. Leona and her sisters did not speak about any of you, so do not blame them.

"Ava, when I saw you this morning for the first time I immediately thought of my sister who was killed two years ago. I could see how you are nervous of me and how vulnerable you are. I do understand how you must feel, Ava, and I think that the best way for you to get over it is with a boy, otherwise the bastards have done you long term damage. I want to stop that. I am that boy for you, Ava. Trust me, I have strong feelings when I look at you. You are so like Wendy, my best friend until she died." John took Ava's hand again and looked into her eyes. "Look at me, Ava, what do you see?"

Ava did not reply, but she saw a boy that had the look of love in his eyes. She was beginning to think she might feel the same, but was not sure she could trust her own judgement.

"Stand up, Ava, please."

She obeyed, and John embraced her. Ava neither tried to get away or respond to him, but secretly enjoyed the intimacy.

"Trust me, please, Ava and let's be friends."

"Yes, John, but just friends do not expect anything more. You can come and visit us here and get to know Lucy as well."

Leona watched from a distance with a satisfied look on her face. They all loved Ava, especially for the way she looked after Lucy. They all realised that only a boy would undo the damage done to her. Leona resolved to keep an eye on things, but she was sure that John was just the right boy to make Ava feel safe and to be able to trust men again, at least enough to lead a normal sociable life, even if she did not form close relationships. This was important if she was to benefit fully from university, she couldn't just have female friends.

James and Elle spent the day sightseeing and shopping for beachwear before having an early supper, for tomorrow they would fly to the Maldives and would have to leave at an early hour in the morning. Finally, to bed, Elle and James lay naked, side by side, both enjoying the feel of their bodies intertwined, but not wanting anything more.

They woke early, checked out of the hotel. The taxi delivered them to Gatwick where they progressed smoothly through the airport to the airline hospitality lounge to enjoy their belated breakfast. They were called to the gate for priority boarding and were soon comfortably seated in the business class cabin. Before long the plane left the docking station and taxied to the runway. This was Elle's first flight and she was both nervous and excited as the plane gathered speed down the runway and lifted into the sky. Her thought turned to Lucy at home as she was jetting away on her honeymoon. She would take her in a plane as soon as possible, she decided, before settling back and dreaming of the holiday to come.

During the flight James described the island that they were heading for, one of a great many in the group of the Maldives. Their island was small, twenty acres at the most. "You can walk around it in half an hour. In the centre of the island is the hotel building with all the services and restaurant, which will be partly open air. The bedrooms are chalets all around the island, on the edge of the beach, spaced out so you do not see the ones on either side. They all have a private spot on the beach with their own thatched umbrellas. The lagoon where we will swim is protected by a reef keeping the water really warm. There are plenty of boat trips and snorkelling for those that want them, but the big treat, my Elle, is the getting there. We go from the international airport to the island by a small seaplane and land in the lagoon, that is fun."

It was the same chaos at breakfast time in the Jefferies' house. Today Lola thought that scrambled eggs might be a good and easy option for her to cook, only to find that they had no eggs. They all settled for cereal and toast again, resolving to go shopping today. While they were thinking of a plan for the day, John arrived. He planted a kiss on Ava's cheek and then, much to her joy, did the same to Lucy. He announced that he was going to take his two girlfriends out for the day. Leona asked him what he had in mind. He replied that he would take them to Peel House, it had a nice garden, a garden centre with a café, also a museum in the house. "What do you think?" he asked Lucy.

"Yes," she shouted, jumping up and down.

"And what about you, Ava?"

She replied with a smile. "Look at Lucy, you are a crafty so and so, how can I refuse now?"

"That's a yes then," said John. "Is that okay with you, Leona?"

"Yes, John, but I warn you, be careful with our girls. They are special to us all and you will have James to reckon with if you upset either of them."

As they were driving through the outskirts, John pulled into the driveway of one of the houses. He opened the door for Ava and Lucy.

"Come in," he said, "this is my home. My mother would like to meet you both."

Ava was surprised and nervous but had little choice but to get out and follow John inside the house. A friendly looking woman in her fifties came up to Ava and put her arms around her.

"I am Anne, John's mother. I am so pleased to meet you, my dear. John has talked of nothing else since he met you, he is so much smitten with you. I can see why, not only are you beautiful you have the look of my daughter that he was so close to."

Ava found all this too much and was on the brink of tears when Anne said, "I am sorry my love, I did not mean to upset you. We all know you have had a very rough time and we just want to help you get over it. Now tell me, who is this dear little girl with you, will you introduce us?"

"Yes, this is Lucy, daughter of my friend, Elle Jefferies. She is my special friend. Lucy, say hello to John's mother."

Lucy shook her hand and said, "I like your son, John; I am his second girlfriend." It sounded so comical they all laughed, and Ava recovered her composure.

John took Ava's hand and they went into the kitchen for a coffee and biscuits. Ava realised that it had been prearranged, that they were expected. When it was time to leave, Anne embraced Ava again and asked her to visit often, maybe this Sunday for lunch with Lucy, this was open house to them from now on. Ava left the house holding John's hand and before getting into the car gave him a kiss on the cheek.

"Thank you, John, your mother was so kind to me."

Anne, watching from the window, was delighted to see the couple so close and intimate. She could see that Ava was not only beautiful but also gentle and very feminine. She realised that she was also very troubled and wondered if her friends realised how much she had been affected by the abuse she had suffered. Anne, as a senior nurse, had seen a lot of suffering and was worried for Ava. She resolved to speak to James, who she had met, and Elle, when they got back from their honeymoon. She would do her best to help by providing a second home. Maybe she could be substitute mother for her. She was confident that John was not going to do anything but good for Ava, but still decided to have a talk with him.

****

The seaplane swooped down towards the island, circled once, then flew into the lagoon, twin waves of surf rising on either side as it skied towards the pontoon, where it came to a standstill against the dock. They were met by a buggy and taken straight to their beachside chalet with their luggage and advised to check in later. Their super-king-sized bed was covered in flower petals and a message wishing them a happy honeymoon. It all looked perfect for a secluded lovers' retreat.

They walked down to the lagoon in their bathing costumes and jumped in. to their surprise it was warm and transparent. they swam about like children, splashing and joking. Then a long sunbathe in the setting sun made a perfect ending to the day. How different from the wet and windy country they left had in the morning.

The lovers checked in and then had a light supper and went to bed, where they lay naked in each other's arms, content again just to be together. They made love slowly and with whispered declarations of their enduring love for each other, ending in little more than a sigh. Both felt anything more energetic would spoil the romance of being alone on an island on honeymoon for the first night.

***

John and his two girlfriends were exploring Peel House and Gardens. They had fun in the main house, which was at best a semi-mansion, then explored the museum before settling in the café with coffee and a milkshake. Lucy then went to explore the garden centre by herself.

Ava turned to ask John why he was taking her out and being so kind when he knew that she was not going to have sex with him; she had already made that clear so what did he really want?

John took her hand and held her eye contact, then he replied that she had answered her own question. He accepted that it was not for sex, therefore she must know the reason why. Yes, he knew full well how she must feel about men. Leona warned him that she did not want a close relationship. Of course he knew that after her experience she was not going to let him or anyone else into her bed for a long time, she had made that clear to him. He pointed out that if that was what he wanted then he had plenty of girlfriends, including the three sisters that she was living with.

"Ava, the answer is simple, I think you know it as well as I do. When I first saw you, you looked up at me and something happened to us both. Yes, you look like my sister, but it was not just that. I could see clearly that you were hurting and vulnerable, but that was not it either, or at least not all of it. Ava, I knew in that eye contact that you were mine and that we were meant to be together. I also knew that you had the same experience, I saw it in your eyes and yes, that is why we are here today. I need to be with you and to look after you while you recover. Love beats lust, Ava. Is that not how you understand it, my love? We are together because we think we love each other and want to be together; it was decided for us."

"Maybe, John. I wanted to hear you say it. Of course I know how you feel about me, I saw it in your eyes then and have done ever since. You think that you love me, maybe I think I love you. But what does that mean for us? I cannot love you physically as you will want, no man can live for long without sex."

"Ava, that is a relatively small issue for now. Never is a long time, love heals many hurts. The simple fact is that we cannot chose not to love each other, so let us take it one day at a time. I think that I know what you are really afraid of, you think that you will feel sorry for me and give in, then be hurt all over again. Well, it will not happen, because I will not allow it too. I will wait until you are completely ready, you will not decide, I will see to that for you. Ava, trust me, I do not want you more damaged, I want to be the one to help mend you. I want the past forgotten for you, replaced by happy times. It may take many months, but whatever you say it will happen. We will not have full sex until I am completely sure you are ready, but you will be one day, Ava, I promise you, then we will have a family together."

"Oh, John, can I believe that, can I really believe that you are my James, that you will stay and help me despite not having a full relationship?"

"Yes, my love, you can rely on me to do just that. We can have some gentle, intimate fun, Ava, when you are ready, kissing, cuddling and maybe later a massage. Time is a great healer. As you get more comfortable and feel safe with me, slowly does it, my special girl. I promise not to go too fast, you can dictate what we do. Now where has my other girlfriend got to? We will go and find a McDonald's and have lunch."

***

Elle awoke feeling happy and contented, she had again slept without any dark shadow or nightmare disturbing her night; still, despite her new life quite a rare occasion. She turned to the reason for her new state of wellbeing. James was watching her.

"Hello, Mrs Jefferies. You look so cosy I did not want to disturb you. I really wanted to kiss every part of you and bury my face in you."

Feel free, Mr Jefferies, it all belongs to you now, where would you like to start?"

"How about here?"

Her lover rolled her over and went to town as he worked his way down Elle's warm, sleepy body. She giggled with pleasure and when he eventually made love to her, she did nothing, simply soaking up the strength of his ardour until she came with a cry forced out by his final thrusts. "I love being married," was all she could say as she climbed on top of her lover and held him tight.

Eventually they rose, showered, and went for a swim before breakfast.

They investigated the several activities based around the lagoon. There was snorkelling, boat trips around the reefs, water sports but not much on the island. This was exactly as they had wanted it. Their main activity was to be the sun, the sand, swimming and bedroom sport. The punker fan did not look strong enough to swing on, but the downdraft was refreshing on their naked bodies, while they played on the super-king-sized bed.

***

Anne had telephoned Ava and invited her, with Lucy, to lunch on Sunday. Ava had been hoping that the casual invitation made during their visit would be repeated and she accepted gratefully. Ava realised that James was the main adult at home with his family. Elle was her close friend and her support since they had met, but of the same generation and with similar problems. Ava needed a mother. She did not have one and after the visit where Anne seemed to understand, she hoped that she would be that older woman that she needed. She might be the missing support, a mother figure who understood what rape does to a young girl, to advise and comfort her, maybe also to make sure that John understood fully.

They were met at the door by Ian Jones, who welcomed them warmly but kept his distance, Ava was relieved to see that he clearly understood. Ian then made a big fuss of Lucy, who loved the attention. They went through to the kitchen where Anne was busy cooking. She took Ava in her arms, gave her a kiss and invited her to help cook lunch. Then, after chatting to Lucy, she drove the others out of the kitchen, closing the door.

Again, she took Ava in her arms and said that she missed her Wendy. "She would be the same age as you. I need someone to mother, Ava. Can I give some of it to you? Since your last visit, I decided I could help you if want me to. John told me that you have no close relations and only your friends, Elle and James." As a possible future mother-in-law, she said she wanted to help care for John's girlfriend, that is if she wanted any support.

Ava, overcome by the sudden offer to be the person she needed most, could not contain her emotion, which was already nearly overwhelming her. She could no longer help it; she sobbed into Anne's shoulder.

"Ava, darling, I will help you. I have been a nurse all my life and seen a lot of girls damaged by abuse of one sort or another. As a nurse and as a woman I completely understand how you must feel after being sexually abused. I will be the friend that I expect you must need to talk to, things that you cannot say to a man, however much he loves you, or you love him. John does love you, Ava, I can promise you that, so trust him, but do not hesitate to stop him going too far or too fast. He is a good boy and not impulsive or selfish. Dry your eyes, my love, is that agreed, I can be your substitute mother?"

"Yes, please, Anne, that is exactly what I need. You are a mother figure. I am so lucky to have you and John. I hope that I will not feel so alone now. Time has not helped me get over the shock. If anything it gets worse. It is strange, but Lucy has been almost my main support for me, she is so wise, and I am sure she understands my troubles. Elle is a real friend, but for some reason does not suffer as I seem to, despite many more times the abuse and rough treatment than I have received, including a sham marriage with a beast of a husband. James helps her and me, he is so kind, I love him, but he is a man. I cannot tell him what they did to me. Elle, she is one tough woman. Her answer is to fight back. She is going to blast those men into hell when they get to court. It is what kept her going before she married, that and of course Lucy, who is her beloved daughter, and she told me her only reason for living when her husband abused and beat her."

"Ava, you and I are going to be the best of friends, I hope very close. Like John, I miss my daughter more than I care to admit, even to myself.

Having you to give some motherly love to I am sure will help me in the future as well as you, hopefully one day as my daughter-in-law. You will share your experience and fears and tell me everything that they did to you. That is important for you, to know that someone knows exactly what you suffered, because a problem shared with me is at least a problem reduced. I understand about Elle. It does not help you if she is apparently not suffering as much as you are. However, Ava, do not assume that she is not. With the trauma that she has experienced, she is almost certainly blocking it out. She might hide it from you, possibly even from James, and keep going, but without Lucy and her new life, she would sooner or later have a breakdown of one sort or another. One thing I can tell you now as a little comfort, you can have your husband's children without conventional sex; fertility treatment is available. But I do not believe it will come to that, whatever you think now. The right man that you completely trust and love will eventually win you over. Now, how are your cooking skills? We're having a joint of beef with Yorkshire pudding and all the vegetables you would expect. Let's start you preparing the carrots."

***

Having chosen to honeymoon on a twenty-acre Indian Ocean island, part of the Maldives group, situated as it is on the equator, the lovers were constrained by the heat during the hours of noon and three o'clock. They either stayed in their air-conditioned beach apartment or the main building. That, of course, was exactly what lovers and others wishing to escape the bustle of modern life were paying for. They had the sun, the sea, luxury accommodation, a gourmet restaurant and a partner that needed their full-time attention, so hiding from the heat during midday was no hardship. Like their fellow holidaymakers, James and Elle very soon established a routine that they followed, give or take a few exceptions, for the ten days of their holiday. The rustic but luxurious chalet of two rooms had, in addition to the punker fan, full air conditioning, and its super-king-sized bed was a refuge from the midday sun and a playground any time of the day as well as their night-time retreat. They needed no other facilities or entertainment and were never bored.

On waking, the lovers laid together, enjoying the comforting sleepy feeling of their partner's body, enhanced by the lingering afterglow from the night's energetic activity. Eventually they would walk across the already warm beach and swim in the lagoon. After showering together, they would stroll the ten minutes to the breakfast area, partly held on the terrace under sunshades. Breakfast from the selection of hot or cold treats was taken in a leisurely fashion, followed by chatting to fellow holidaymakers. The rest of the morning was their activity time, selecting books from the library, putting, tennis for the energetic. A walk around the island with visits to the various pontoons and communal swimming beaches, this was also the time for boat trips outside the reef and snorkelling. For golfers you could buy expensive golf balls and drive them out to sea, no doubt to be rescued by a diver and resold. After all this activity it was time for a swim and a sunbathe before it got too hot, when it would be time to retreat back to the airconditioned chalet playroom.

Lunch was either taken from room service or in the restaurant, usually seafood or cold meat and salad washed down with Champagne for Elle or expensive Sancerre wine, which James preferred. As the sun moved overhead and crossed the meridian, it lost its most intense heat. It was time to sunbath and swim again. Evening came suddenly on the equator, so relaxing with a cold drink while watching the sun go down was a satisfying way end the day's activities.

Dinner was a significant feature of the holiday for most guests, taken in the evening cool, with a breeze gently wafting through the open sided restaurant. The food of international five-star standard was eaten slowly, as many courses as it took to satisfy the appetite of the guests. On the first night Elle and James shared a chateaubriand cooked rare and eaten with only a few fresh vegetables as the main course, on another night lobster with a rich sauce, five courses in two leisurely hours, coffee and a couple of brandies. Later they would stroll through the woods back to their lovers' retreat.

Another hour sitting on the terrace of the chalet with further encouragement, usually from a vintage brandy, and they would be ready for the air-conditioned bedroom, the serious lovers' fun time, the main point of a honeymoon taken on a remote island.

Without any suggestion that the natural order of their relationship was being altered, it was not unusual at this stage for Elle to take the lead and guide James. He understood that she was letting him know early in their marriage that the type of sex that she was forced to provide in the recent past was to be avoided. He very soon got the message and the preferred order of dominance was restored. James became a very gentle lover with plenty of foreplay to start each session, then, with Elle fully relaxed, he could be his usual robust self.

That was especially true one night after they had been there for a week. Elle thought that she saw her opportunity to give James some real fun. She launched herself at her lover, hoping that with the surprise and the extra brandy she had fed him she might be able to pin him down long enough to make him submit. She got him flat on his back with her legs locked around his middle and her arms around his neck, trapping his face in her breasts.

"Got you!" she cried. "Do you give in?"

It was always a lost cause. Elle held on for a while until James stood up with her still clinging on like a leach. James sucked her nipples and whispered, "You sexy little madam, you are so adorable but that was a big mistake. Not nearly enough brandy for that to work, tiger, now you really are for it. I will have to teach you just who is the boss in this bedroom. "

The next ten minutes went some way to rearranging the bedroom. Elle did not give up the fight that easily. She wriggled and squirmed as James struggled to turn her over his knee and keep her there. They finished up on the floor more than once before he finally got his leg over hers, trapping them. He got and held both her hands behind her back with one of his. Finally she was unable to move.

"Now I have got you, are you sorry yet, you naughty little girl?" His hand fitted nicely over her cute, shapely little rear. James began to give the firm warm cheeks a good spanking, turning them nice and pink, with more fingering to add pleasure to the stinging, before he dumped her unceremoniously on to the bed. "Elle, baby, you drive me insane with lust. I am sorry, but you asked for it. I am going to give you my full attention."

"Promises, promises," Elle goaded him. "Take care, old man, not to have a heart attack. I don't want to have to take you home in the luggage, they will charge me extra."

James nearly lost it laughing, but proceeded to give her an extremely vigorous shagging. "Take that, you little monkey, and let it be a lesson to you, and no more of your cheek. You are just a weak and feeble woman and I love you to pieces, my little angel."

"Oh, James, my lord and master, you are so strong and virile," she mocked as she threw herself back on to his exhausted body, this time to kiss and hug him. "James, I have never imagined that anyone could be as happy as I am now. I know that you will look after me and Lucy and I feel so safe. please tell me if I am not giving you everything you need from me."

"Elle, baby, you must be joking. Look at the state you have got me in, you give me more fun than all my previous women put together. I am going to have to join a gym to be fit enough to cope with you. Come here, tiger, and cuddle up."

Elle giggled and thought, one day I will win a fight by fair means or foul, then I will spank your bottom, my lord and master.

ELLE

That really was fun. I am not too sure why I did it, but it had to do with the overwhelming love I feel for James, my husband of a week. He is so handsome when dressed for dinner. Sitting with him over a luxury meal on an island in the middle of I do not know where, just gives me goose bumps. I feel so emotional, he has a Hollywood look about him, suave and mature. I feel so safe with him beside me, so why me, I ask myself again. What was fate up to on that road that awful day? When naked in the bedroom, my man is everything a woman could want, sexy, confident, loving but dominant, a girl knows she is going to be well treated and fully satisfied. It just all too much for me, I need to spoil him. I wanted to give him a special treat, I do know what men want. For this man that I love above everything else in the world, I will do anything.

Tonight, I wanted to give a real boost to his caveman ego. He loves my body, so I wrapped it all around him, smothered his face in my breasts, then pinned him to the bed and let him fight his way back out. I did not make it easy, then when he finally subdued me, he did exactly what I expected him to. He loves my bottom so I was pretty sure I knew what that would be. I wanted to tease him so that when he finally hammered me into the bed, as I knew he would in a passion of lust, his orgasm would be as good as he has ever experienced. I was spot on. I had fun, but my lover has never worked so hard for his sex or enjoyed it so much, of that I am certain. I have never felt happier or safer. I know James so well now, he will take care of me and Lucy, whatever it takes.

JAMES

My god, what is she up to now? the adorable little minx jumped me, now I am flat on my back smothered in her body and mainly her breasts, the little Tiger is wrapped around me. I can feel her pubic hair. I will suck her nipples, especially the one up my nose. Now what, I will stand up and put her across my knee, well maybe not without a struggle, she wriggles and fights like a fish, I cannot hold on to her. We are on the floor then back on the bed. I am knackered but she is more so. Now I have her over my knee face down, her back, her bum and legs send me wild with love and lust. That will teach her, a nice pink cute sexy bottom. I turn her over. She is on her back, legs wide open, watching me with a mischievous smile, telling me not to have a heart attack, cheeky monkey. Now I will fuck her into the bed as hard as I can, we both need that. That was fantastic, I have never had an experience like that before. I think the little minx she knew exactly how it would all work out. How many women can do that to a man? I will cuddle my baby girl, I love her so much, we will stay close and sleep.

****

In the morning Elle kissed James and said, "You were fantastic last night, my love. I have never experienced anything like it before. The fight, the spanking, the sex—I will remember this honeymoon last night all my life. It could not have been more special, thank you, my love."

"No, Elle, thank you, you organised it all, I just reacted exactly as you wanted me to, you are the special one, darling. I too will never forget last night or this honeymoon. You really are an incredibly special woman." They showered, then swam before breakfast. The time soon passed, and it was the last day.

By the final night of their holiday, the lovers were so relaxed that they were content with a long build up to arousal, intertwined on the bed kissing, with a final flourish with them taking turns to be on top. They slept contented until it was time to shower, dress and grab a breakfast before being checking out and buggying to the pontoon, where the seaplane was waiting for them. They were again the only passengers. With a roar the plane taxied from the dock; at increasing speed it turned, raced across the lagoon, the twin wakes rising, then diminishing as the plane lifted clear of the water and climbed up over the reef. They soared into the sky, turned, and flew back over the island for a last look before heading for the airport. At the international airport they transferred to the flight that was to take them home. They settled back in business class and prepared themselves for the long journey.

CHAPTER TWELVE

Gatwick was the usual hustle and bustle of holidaymakers returning at peak time. They joined the solid flow that was delivering the travellers and their luggage into the arrivals hall, where they looked for the taxi that was to be booked for them by Joan. They were standing and looking around when Lucy ran up and grabbed her mother. Elle was surprised and delighted, picking her daughter up. James gave her a welcome kiss and asked, "Who brought you here baby?"

The question was soon answered when Ava arrived and welcomed them home. John followed on behind and was introduced with the explanation that he had borrowed his father's car to collect them.

Lucy was dancing around, wanting to tell her mother something. Eventually she could get Elle's attention and announced proudly, "I am John's second girlfriend."

"Are you?" her mother asked. "And who is the first then?"

"Ava is first because John loves her the best."

They all laughed as Elle gave her daughter a hug. "You are the lucky girl, Lucy."

Ava had gone red and was clearly embarrassed. James gave her a hug and said, "Well done, Ava, he must be a special boy, we must meet him properly."

On the journey home it was not hard to tell them all about the holiday which, leaving out the night-time activity, was soon covered. It was, however, obvious to Ava and John that it had been just what they needed. The happy couple were bronzed and relaxed, they had no trouble filling in the missing activity for themselves, it was after all a honeymoon.

Elle and Ava had a long conversation in Polish, Ava explaining how John's mother had become her friend and that she was going to stay with them tonight. She also explained how she became involved with John and how she hoped he was to be her James. Ava wanted them all to meet soon so she could introduce Anne, who was keen to talk to Elle to understand more about the men and their trial, especially if Ava was involved in the evidence. Elle agreed to meet soon and would like to bring James as well. After they had unloaded the car, Elle thanked John with a kiss and said she looked forward to seeing him again soon. She explained to James that they were going straight to his house. James shook John's hand and thanked him for fetching them, and he asked if they could meet to have a beer and talk.

The honeymooners were happy to be back with the family, four daughters with ages ranging from seven to twenty. They missed their adopted daughter, Ava, but were pleased that she was with friends, a major step forward for her. Lucy knew that it had all changed with the wedding, but was not quite sure how it would affect her. She asked her mother what it meant that she had swapped George, her father, for James.

Elle took her up to bed to explain it. "Lucy, my darling girl, you are very bright so I will tell you the truth, so that in future you will understand that I was always honest with you. George Wheeler is your father, he always will be, but it is unlikely that you will see him again for many years, in fact until you are grown up yourself. He has been a bad man, Lucy, and I think he is going to prison for a long time. I thought that George was my husband, Lucy, but he tricked me, the marriage was not legal, so I never was properly married. Do you understand all that, my love? You are still our daughter, but we were not married to each other."

"Yes, but why did he trick you, Mummy?"

"That is harder for me to explain, you will have to accept that he did, for reasons that only he really knows. For me, Lucy, it is lucky because I was able to marry James without having to divorce your father, who did not love me. James loves me very much and we are so happy together. You know that James also loves you very much, Lucy. He will look after you as well as he did his big daughters. James will make sure you have everything you need for your education, including expensive schools and university. He will be more than just a good father to you, he will be a special loving father, you know that already, Lucy, don't you?"

"Yes, Mummy, James is a special father to me. He does sums, he took us to see dolphins and he talks to me like he is my friend. I love him, and I love you, Mummy."

"Good girl we are all going to be one big family with your new sisters. Lucy, I am not going to tell you why your father is a bad man, so forget him for now and when you are grown up I will explain it to you."

***

Elle was up early the next morning and pleased to find that the house and kitchen were clean and tidy. Leona was sitting at the table drinking coffee and made one for Elle. She described the initial chaos when they found themselves in charge; none of them had done any housework before. Like their mother, they thought that was for paid staff or, in this house, James and his girlfriends. "Like you, Elle." Leona said she eventually took charge and enjoyed making her sisters knuckle down and help. She took responsibility, but Ava looked after Lucy on a day-to-day basis as they were such good friends.

She thought her friend John was serious about Ava and he was a thoroughly nice boy from a good home. She had watched them both and thought it was a romance in the making. She was now going back to stay at her mother's house and start work experience in her office. Her sisters were going to visit friends later, and they would leave her alone to settle in with her father and organise the move to their new house.

James soon joined them and thanked his eldest and most responsible daughter for taking control and looking after the family, particularly Lucy. He told Leona that he was a new man and in future his family including her and her sisters, was to be his full-time occupation. Leona could see that he was a different man and secretly thanked Elle for bring him to heel. He was in danger of going off the rails altogether before he married her. She could see he now had a new lease of life getting back to the man she knew, with a family to look after. In her opinion there was no better father; Lucy and Ava were lucky to have him and Elle.

The following Saturday Elle and James were invited to tea with the Jones's. Ava, who now seemed to have a full command of the English language, introduced them all. Anne was fascinated by the now locally famous Elle, the exotic, ex-captive sex worker who, according to the local press, was credited with bringing down the perpetrators with her denouncements and police evidence. She was captivated by her astonishing beauty, short dark and shapely, with a pretty face and black hair framing it. James she also knew by reputation; following the wedding, several of their friends that had been there described the talk given by the judge. Ian was nervous, and well he might be. Elle kept her composure, but both knew that although they had not met intimately, he was a visitor to the brothel. Elle smiled at him reassuringly.

After the meal, Anne suggested that the men go to the pub and have a chat while the girls did the same here. Lucy was given some sums to do by James and a book to read.

When they were settled in the living room Anne asked Elle if she was prepared to share her experiences with them, in the hope that it might help her to understand the suffering they had both experienced; so that she might be more use in supporting Ava, and even Elle herself if she ever needed someone to talk to.

Elle considered her reply in silence for a while. She liked Anne and realised that she might turn to her if she ever needed a sympatric councillor. Eventually she addressed Ava. "My experience and yours have been very different, but the end result will be the same if you come to see the abuse we suffered for what it is, and what it stands for, which is not just a sex act. I will try to explain how I eventually dealt with it. Sex is the common factor in our experience, but for me it is not now the issue. I understand that you cannot contemplate sex with a man and most people would agree that is a reasonable reaction.

"Today I do not see it that way. For me the issue soon became not the rape, but one of power and subjugation. I could not accept being captured, kidnapped, held down as I was abused, humiliated, and imprisoned in the brothel. Sex was their weapon, but it was in fact for me all about their power and my helplessness. It was not just men; women were involved. In fact, one of the worst perpetrators was a woman, the one who allocated girls. She was jealous of my popularity and saw to it that I met the least liked customers.. Apart from being raped, I assume that unlike me you were not a virgin before you were abused. I see you nod, so you do know what sex with a freely chosen partner can be like, good or not so good, but shared willingly."

Elle paused and thought.

"I will give you both a brief history of my experience. You know some of this, Ava, but not all of it. Please be clear, I am telling you as girl talk, in the hope that it benefits you, Ava. It is strictly between us three. Some of this I would not tell any man, especially not the one that I love as I do James."

They both agreed.

"For me, a virgin, being raped was traumatic. I fought back, and it took two men to hold me down and rape me. The sex was unpleasant and painful, but I was so incensed that two men should overpower and strip me. I was helpless. I felt so insignificant in their hands, that the sex was almost an added insult rather than the main event. I vowed as I struggled that I would one day get even with these criminals. I still feel as strongly today as I did then. James has to watch me because he knows that if any of them walk free now that I have escaped their clutches, I will do them serious injury. He had to almost lock me in my bedroom when the committal hearing took place. I was going, possibly to cause trouble. He refused to allow me out of the house. But my day will come, my evidence to the police is so strong that they say the perpetrators will be advised to plead guilty, to try to reduce their inevitable sentence. Believe me, I will stand up in court and give a victim impact statement before sentencing that will double their time in jail, or at least get it up to the maximum permitted.

"I was then kept prisoner and forced to work in the brothel. Surprisingly, believe it or not, a brothel can be quite a fun place, or is to free women earning a living. There were always several girls, much like you and me. The men were mostly kind and considerate, often husbands that for some reason or another were not getting what they needed at home and perhaps did not want to have an affair, easier and safer to pay. These men know how to treat a young girl, many have daughters our age, so it was not all bad.

"As it happens, I found that I enjoyed much of the sex and I am good at it. I learnt a lot from the experience, mature men who usually respected the young girls and taught us all there is to know about sex. I gave most of these men what they wanted. Some came with gifts and flowers, sometimes men only wanted to talk and perhaps a cuddle, a friendly female. Some were regulars and we became friends. I learnt to respect men and their weaknesses. "We all have needs, for a lot of men it is sex with a woman and no emotional hassle. You look shocked and wonder why we did not escape, but we did not believe we could. They convinced us that we were illegal and would be deported back home to the gang and recycled somewhere worse. There are of course unpleasant sadistic men that visited and abused and humiliated me for their pleasure and that of Janet our sadistic supervisor. Two are in jail now, being prosecuted for assault and aggravated rape on my evidence. I want them to get fifteen years."

Elle continued. "We did actually have a plan to escape but it all changed for me before we could put the plan into action. That was when George Wheeler, one of the main culprits also got jealous of my popularity and decided to take me home for himself and marry me, or so I thought. I went along with him as I calculated that it would be easier to escape once married to an Englishman and living outside the brothel. I almost immediately, accidently I can assure you, got pregnant, so Lucy put that plan on hold as well. As it has turned out, it was in fact a sham marriage, but I did not know that. At the time I put up with it as many married women do. He was often unpleasant, even abusive, and had no love for me, but when my Lucy arrived that was my reason for living with George who provided the basics, like medical care, and was not a bad father to Lucy, that is until he assaulted her by kicking her across the room. He also punched me on the side of my head which gave me concussion. Abusing Lucy was the final straw. I decided she was old enough and that we should go at once, so I packed two suitcases and went to the cashpoint. There was no money. George got there first. I was trying to get back home before he found we were missing when I collapsed beside the road.

"Enter James to our rescue. I was too concussed to know what was happening, but he took us home and gave me brandy which brought me round."

Ava said, "James told me he was driving along when he saw the most beautiful girl like an angel, that he had ever seen, sitting on a suitcase beside the road crying, He fell in love immediately and you with him, it sounded so romantic."

"It is true," Elle said. "When I recovered and looked into his eyes there was magic between us. I knew immediately that he was safe and would not hurt us. I loved him, and it has grown ever since. James is really a naughty boy. He has had plenty of women that did not belong to him. I spotted two looking lovingly at him during our reception and he admitted comforting them while their husbands were away. Don't let on. Also I did not tell him that there was a man that I have seen in the brothel at the reception. I will keep his secret, I have no quarrel with most of the men who came and paid for sex, it might have saved many marriages and families.

"I was not sure of James's motives at first. Since I was fifteen, men have only wanted me for one thing. Until I was raped I always refused and remained a virgin. I ran away from home when my stepfather tried it on. James took me to bed with him on the second night after Lucy told him about my nightmares and crying. But we formed a no sex pact for one month to prove it was love not simply lust; this remained in place until we were engaged. Despite all my experience, when it happened, the sex with the man I loved was in a class apart, it was the same for James despite all his lovers.

"So, as you see, Ava, in the end whatever has happened to us, it is the sex that matters. As real lovers we are completely as one, however not for our skill in bed, but because we are as one person with our love for each other. That, Ava, is what will eventually give you your life back. Intimacy with a man you trust and love completely and one that loves you the same. If and when you find such a man, take your time, go slowly but keep going. It will end well for you both. It is completely different to any other sex; you act as one person to satisfy each other, not for your own gratification or his. It reaches a level you cannot experience without love, it is more than a just a sex act, the afterglow when you cuddle up together and just enjoy the warm of his body is special, as is waking up in each other's arms the next morning. You will find love, Ava, and marry, so try to forget the rape sex, think only of the men or boys you knew before. Ava, don't tar all men with the same brush." Elle said slyly, "I bet James could get you to bed if he tried. I see you blush, don't because I know you love him and that is good for you both. Show your love, I promise that he will not try to take advantage. He will take care of you like a father, as he does his own daughters and now Lucy. I will love you as a sister, Ava. Here it seems you also have a mother, so that only leaves a boyfriend that really loves you.

"I will tell you another honeymoon secret, Ava, to cheer you up. You can also have fun with a loving husband, not always possible with a casual lover. One evening on holiday I thought James was very mellow, so I saw my chance to have some fun and be dominant for once, I fed him more brandy, then I attacked him to try and make him submit." Elle gave them a version of her fight with James with some poetic licence and exaggeration. "I can still hear it and smile. He said to me, big mistake, tiger, not nearly enough brandy, now you are for it. I see you laugh. I must have looked stupid but it was fun, trust me. I did not give in that easily, I never do, so we fought on the bed, on the floor nearly wrecking the bedroom. Eventually he got me trapped over his knee and spanked my bottom, then he dumped me on the bed and finished me off, shall we say rather robustly, he was going to show me who was the boss. I tell you, Ava, when we cuddled up together to sleep, both quite exhausted, I have never been happier in my life or felt as safe, as I was then, in the arms of my strong man, a man that I know can and will take care of me and Lucy. That sort of fun you can only have with the man you love and know exactly how he will react and the worst thing that can happen to you. So strange, when you think of it, that I was just as helpless as when I was raped, but I asked for it this time and loved my man for being able to do it to me. The lesson to you, Ava, is move on, put it behind you, find the right man and live again, have fun ,that is the way to recover." Elle lapsed into Polish. "Let your boyfriend into your knickers, Ava, you will soon forget the past."

Ava and Anne were looking astonished as they were laughing.

"Elle, you are quite impossible, poor James how does keep up with you, really you are a fighter, I almost feel sorry for your enemies."

Elle said, "Yes, I am small and submissive by nature, but only to the man that I love, not just to any man. I urge you, Ava, to think as I do, join me in getting even, maybe even stand with me and tell them what you think of them, or just be there to show you are not afraid of what people think. It will help you. I am not afraid to tell my story, I was innocent, abused in this town. It is not me that should be ashamed.

However, neither of you need to feel sorry for James, he is a really naughty, lovable alpha male boy, he will always eventually win with me, I will of course make sure of that, but trust me I won't make it easy and there will be nothing left over when I have finished with him for any other lovesick admirer that he might have, that I will also make quite sure of. I will keep my James happy, that is my pleasure and duty as his wife and lover, just as he takes care of me and my Lucy as our father, husband and lover. But our relationship is not all sex, we enjoy each other's company and are united in wanting to look after our extended family, including you, Ava. We will always be there for you, we both want you to go to university. James has spoken to them as you know, so it is there if you want it, all free. They have made arrangements for you as compensation for your treatment in their town.

"My James is special, he has a way with women because it seems he loves us all, it is just as well with three daughters, one stepdaughter, one adopted daughter, one ex-wife and one new wife. He has a particular desire to see we are educated and have the best chance to get on in life, he is working on Lucy's special needs and even wants me to do evening classes. I love being his wife, Ava, you will too one day love being a wife."

Ava was looking at her friend for some time before she said, "Elle, you are so amazing." She broke into Polish to express herself properly. "How you are not completely traumatised by what has happened to you I do not know. You say you had nightmares and cried at night, how then could you live in the brothel and then with an abusive husband and now be so normal." In English again, she continued, "You did not hate those men that paid for sex and loved James at first sight, surely this cannot be normal, is it Anne?"

Anne was also looking at Elle. "No, Ava, I do not think it is, but clearly Elle is an exceptional woman, driven by her will and desire for revenge. James is right to watch out, I would not put anything past this girl. Please, Elle, do not get yourself into trouble, think how your enemies would love you to get into difficulties with the law, it would be a victory for them. Ava, there is a lesson for you here. Do not let you enemies ruin your whole life, that lets them win again, try to adopt some of Elle's fighting spirit and let's all plot a celebration when they get their just deserts."

"Yes, girl power," said Elle.

"Yes," cried Ava, "I will come with you to court and stand with you, not to speak but as public support."

"Thank you, Ava, I appreciate that, it will help me. Now, where are our lovely men? I want to hug mine."

"I will too," said Ava, "hug yours and mine."

The men returned and were surprised to be hugged and kissed by their womenfolk.

James held on to Ava. "Good girl," he whispered. "You are looking happier every day. Elle and I like John, we think he loves you and is very suitable. His mother will help and keep an eye on you both, so good luck, take it slowly but don't be afraid, your future is as good as you want it to be and our house is your home as long as you want to live with us because you are family as far as we are concerned."

Ava gave him a kiss and thanked them very much for coming to her rescue. They were her family now and she looked on Lucy as her sister.

Anne watched this show of intimacy with satisfaction, clearly the right man could get Ava to respond. As Elle said, James was a lover and easy to love. With luck she was sure John would do the same for Ava over time if he was careful not to frighten her. She also noted that James's reputation with women was not just a rumour, it seemed they all loved him. Anyone that could make these two Polish girls and some of her friends fall at his feet must be pretty special; she decided to get to know him better and see for herself.

Ava stayed with John as the girls were all away. The three Jefferies went home as a family, for that name now included Lucy. Elle had decided she would change her name legally. In future she was to be known as Lucy Jefferies and eventually she hoped that James would be able to become her legal father in some form or other. Elle wanted to wipe George from her daughter's life and from her own forever. She would always know who her biological father was and could chose to meet him when he got out of jail, if she wanted too.

They had supper in the kitchen, then played I spy until it was time for Lucy to go to bed. James produced a bottle of brandy and they sat together on the sitting room sofa, fully relaxed, and made plans for the new house. They also discussed Ava. They were agreed that John was likely, with luck, to be the one for her and that Anne was exactly what she needed as the mother she never had. She herself had looked on Joan as her mother type and would always be grateful for her advice and emotional support, apart from her legal efforts on her behalf.

Elle said, "It is strange, James, is it not, how we both rely on your ex-wife for advice and support. She and I almost share you; I do the house and bed duty, she does advice and legal work."

James laughed. "Sounds like the perfect ménage à trois," he said. "We never fell out, we just decided we were not compatible as a married couple. Simon is right for her. I have sometimes wondered how we found ourselves married in the first place. I think when we first met we were young and Joan had not embarked on her legal career, we were in love as I think we still are. But once the novelty wore off and Joan qualified as a solicitor she found my bedtime needs too much and too often. Joan never wanted to be domestic in any way, she was a good mother as long as we had a nanny to do the actual work and the caring. She provided the role model for our independent minded gang of girls, who learnt to love to tease me. They are modern girls and will never tolerate sexist behaviour from any man. They will never be to their husbands a domestic wife; sex, yes, but not housekeeping, at least certainly not Leona."

They drifted to bed still fully relaxed, made love without any high jinks or drama and fell asleep, together in their own bed for the first time as a married couple.

After breakfast, James phoned an architect friend of his and arranged to meet them at Dunwood House. They gave up the idea of doing the renovation themselves. Elle was now fully into mode as a wealthy man's wife and no longer had the desire or time for DIY activities. The three of them did a walk around for a general survey and then got down to the details.

Starting on the ground floor, they decided that they did not need a formal dining room. They would create a large living in kitchen day room. To make that they intended to knock the existing kitchen, the dining room, the study, and scullery into one large farmhouse kitchen, with an old pine table big enough to seat ten or better still twelve, if they could find one. This would be the sitting area, set at one end, complete with suitable sofas and easy chairs for the kitchen setting. Off this living end they would build a conservatory sunroom, all glass, but with a solid wooden, open pitched roof. Glass roofs, they were advised, are too hot in the summer and too cold in the winter. This kitchen cum living room plus sunroom would be the heart of the house where they would all spend their time together. For the kitchen end itself, they would get specialist firms to advise and quote. There would also be a new annex off the kitchen to house the pantry larder, scullery, laundry, and boot room with a walk-in heated extension for outdoor clothes storage and hanging space. A back door through the annex led into the kitchen garden and on to the lawns beyond. A second door, the official back door, would lead directly from the kitchen onto the driveway for deliveries and access to the garage.

The existing sitting room on the south side of the house was a good size with a large fireplace, so there was only decorating and the addition of French windows and larger picture windows for the builders' attention, these to be made locally in wood. A second even larger room on the north east of the house was currently being used as a playroom. This was now planned to have at one end a television, almost cinema area with surround sound, and facilities to play music and DVDs, speakers throughout the house would work together with this system, all controlled by iPad or any iPhone. A corner of the room would have a desk for Lucy to work at, with bookcases built around it to form a library area, complete with leather chairs to sit and read in peace and quiet. A table and chairs in the middle of the room would be used for an adult desk space and a place for the family to have supper while watching television. The ground floor was to be completed with a small snug come office, a bathroom with shower area and a large walk-in coat room. All these areas would be gutted and refitted.

Upstairs the existing layout was six bedrooms, two with bathrooms, one family bathroom and one separate loo. After much discussion and drawing of rough sketches, it came down to either four bedrooms all with bathrooms, or five bedrooms, with two sharing a bathroom that was between them, having connecting lockable doors. This would also have a door into the hallway for visitors to use. In both cases the separate loo remained. It was agreed by all after much discussion that the extra bedroom might be needed with all the potential visitors, so five it would be.

James agreed terms with his friend, Tom Nuttall, to draw the plans, obtain the necessary approval and go out to tender from local builders, then to supervise the work.

Elle was beside herself with excitement, she owned half this grand family house. She hugged James much to Tom's amusement. He, like so many before him, was already half under her spell and looking forward to working for her.

While all this was going on Lucy was wandering around the extensive gardens following butterflies; they seemed to fascinate her and she asked if she could have a book on them to look at. She asked questions that neither of her parents knew the answer to. Like dolphins, it was to become an interest that would grow into an important part of her future study.

James asked Elle if she liked gardening as he was not particularly green fingered. Elle said that she had no experience but had always wanted a garden and would like to learn to look after this one. She was sure that Lucy was an outdoor girl and interested in nature as well.

"Good," said James, "then you shall be in charge of our garden. We have a man that comes in two days a week called Jonathan. He will teach you and there is a garden club that we can join which will help. So, let us go and walk around the garden. Come on, Lucy, we are going to explore the garden."

Going out of the front door, they walked around to the south and on to the large paving stone terrace in front of the sitting room. This was surrounded by a stone balustrade, the other side of which was a full length rose bed in full bloom. "That is so pretty," said Elle, examining the multicoloured blooms, but not too sure what they were. Walking to the end of the terrace, they found two steps down on to the manicured lawn that surrounded the rose bed and extended around the house and outwards to an orchard full of mature trees. They walked across the grass.

"We must have a mower," commented James, then looking at the trees he said, "I am not too sure what all these are, but they all look well cared for."

The rest of garden, which totalled three acres, went beyond the orchard and back towards the gate. It was mature shrubs and trees in a woodland setting with open spaces and a walkway wending its way through.

"I like this," said Lucy. "We can explore here and maybe make a camp."

Walking back across the lawn and further around the house, they found the kitchen garden and various sheds and green houses. It was all in good order, but there were no vegetables to be seen. There was an enclosed area with netting around full of what were obviously fruit shrubs.

"Well, girls," said James, "you have got a lot to learn, then you can explain it all to me. We will meet Jonathan tomorrow as that is one of his days."

Elle picked up Lucy and together they embraced the man that had changed their lives and given them so much. Elle kissed her husband and said, "Thank you, James, we are so lucky, aren't we, Lucy?"

"Yes," she said and also kissed her new father.

"I am just as lucky to have you both," he replied. "You have changed my life as well. I will love living here with you. I was a lonely man before I met you two girls."

They shut the house and went back to their other house.

Ava returned to what was now established as her permanent home. She was part of the family as an adopted sister for Lucy. Their relationship was getting ever stronger, hard to accept the age difference as they were so close. Lucy gave Ava moral courage and strength; she appeared to understand her needs. Maybe because she had seen at first hand her mother's suffering and her rescue by a loving James.

Ava also looked upon James as a father figure. She saw all the good he did for Elle, Lucy, and for herself. She loved and trusted him. She knew that he was there for her if she needed any help.

The following morning, they all went back to Dunwood House. Lucy took Ava on a tour of the house while James went to find Jonathan with Elle. He had already met their gardener and agreed a new contract of employment on better terms than he had before, so he was content with his situation. Of course, he knew all about Elle Jefferies, most people locally had seen the reports in the local paper and on the regional television news. He was a red blooded forty-year-old male and looking forward to meeting his new employer's exotic wife.

Neither the stories, nor the picture in the paper, prepared him for the real thing. Like so many men since Elle was a teenager, he was mesmerised by her in person and this was only magnified by her reputation as a sex worker, all be it an unwilling one. Seeing her in real life, dressed in tight jeans and jumper, he was temporally struck dumb.

James took it all in and said, "Hi, Jonathan, this is my wife, Elle. She is going to be in charge of the garden so I will leave you two to get to know each other." Then he diplomatically walked away, quietly grinning to himself. He fully understood the situation. He knew what Jonathan was feeling, and enjoyed the effect his Elle had on men. He thought it best to let Elle put him at his ease.

"Hello, Jonathan," she said. "Don't be embarrassed. I know that I have something of a reputation but in fact you will soon find that I am just a normal wife with a husband and daughter to look after, now also a garden, so I am hoping that we will work together while I learn. It is all new and exciting for me, but I know nothing about gardening so would you mind helping me to understand what you do? Shall we walk around, then I can ask you questions." Elle waited for him to recover then asked how often he had to cut the lawn.

Rapidly getting his composure back, Jonathan explained that it depended on the weather, the time of year and if he had fertilized it or not. They strolled around the garden, Elle asking anything she could think of, realising that even her questions were a display of ignorance and simplistic. She resolved to do some homework before they met again so as not to look quite so stupid.

"Thank you, Jonathan, for being so patient. I am sure we will get on fine when I learn a little more about what gardening is all about. Please also talk to my daughter, Lucy, when you can. She is not an ordinary little girl and learns fast."

Jonathan watched his new boss go back towards the house. He had really mixed feelings. She was everything he expected and so much more, small and vulnerable; his instinct was to hug her and take care of her, but her reputation and her marriage to a wealthy man told a different story. She did not need any help, except with the garden. He could not wait to meet his mates in the pub. He would talk up her looks and pure sex appeal, but also tell them that she was a kind and considerate woman. He knew she had gone out of her way to put him at his ease and not tease him and show off as many women would. Her questions were completely irrelevant to the garden but he suspected that would change quickly once they moved in.

CHAPTER THIRTEEN

On arrival back home, James called Ava to have chat. "Ava, I am going to make you an allowance. you cannot exist without money. This is not a wage as we paid you at first for working, this is an allowance as I make to all my daughters. To Elle and me you are family now. You do plenty to help us, and especially we value the way you take care of Lucy and help her to learn, so I have opened a credit card account for you with a standing order to pay into it £2000 every month. There is credit limit of £10,000. It is all on this envelope. But don't worry if you overspend, it will not bounce. Do you understand that, or shall I call Elle to explain it?"

"James, I think I understand but I will check with Elle. James, you are so kind to me, you always have been. I do not know why you should adopt a strange girl like me. I love you so much, James, I really do."

James embraced her and said, "I know you do, Ava, and you know that I love you too. You are like a daughter to me. I love all my daughters they are fun, you always will be one of them, we will always be here for you. Dunwood House is your home to come back to with your family when you get married, and you will, Ava, your love for me proves that you will, when you love another man enough, and he loves you. I think you also love John and I approve of that; believe me I would say if I did not think him good enough for you. Go carefully and take your time to be quite sure. If you love each other as Elle and I love each other, then everything will fall into place and you will enjoy a normal married life. If not there will be many more good men, especially at university, with the same interests as you.".

Sex as a married couple was evolving for Elle and James. The excitement and surprises of strangers has been replaced by a deep understanding of each other's needs, emotions and ability, a full range of activities has developed and is being refined and expanded, based on their love and desire to please each other. James still had to be careful;

when Elle was in an exuberant, happy mood she was still capable of wild and unusual surprises, but not another attempt to dominate her lover. Elle had to be prepared for James's occasional lust driven assault, mainly after a night out with drink and good food. His impatient, no foreplay sex gave Elle no satisfaction at all, but she did appreciate his lust for her body. She had always loved this weakness in men, this overwhelming lust; it was fun to watch his face. She also enjoyed his remorse when he was spent and exhausted.

Later in the night, when they were both mellow, James reminded his lover that it was her driving test in two days' time, so they should go and look for a car for her, does she know what she wants.

"I don't need much of a car just for shopping and school, a second hand run about will do."

James pulled his lover into an embrace then held her face in his hands. "You are the most special person I know. You are a cuddly baby, clever, strong, kind and generous, the best thing that has ever happened to me. You are way better than any of my friends' wives. They're all jealous of me, so why would you have a car that was not as good as they have? Are you going to turn up at their houses or school in an old banger alongside their BMWs and Range Rovers? No, you are not. You are my wife, I am proud of you and you will have nothing but the best to be seen in. If you say something is good enough for you ever again, you will be in real trouble. Do you understand that, Elle, baby?"

"Oh no, master, don't scare me. I'm just a weak and feeble woman. I'm frightened, what will you do to me?"

"You know very well what I will do to you. I will turn your sexy little bottom pink."

"No, no, not that again. You might finger me as well. I cannot take any more of that brutal treatment. I will have to go and sit beside the road again and cry until a nicer, kinder and more generous man comes along and saves me."

James gave her bottom a good smack, then kissed it better. They went to sleep content and satisfied, all Elle's nightmares long forgotten.

***

The following morning, John called to fetch Ava in his mother's car. They were going for a drive then having lunch, before going to his house to stay the night. They drove down to the coast and walked along the beach, paddling in the sea, throwing stones to see who could skim one the farthest. They found a beach café and settled down to fish and chips. "You look especially beautiful today, Ava. Is it just the sea air or are you feeling better now? You look happy."

"I am happy, John. I like having Elle and James back. We went to see the new house yesterday. James said I was part of the family and it would be my home to come back to when I am married. He also gave me a credit card and an allowance. He is so kind. He said he approves of you, John, but take it slowly. "

"That is a relief because you take notice of what James says. I think that you must love him, Ava."

"Maybe I do. I love it when he holds me. He says he loves me just as much as his other daughters and I am now one of them. I never really had a father. I feel safe when he is near me. I am lucky, John. Your mother is a mother to me now and James is a father, that is why I am happy. I am loved by them and by Elle, but also Lucy, my special little sister."

"That only leaves a husband then, Ava. May I apply for that, because I love you too."

"Yes, John, I know you do. You can apply but it is much too soon for me to give you the answer. James was very careful to work up slowly before I trusted him. You are doing the same. I do love you, John, but the future as a couple for life is a very big step, not one I will take quickly. For now we are good friends."

They drove home in time for tea, Ava asked if she could speak to Anne. They took a pot of tea into the sitting room and settled down in easy chairs. "Anne, I am confused. As I told John, James gave me a credit card and an allowance. I hugged him and told him that I loved him, he said that he knew, that he loved me too just like all his daughters, that the new house is to be my home, somewhere to come back to with my family when I am married. He was lovely and so kind, as he has been ever since Elle took me home to his house when I had nowhere else to go and no friends. He also said he approves of John."

"James is a good man, Ava. What's the problem?"

"The problem, Anne, is that I should hate having a middle aged man like James anywhere near me, but when I said I loved him I did not mean as a daughter. I love him and I might do whatever he wanted me to. Do you remember Elle said I would go to James if he asked me? It's true, Anne, had we been alone I would have gone upstairs with him. I think that Elle knows that; she said it was a good sign, that I was still able to love the right man. What is the matter with me, Anne? It doesn't make any sense, me loving a man James's age."

"Ava, darling, you're confused. The trauma has upset your emotional compass. James is very lovable man. You just have to know his reputation and the number of women who still love him to know that. He knows that you love him; he made it clear that to him you are a daughter. Cool it down, Ava, don't tempt the poor man, be his daughter as he wants you to be. Any man can stray and act impulsively if a girl wants him badly enough, that would be a disaster for everyone, but you know that well enough. I am sure you would come to your senses long before you got to the bedroom. You're more worried about why you feel like this, that I can understand. I think you just badly needed some love and he gave it to you, and a home and more besides, I think that you, despite what you say, really needed a father, not a lover. You have confused the two. He is that father, not your lover, Ava, so just think of that. Sex is uppermost in your mind when you think of any man, since you bad experience, that is quite understandable, but you need to sort things out in your head. Elle told you not to associate all men with the rape—that's good advice. But Elle also told you that when you love a man enough you would go with him; this proves that what she said is true. I have no doubt Elle had already seen that in you with James, she would not be worried that you two might do something silly. Elle is smart, especially with men. Her James is safe and has plenty to cope with already without trying to add you to the list of his lovers."

"I know all that, Anne. I just could not understand how I was able to want to go to bed with a middle aged man, it still does not make sense to me. Was it like someone afraid of heights wanting to jump off a tall building when looking down? But I will take care, it is not fair to either

James or Elle for me to make James's life difficult, I have never been a bad girl, Anne. I just don't understand what is happening to me."

"Come on, my love, let's find the men, I think we will all go out to supper. One of those men loves you as well as, James, Ava, you're a lucky girl: two men, one a father and one wanting to love you for a wife."

Later at bedtime, John asked if he could come to Ava's bedroom for a cuddle. She agreed, so when all was quiet he crept into the main guest room where Ava was in bed, wearing pyjamas. John got into bed and took Ava in his arms.

"That's good. I love you, Ava, let me hold you," he said. "You are so cuddly and warm. I can feel your breasts and your nipples. Do you like this feeling against me, my sexy little Polish girl?"

"Yes, John, of course I do, I love to be cuddled, but be careful, don't push yourself against me. I'm not ready to feel quite all of you yet."

John deliberately undid Ava's top and, when she did not stop him, he put his hand on her breast and gently massaged it. He took off his top and cuddled up again to feel her breasts against his bare chest, kissing his lover fully on her lips and getting the response he hoped for.

Ava pulled away. "Enough now, John. That was good for me, but stop now and go back to your bed. I don't want to get carried away and do something I might regret. It would set us back. I'm not ready yet, so let's agree now, topless and no more for some time. Maybe a long time, I am still confused and have flashbacks and nightmares, it could go horribly wrong for us."

John agreed and gave her a goodnight kiss and went back to his room, content with the progress he had made.

The following morning after breakfast, Anne poured two cups of coffee and settled down for another chat with Ava. "I have given it a great deal of thought during the night, Ava, and I am quite sure that you always loved James as a father, never as a lover, from the time Elle took you home to his house, they were not married, so it was his house. Until today you have grown to love James as any girl given such generosity would have done. Many men would have given you shelter in the circumstances, but from the start James gave you so much more than just a refuge; he gave you love, he gave long term security and helped to get you an education, he has given you an allowance. He has adopted you as another daughter. You have a home for life. This would be enough to disorientate any girl, let alone one traumatised by abuse. In your mind you might have confused his motives and mixed up your love, perhaps wanting to please him and give something back. In reality, in all the circumstances, you cannot ever have really wanted sex with James can you. It's clear you needed a father and he wanted you as another daughter. It seems he just loves his daughters, especially, I understand, his new stepdaughter, Lucy. Be that daughter for him, Ava. Make him proud of you, get the education he wants you to have, try to forget the rape and make a good life for yourself. We are all here for you to help. Now, John is ready to take you to meet more of his friends. They are your future friends, have fun."

***

James fetched the car from the garage, collected Elle and Lucy and set off for a tour of the car showrooms. "First stop Jaguar Land Rover," he said. "I would like it if you chose British now that we have left the EU." As they walked into the showroom, James said, "Don't look at the price. We're going to get the most suitable car, provided it is the one that you like."

A salesman came to help them. On hearing their requirements, he showed them the Range Rover. "This is big and strong and has everything you might need; it is about the safest car on the road," he boasted. It was James's preferred choice, so he had already removed the price tag from the bonnet."

"This is very grand," was Elle's comment as she sat in the car and looked around. "I'm not sure about parking it, though, it is big."

"We can come back later," said James, "but first have a look at the Discovery. That's a little smaller, see how that feels."

Elle and Lucy climbed into the dark blue showroom Discovery. "This is better," Elle called. "I can see myself in this, not as big and grand but it has plenty of room inside, yes, I like this one."

"Bad luck," James said in an aside to the salesman."

"Never mind," he said, "this is my favourite as well."

"Do you want to look at any more makes or models, darling?"

"Not if you want me to like the Land Rover, James, because I do like this one. I would be happy driving this car around."

"Well, let's see what sort of a deal we can get for a cash purchase."

After twenty minutes with the salesman and his manager, James came to an agreement for the actual car in the showroom. He did not intend to reveal the price to Elle.

"Well, Lucy, what do you think? That is now your mother's new car."

Lucy was surprised by the whole notion of her mother driving a car. "Can mummy drive a car? She never has."

"Yes, my love, I have been learning to drive and can drive this one when I pass my test, and before then with another driver in the car. I can take you for a ride on my own when I pass my test. I hope that will be tomorrow."

The driving instructor dropped a smiling Elle off after she had passed her test. He was pleased that another student had passed first time but disappointed that he would no longer be sitting beside and instructing Elle Jefferies. She blew him a kiss, to which he responded with a wave and drove out of her life.

"Lucy, James, where are you? I passed."

James said, "Who's a clever girl, then. This is like the key for the door, you are free to go where you please. You must take us for a drive then, in my car, Elle. Yours will not be ready for a couple more days, they have to predelivery service it for the road." James fetched his rather old Range Rover and off they went. Elle was unfazed by a different car, her passengers were impressed.

Elle drove Lucy to Dunwood House in James's car to meet Jonathan. She had spent several hours on the internet with Lucy as they took a crash course in garden plants. They'd also watched a year's worth of *Gardeners' World* with Monty Don.

"Good morning, Jonathan, this is Lucy." With the introduction made, they found a rustic seat and table to sit at and have a chat. Elle produced a basket of coffee and biscuits. "Now, Jonathan, tell me, did the last owners take an interest in the garden or leave you to get on with it on your own?"

"Actually, Elle, they did take an interest until they both got serious medical problems—they were in their eighties—so for the past couple of years I have been on my own working for an agent appointed by the family."

"Are you happy to have me following you around learning, because I am keen to become a gardener, so is Lucy. Although her main interest is the bug and bird population."

"Mrs Jefferies, you must be joking. I'm bored stiff here on my own with no one taking an interest in my work or the garden. All my friends are jealous that I'm working for you. Sorry, I did not mean to be rude; I mean that working for you will be a privilege., I will do anything I can to help you both."

"No need to apologise, Jonathan," Elle said with a laugh. "I can guess the teasing that you might be subjected to down the pub. Now tell me, is there anything you would like to do or buy to improve our garden? I would like to make a difference over the next year or two. Think about it and we will talk again, another time. Money will not be a problem. My husband is determined to make this family home as comfortable as possible and has given me a generous budget, so let's have fun. We will rely on you to help with all the outside areas. Now can we do another tour and then maybe you can find some weeding or other work for us to start on."

Jonathan was impressed with the amount that both his pupils had learnt since the last walkabout. "Well done, you two, you really are taking it seriously; it is so much nicer for me when the owner takes an interest in what I am doing for them." He set them to work weeding the rose bed and gave them the job of trimming the lawn edge every week, and showed them how to dead head the roses and other perennials. Jonathan was a happy gardener as he watched his new apprentices: his new boss in jeans, with her miniature version daughter, both busy in his garden. It suddenly did not look like he was the only one who cared. Even his wife was impressed and wanted to hear all about his famous new employer. Elle, sensing that this was likely to be the case, invited Jonathan and his family to visit and have tea one afternoon.

After a good session in the garden, mother and daughter went into the house to see the progress the builders were making. All the structural work had been completed. This was no big deal as it only required the demolition or alteration of non-load bearing internal walls. The annex was being built at some risk as planning permission had not yet been obtained. Building regulations has been applied for and they were taking care to comply with the rules and had the foundations inspected to be on the safe side. Replacement windows and doors, together with fittings such as bookcases, were all in hand as the work progressed at a pace. The kitchen had been agreed and orders placed. The hope was that they would move in in two or three weeks' time.

Life in the Jefferies household was fun and exciting. Everything seemed to be happening at once. In addition to the new house and garden, Elle's car was ready to collect and Lucy was to start her new school in two days' time.

That evening, as Elle was helping Lucy to bed and having a mother and daughter heart to heart talk, Lucy asked the question that Elle was hoping to avoid. "Mummy, why did Daddy hurt you? Didn't he love you? James has given you a car and a house, he loves you, doesn't he? Why, Mummy, why does he love you and give you things and not Daddy?"

"Lucy, darling, I am not going to talk about Daddy. It is complicated and not something you need to think about. When you are older I will explain it to you, but now you can remember the good times we had and forget the bad times. Daddy will be away for a long time, so we must concentrate on making our new house and garden a special place. You will go to your new school and learn as much as you can then decide what you want to be when you grow up. James will look after us both and Ava. We must all look after James and love him as much as we can. He is a very special, kind man, Lucy. We are lucky to have him as my husband and your new father."

"Yes, Mummy, I will, but why does he love us and give us things, not another mummy and her daughter?"

" Lucy, it's hard to explain. When two people, a man and a woman, love each other, as James and I do, we cannot help it, it just happens to us. It's nature's way of saying this is a special person just for you to love then you can have children. It's the same with birds and animals, too. When they find a mate to love they have babies. Without this, there would be no new babies and then no animals or people. James and I loved each other as soon as we met. We knew we were meant to live together and look after you. We both already have our babies so we can love them all and help them grow up. You are our baby, a big baby, darling. Do you understand what I am saying, Lucy?"

"I think so. We did learn about how babies are made at school when people love each other. Are you and James going to have babies, Mummy?"

"You mean as well as you and his girls? I cannot answer that, Lucy, but it is possible. Would you like us to?"

"Yes please, Mummy, I would love a sister or brother."

Later in bed Elle recounted the conversation to James.

"I wonder just how much she understands," he said.

"More than we realise, I think."

"Remind me, Elle, when did you stop taking the pill?"

"A week before we married," Elle replied. "I finished a course and have not restarted as we agreed."

"Good, then we will have another go at making a baby, shall we? You never know your luck."

"Wait, not so frisky, lover, lie still darling," Elle said as she lay on top of James. He was on his back and she held his head in her hands and kissed his rugged face. "James, Lucy is right, you love me and give me so much. I want you to know just how special I think you are. No, James, I don't want to hear about me, be quiet, lie still and listen." Elle put her finger on his lips. "You, James, are a very special and loving man. You are everything a real man should be, strong dependable and handsome. All my doubts and trauma are gone, no more nightmares. I am living a dream being married to you. I have to pinch myself to make sure I am real. But it is not just me. Lucy, too, is free from all stress and growing up at an amazing rate, due to your love and the interest you take in her. Then there is Ava. You have saved her. She was lost in this country with no friends, now you have given her a family, a home and a lover, all because you are a very special, generous and loving man and all mine. I am the luckiest girl, thank you, James, from us all."

Elle held on to his face kissing him again. "We will all pay you back in our own way. I will take care of you, James, spoil you as much as I can and give you everything that I humanly can with my body and my love. No, don't say a word, my darling. Relax as I give you my version of a full body massage. By the way, Ava was certain that she would never have sex with a man again. I always knew that was more of a superficial mental reaction, due to the humiliation and helplessness rather than not wanting any actual love and sex. I was the same at first. I can promise you that it will not be years, not even months; she will let John love her in weeks at the most. She loves quite easily, does our Ava. She is no innocent, her resistance will disappear when she can do so without losing face, after all her never any man talk. I could see it with you, James. She needs a man of her own, even if she has not yet admitted it. So, James, tell her to get on with it and stop teasing poor John. It will be fun to watch her give in to her inner needs and John. It will not be long if he plays his cards right. I might give him a few hints how best to put Ava at her ease and get what he must be desperate for."

Elle then took charge and was as good as her promise to spoil her lover using all her massage skills. James remained silent as instructed, then he took Elle into his embrace, having recovered from having one of the best orgasms he could remember. He knew that he was just as fortunate. His new wife was a woman in a million and his own for life. Both Lucy and Ava were daughters to be proud of; he would do everything he could to steer them into adulthood and fulfil their ambitions, to him that was satisfying. A new woman grown up and educated, ready to take on the world as an equal, never to play second fiddle to anyone. Also, he did love all his women, he always hoped that they would strike the balance between being feminine and high achieving and hard bitten feminist demanding just demanding equal rights before they have earned them.

"Now, Elle, that's it," he said firmly. "No more praising each other, we are now team Jefferies. We are equally responsible and make our own unique contributions to our union, we share everything in our marriage. I fully understand the change that has happened to you since you arrived in England, but that is it, we are one person now, agreed?"

Elle lifted his head and kissed him. "Agreed," she said. "I have taken time to adjust to my situation but will not look back any more."

***

At breakfast James asked Ava what she was going to do that day. She said that she was expecting John to come to take her to meet his aunt and family, then she was going to stay the night with him. "Good, then you can drop us off at the garage to collect Elle's new car."

The salesman that sold them the Discovery met them and sat them down to watch a film of the Land Rover being put through its paces.

"I had no idea that I would be able to drive up a mountain or across country," said an excited Elle. "That might be fun, James." Next they spent some time learning the controls and features, Elle and James taking it in turns to drive up the road and back. When they were all satisfied that they had both mastered the Land Rover Discovery, Elle drove them home with Lucy in the front and James in the back.

***

That night Ava and John were lying in bed together discussing their day. Ava had been welcomed by John's family and was in a happy and relaxed mood. Pressed up against John, she could feel his erection and realised with something of a shock that there was no way she was going to resist having sex with him for very much longer; she had an urge to get his cock out and climb onto it. She had a rush of love for John as she understood the full extent of his sacrifice for her, waiting with no end in sight while she came to her senses. She felt very selfish. Now, despite all she had told everybody, she wanted John badly. She could not quite understand why, but she did not in any way associate sex with John with the rape. It was not sex she was afraid of—she had always loved sex. She realised that this was exactly what Elle had told her; it was the humiliation and helpless feeling of being held down by dirty old men and raped that traumatised her. She guessed that Elle had watched her with James and John and was hinting that it was time that she should react as she was now towards John, who clearly loved her as she loved him. She knew he was not going to, but if John demanded sex now she would agree and enjoy it, so what was she to do to normalise her affair and save face?

Ava decided that if they were to go away together for the weekend or a holiday then they could come back and declare their love and possibly their engagement. No one, including John, would be surprised.

Well done, John, they would say. Later in the night she asked John if they could go on holiday; she had money from James. He jumped at the idea and they decided to mention it to his mother at breakfast.

At breakfast, John brought the subject up, asking his mother if she thought it was acceptable for him to take Ava on holiday to get away from everyone and be on their own for a while.

"Good idea," she said. "Why not go to the seaside? The air will do you both good."

Later, after John had driven Ava home, they joined Elle and James for coffee. Ava told them that they were going to the seaside together for a few days to spend time together by themselves. Elle looked at Ava and spoke to her in Polish, Ava looked back at her surprised, then burst out laughing and replied in Polish.

"Good plan, Ava," Elle said, again in their own language. "Anne is going to be proud of her son," she said, "John the great seducer."

"Yes," Ava replied. "I will struggle for all of half an hour on the second night before slipping off my knickers and giving in to him. He will think it was all his doing, as I suppose it is, to be fair. I love him, Elle, and want to marry him eventually, but not for at least a year to be quite sure, to get over this feeling of dread and fear I still have at times, and to start university." They giggled together, like schoolgirls while the men looked, on wondering what it was all about. It was Ava's secret and Elle would keep it for her, much to James's annoyance, but he more or less guessed. He was well aware that Ava could be seduced, and respected Elle's loyalty to her adopted sister.

Later, James found himself alone with Ava while Elle was upstairs with Lucy, having their evening bedtime talk together. As Elle had suggested, he held her hand and said, "Elle has not betrayed your secret, Ava, but I can guess more or less what you two said to each other earlier on. You are a beautiful, passionate girl, Ava, with a bright future. It is time for you to put the past behind you. I have known for some time that you would soon do this, I fully expect that you will return from holiday with John all sparkling and full of love for each other, am I right? Is that what it was all about?"

"Yes, James, I know you understand me, but keep my secret too. I do not want John to guess. I can thank you because it is you that has helped me to change, your generosity and love made me realise that not all men are the enemy, even middle aged ones," she teased. "I know that I too can love again, because I love you."

James interrupted her. "No, Ava, do not say any more, or even think it, to me you are an adopted daughter. I am and always will be like a father to you. I will watch you marry, and have a family, just as I watch and help my own daughters. I know you are an emotional girl full of love, so give it all to John. Ava, my love, it is time to move on and live a full life with the boy that loves you, he deserves it, he has been so patiently waiting. Please tell me the dates and where you want to go, I will book and pay for your holiday."

Ava kissed him. "Thank you for being a father for me when I needed one, and taking care of me. But I cannot help it I do love you, James, and not just as a daughter. Elle is a lucky girl, but she deserves you, she is a strong woman and my friend, she will look after you for all of your daughters. When I have a family they will call you Grandpa James, if you let them. I will explain to them how you adopted me when I needed someone to care for me. I don't think Elle will want to be Granny, that will be Anne. Elle will be Aunty Elle, then Lucy will be big sister or another auntie. I have a family, thanks to you taking me into your house."

"Yes, Ava, I will be a grandpa to your children but no more talk of love, you know it is not me you need now, so please take your time, but move on with John and friends of your own age, that is the way to thank Elle and me."

CHAPTER FOURTEEN

Back to school time for Lucy. They had taken her for an interview and had a tour of Cedar Hall. Lucy was overjoyed when Elle said she could go there. The building was a country house, a family home from the last century, a small stately home extended to have facilities for girls of all ages. Some were boarders but many were day girls as Lucy would be for now. The uniform in green was typically expensive as was everything else. In total there were six hundred girls in classes of ten or less. The school had a reputation for academic excellence. Lucy was given a test for entry and passed easily; following the test the headmistress was noticeably more keen to accept Lucy. Before that she was, James thought, rather cool and stuck up. James was prepared to tell them to keep their school if he thought his wife's notoriety was a factor.

Today, for her first day, Elle drove her daughter to school with pride and deep satisfaction. Nothing confirmed her new life and status more than this journey, mother and daughter both impeccably dressed, driving a new Land Rover Discovery, James, her husband, with them to make sure his stepdaughter was happy and well treated. They parked amid the chaos of all the other girls arriving for the new term. They were met in the building by Miss Jane Terode who would be her head of year. Lucy kissed her mother and ran into the great hall without a backward glance, eager to start her new school life. Elle stood watching, overwhelmed with pride and love until James took her by the arm and led her back to the car. There were tears in her eyes and James held her as she composed herself.

"James, I know there have been many good days, but this is as important to me as any, other than our wedding day, my Lucy running into that great building, eager to learn and without a trace of fear. I could not do that. How can she be so different, what gives her that self confidence and drives her on so?"

James kissed her. "I do not know, darling. She has some inner motivation and stability that I have never seen before. My Leona was always clever and keen to get on, but nothing like Lucy. Come now, we will go and see Joan and have coffee with her."

Leona took orders for refreshments and went to buy them at the nearby coffee shop. Having returned, she distributed the various orders, then sat down laughing quietly to herself.

Joan looked at her curiously and asked, "What is amusing you, Leona?"

"You three are," she replied. "It struck me suddenly that you are like a mini harem, two wives chatting together, the older one having handed over marital duties to the younger one and his excellency sitting up like a sultan smiling benignly at the two of you."

"Very funny, dear, but not accurate. His smugness and I separated many years ago and there have been dozens of applicants trying out for the job since then. Elle came and took on the role, for her sins. Now his mightiness may be the sultan, but he may well have bitten off more than he can chew. I have a suspicion that submissive little wife number two is, in fact, more than a match for him, is that not so, master?"

"No, it is not so, actually, wife. I am firmly master of the harem as you call it. I am off to the loo. While I am gone get Elle to explain what happened when she thought she would take control and make me submit, assaulting me and trying to hold me down on the bed, having got me sufficiently drunk, I might add, or so she thought."

Elle gave a brief account of her attempt to subdue James and the punishment he dished out after winning the fight. Joan, and Leona both looked at her in amazement.

Leona said, "I have never heard of anything like that before. I cannot think of any of my friends that would fight their boyfriend, especially anyone as small as you Elle."

Joan said, "Leona, you should listen to Elle, she knows more about keeping her man happy than anyone else I have ever met. Be honest, Elle, you were never seriously trying to subdue James. You were boosting his ego, making him feel masterful, which we can all see he clearly does."

"You are right, I had no expectation of winning the fight, but it was not to boost his ego, that needs no boost. I suppose it was to confirm our relationship to each other, and frankly to have some fun. I loved it, very hands on and physical, most satisfying. Excuse me saying it, but the sex was exceptional when we finished the fight. We were both all roused up full of love for each other, then after that I have never felt happier or safer, sleeping in the arms of my strong man.

"That, Leona, if anything, is my lesson to you: decide in advance what sort of man you want to marry. They do not come any better than your father, but you have to let him wear the trousers if you are not to spend your life in arguments. As it happens, that is also the best way to get what you want. James will always make sure that I am happy, I do not have to ask for anything, it goes with his love and being in charge. You will manipulate that to your advantage, of course. Then there are areas and times when I take charge or make the decisions, like our new house, or the children. There is nothing wrong with equal responsibility, or a dominant wife, but sort it out before you ever marry someone like your father, understand what he needs. You will not change a man, however much you think you can, so do not love someone that is not compatible with your long term needs in the relationship."

Elle went to the loo. "She is perfectly right, Leona, that is why your father and I are good friends but no longer married. Elle is going to get the best out of him and they both come out winners."

James returned and Leona asked if her account of the event was accurate. Having heard her version he agreed it was broadly accurate.

Leona asked, "Why did she do it, Dad? I was not at all sure about her explanation."

"Well now, girls, my Elle is a bundle of fun. I never know what she will do next. She may be small, but she is brave and determined when she wants to be. But she has deep insecurities, or she did have, now I hope largely gone. When she first came to me, she slept with Lucy, but she had nightmares and Lucy told me she was crying at night. I took her into my bed and right up to our honeymoon she continued to wake up with horrible nightmares, shivering and sobbing in my arms. It brought us very close together, those moments in the middle of the night.

"Testing me might have had something to do with her antics that evening, to see how strong I was, and what I would do to her in return. But honestly, she does not need an excuse to surprise me with this sort of stunt. She did tell me afterwards that she had never felt so safe or happy, as she did when we lay together to go to sleep after it was all over. Her nightmares finally went around that time, on honeymoon, her security in marriage and knowing I am strong enough to look after not just her, but her beloved Lucy is what she needed to be sure of. But I do not expect much to change in the future. My Elle is full of trouble and mischief. I love it not knowing what she will do next. Look, here she comes, my trouble and strife, have you ever seen anything more beautiful? I know I never have."

Elle and James left for the golf club. Joan and Leona sat in silence for some time.

Leona said to her mother, "I knew they were in love, but Dad is absolutely besotted with Elle and she is with him. What do you make of that story? Is there more to it than Elle admits?"

"You are right, dear; I had not realised the full depth of their relationship or that Elle was ever so insecure. I think it puts the story of their fight into a different light. From what they both said, I think she may well have been testing him to make sure their relationship was strong and that he would be able to look after her and Lucy. Maybe not consciously, but that was what she wanted to be sure of. Sad on the one hand to feel the need to test him, but lovely on the other, your father has a wife that loves him to the hilt, much more than anyone without a history of trauma and rescue by her lover could. Elle will do everything in her power to keep him fit and happy. Your father is equally in love with the woman that was so traumatised and perhaps still insecure, he will do everything he can to make her feel safe and loved. That, Leona, is a perfect match. Take her advice and ask for more; that girl knows all about men, their needs and weaknesses. Your father may be the boss, but she will be quietly pulling the strings. It was good advice to work out what sort of a man you want before you fall in love with the wrong one. Elle is right you cannot change a man, or woman come to that, much as people think they will when the decide to make a life together."

***

James introduced Elle to one of the professionals at the golf club. They met at the driving range. This was a long, open, stable type building with ten-foot bays for golfers to stand in the dry and hit balls down the range to various targets, with distance measurements in bold numbers. At one end of the range was the teaching bay with video equipment for the professional to demonstrate the golfers' faults. Before the lesson could begin, they went to the golf shop to buy Elle a pair of shoes and a left hand glove. The pro produced two ladies clubs for the lesson as Elle had no golf equipment of her own. Most of the next hour was taken up with theory of the golf swing, learning how to grip the club and taking a stance. Towards the end of the lesson Elle was shown how to swing the club at a ball; she hit a few balls and was very satisfied with the result. The pro congratulated her and hoped to see her again soon.

Elle then joined James in his booth and had a go with one of his wedges at a green one hundred yards in front of them. Elle managed to get several balls on the green and was hooked; golf was to be her sport. James was delighted; golf was an excellent family pastime and sociable, based at the clubhouse with its facilities. Golf friends meet to play once or twice a week if they were not working, that included many of the wives among James's group; men usually played at weekends. They formed groups of likeminded friends, entertaining at home and meeting for drinks in pubs and at events in the club itself.

Elle and James, both pleased with the morning's introduction of Elle to the golf scene, changed their shoes and James put his clubs in the boot of the Defender. They made their way into the clubhouse to have lunch. A group of golfers, both men and women, friends of James, waved them over. Introductions were made all round, with several, while giving Elle a close scrutiny, saying how pleased they were to meet James's new wife. Elle explained that she was a beginner but would like to walk round to watch others play and learn the rules. It was arranged that a mixed foursome including James would play on Friday morning and Elle would caddy for her husband.

After lunch they made a stop at the supermarket to do the weekly shop and fill the time before going to fetch Lucy. They arrived at Cedar Hall and parked in front of the entrance that the girls should appear from. Eventually, in an exodus of schoolgirls, Lucy appeared accompanied by

Miss Terode. Lucy ran up to her mother excited and wanting to tell her about her first day at her new school, but was interrupted by Miss Terode.

"Hello, may I have a quiet word please, Mrs Jefferies?"

James took Lucy by the hand saying, "Come on, we will go to the car."

"Is there a problem, Miss Terode?"

"Not a problem in that sense, Mrs Jefferies, but we would like you to make an appointment with the headmistress and myself to discuss Lucy's education. We have had great difficulty assessing where Lucy fits in our streamed classes. It is only the first day but it is already clear that in some subjects she is average or even behind her age group, but in others she is so far ahead that we cannot decide which class she will fit into, in maths for example. As I say, this is, of course, the first day so we will have to conduct more tests in several subjects. But it would be helpful for us to know what her previous school said about her, and anything else that you can tell us."

"I see," said Elle. "We did take her to the university to be tested by some friends of my husband, they had the same problem and recommended we find the best school possible for now then look again in a year or two, she certainly surprised them in maths. That is the reason we chose Cedar Hall; you have a reputation for academic learning. I will telephone later after I talk to my husband. He takes a keen interest in Lucy's education."

"Thank you, Mrs. Jefferies, we will look forward to meeting you both to discuss your daughter. I think we are going to have our work cut out with Lucy, but it will be rewarding for us if she turns out to be as talented in some subjects as we think she might be, thank you for choosing Cedar Hall. She is a very assured and independent young lady and very well behaved. Lucy is a credit to you, Mrs. Jefferies."

Elle smiled to herself as she drove her family home. James looked at her, wondering what the teacher had said that gave Elle such obvious satisfaction.

"Right," James said when they were inside, and Elle was parking her car in the carport behind the house. "Did you have fun at school, Lucy?"

"Yes, thank you, James, I had tests, but some were easy, so I am not sure which class I'm supposedto be in." She ran upstairs to change as

Elle came in. "Spill the beans then, what did she say that made you smile?"

"The headmistress wants us to go and discuss Lucy. She is behind in some subjects but so far ahead in others like maths that they do not know what to do with her. They are pleased to have her in their school. She is, I was told, independent and well behaved. Miss Terode told me that she was a credit to me, that is what made me smile. A change of tone from the interview."

"Ah, you noticed that too, did you? I nearly told them to stuff their school. I think we are going to get our money's worth from that school as they get to grips with our Lucy. After tea, let's all go to Dunwood. The builders have more or less finished, yesterday I did a tour with Tom and the kitchen was being installed."

Ava and John arrived and joined them as they were having tea. "We are going to Dunwood," said Lucy. "Are you two coming to explore with us?"

"Not me," said John. "My mother needs me to help with a dinner she has arranged for some of their friends."

"I will come with you, please," said Ava. "I want to see the house now it is nearly finished. I am so happy that I can come with you, I will do all the housework to earn my keep."

"No, you will not," said James. "Elle will have a plenty of hired help in the house to take care of that, as she is going to play golf and do the garden. You, Ava, will be too busy studying at university, I hope."

"Yes, James, I will, thank you, I want to be a teacher. I speak four languages now. I will be a translator and a teacher for special needs among the ethnic community, so many wives do not speak English, and many are abused. I will help just as I have been helped myself by you two and Joan."

This time, for a change, they went in James car.

The inside of Dunwood House had a completely different feel now that the renovations were nearly complete. The kitchen and day room was now one large living space with the working kitchen at one end, featuring a marble topped central workstation with an eight burner hob and a wooden chopping block built in. A breakfast bar to seat four was fitted along one side. An AGA cooker with four ovens would keep the room warm, giving the farmhouse effect. In addition, there was also vertical stack of two more ovens, one a combi multi-function unit with microwave, the other a modern top of the range electric oven with WI FI temperature control and a steam function. A full range of country style units with matching marble tops surround the kitchen area, with a space left for a fridge freezer. Leading off the kitchen was the new annex containing the larder, a sink unit, the laundry, a broom cupboard and work tops with drawers. Coats would hang in the passageway to the door that led to the garden and driveway.

The living end of the room was bare, ready for the new furniture that Elle and James had ordered with the help of an interior designer from Tom's office. She was commissioned to furnish and decorate the house to the detailed instructions that Elle and James had given her. The sunroom on the south side was now complete and full of sun, again waiting to be furnished. Upstairs, all the bedrooms were completed in the new layout, walls rebuilt to form bathrooms that had yet to be installed. The master bedroom was an impressive, large, corner room on the south west of the house, with French windows on to a new balcony. The bathrooms with windows on the west side had his and her ends with a double spa bath in a wet area between the two. It all looked perfect for a newly married couple. The bedroom was complete and ready for the bed and other furniture.

Most of James's existing furniture would stay in the old house, which would remain fully furnished, for the girls, their friends and as an overflow for guests if there was not enough room at Dunwood. Ava had been given the choice of which house she wanted to make her home: with the girls, who were away most of the time, or as family at Dunwood. James confided to Elle that he expected her to ask for the master bedroom in the old house, if or when she finally overcame her reservations about sleeping with John, and should they decide to move in together. Elle agreed it would be ideal for Ava's full recovery and also that the independence that this gave her might outweigh the benefit of living as family. Elle said that she would talk to her as her friend to say it would be available for her to choose, as none of James's daughters showed any signs of having a regular boyfriend; they were having too much fun playing the field.

Of the four remaining bedrooms, the biggest and best would be kept as a guest room. That left one with its own bathroom and two using the main and visitors' bathroom. Elle allocated one of these for Lucy, as she went to bed early and could always come and use the bathroom in her mother's bedroom if she wanted to. Ava said that if she stayed in this house, she would be happy to share with Lucy and have next door bedrooms, leaving the final bedroom with bath available for visitors.

John and Ava, planning their holiday break, were deciding how they might best get to the hotel in Sidmouth that they had chosen. To hire a car so they could explore the Jurassic Coast or go by train to Exeter and taxi and stay in the town? In the end, James intervened to solve the problem by putting John on his insurance and lending them the Range Rover, declaring, "I am happy to be chauffeured about by Elle in her new car for a few days."

Excited by their adventure, the holiday couple set off and enjoyed a sedate drive across country to the Dorset coast, then west into Devon and Sidmouth's harbour hotel. They each had their own expectations for the four-day break. John hoped to make progress towards a normal relationship sometime soon, or at least in the not too distant future. Ava worried that she might not be able to convince John that he had actually seduced her, rather than she had wanted to be seduced and given in rather too easily, especially if she let herself go and gave John the sort of sex she had enjoyed before the rape. She rather suspected he was less experienced than she was. He was loving, kind and gentle; her needs were for him to use the opportunity to force the pace and make her give in. She was ashamed that, much as she loved John, she could not shake off the deep feeling that she wanted James to take her to bed and drive away her demons with the sort of domination and shagging that she just knew he would give her. She fought against it but could not shake the longing, off especially at night.

John was fully aware of Ava's feelings for James. He had already discussed James's generosity towards his girlfriend with his mother. He wondered if there was more to their friendship than he knew. He thought it strange that someone would take in a stray girl and spoil her as James did Ava. He suspected that Ava loved him, and not as a father, despite her experience with men his age. His mother told him not to worry; it was a lot to do with his love for his new wife as she was herself in Ava's position once and James, as her rescuer, was supporting Elle who had, in turn, rescued Ava. He also loved all his other girls and she fitted into the gang. Of course, neither knew just how well off James really was. Had they known that the appreciation and interest on his investments was more than he could spend, including buying and fitting out a new house, they would have been less concerned. Nonetheless, it did not really answer John's question as to why Ava appeared to love James as much as she did; it was Elle that was her benefactor.

They checked in as James had booked them, Mr. and Mrs. John Jones, and went up to their bedroom with its large windows giving views over the coast. Having tipped the porter, they walked on to the full length balcony overlooking the swimming pool and the sea beyond. As a Polish girl, Ava had not been to the seaside very often before, other than day trips. She did not possess a bathing costume, so, their first trip was to the hotel shop to buy a bikini and a sun dress. *Thank you again, James*, she thought, as she produced her credit card and it went through without any hitch. They next explored the hotel, had lunch in the main bar then went back to their room. They changed into swimming costumes for a dip in the pool, but first Ava lay on the bed and held out her arms.

John came and embraced her, kissing her full on the mouth. Ava slipped her leg between his and felt his erection with her knee, well satisfied and aroused with what she felt. She waited for John to rub his knee between her legs where she had a hot feeling that needed itching, but it did not happen. *I have frightened him too much*, she thought.

Later, after swimming, they had their first gourmet dinner as a couple, or indeed ever, sitting in the window seating that went with the prime bedroom they were occupying. The whole experience was new to both of them. Neither had holidayed in such luxury before, candles on the tables and exceptional service with food to match; they felt fully relaxed and happy. They had eaten well and drank much more than either was accustomed to, finishing off with liqueurs. The staff seemed eager to please them, suspecting that they were newly married.

Back in the bedroom, they played for time having a final drink from the mini bar. By consent they used the bathroom separately, showering and putting on their night clothes and getting into bed. Ava was wearing her smallest pair of briefs that covered almost nothing under a short nightdress. It would not be necessary for John to take them off if he got very bold; just to push them to one side to get what she was sure he must be desperate for… She hoped he would try and save her the trouble of making it happen tomorrow while convincing John that he had actually seduced her. Ava would, however, stick to her plan and wait for the second night before forcing the issue by taking control. After fumbling and kissing, John was not sure what more he was allowed to do. Getting no help from Ava, he gave up and they went to sleep.

Later in the night, James came to Ava. He said to her, "It is high time you had proper sex, Ava, and stopped just dreaming about it. L have come to sort you out. Take your knickers off and open your legs." James pulled her nightdress up and fondled her breasts, then he pushed her back on the bed and was about to enter her.

As he paused, she shouted, "Yes, James, fuck me now, fuck me hard, please, James, make me cum."

Then she woke up in John's arms with his hand on her breast. There was silence. She said, "My god, what has happened? I had a nightmare."

John intervened. "Wait, Ava, do not say anything, think for a while then tell me the truth about you and James." Ava was devastated by what had happened and started to cry. John held her and said again, "Tell me the truth, Ava, please, it is only fair. I love you and must know how I stand."

"I will be completely honest with you, John, as long as you promise to keep it all secret. Whatever you decide to do, promise not to tell anyone what just happened, no one, especially your mother and Elle."

"I promise you, Ava."

"I can tell you, John, that I love you and there is nothing going on between James and me. Quite the reverse, just last week he told me that I was a daughter to him and that I should get over my abuse, give all my love to you and get married, our children would call him Grandpa James. He loves me as a daughter, he told me, just as he loves his own, and Lucy. Elle, who knows more about men than anyone, would know immediately if anything happened between her James and me, so you need have no worries on that score."

"Then, Ava, why are you shouting his name in the middle of the night?"

"John, I will be as honest as I can be, you deserve that, but I do not understand it all myself. I can only guess, and it may not reflect well on me. Firstly, I am no innocent little girl. I lost my virginity soon after my fifteenth birthday, I will need to tell you more about this another time. From then up until the time of the rape, I was very sexually active and had affairs with all sorts of men, many much older than me. I was then genuinely traumatised by the rape, here in a strange country whose language I did not speak, by revolting middle aged men. Two things have happened to change me from the pathetic little girl you first met and fell in love with back to something more like my old self. The first was Elle telling me and your mother that it was not the sex in rape that upset her, and she was a virgin, it was the helpless feeling of being held down, stripped naked while men took turns to have sex with her. I began to realise that for me as well it was not the actual sex that traumatised me; it was the helplessness while being abused. Elle urged me not to associate all men with my rape, she meant you, of course, John. The second thing that happened was that when we were last in bed and I felt your erection, I suddenly really wanted it in me. I realised that I needed sex, you could have had me then, John. You remember, that was when I suggested a holiday.

"I made the suggestion because I felt that I could not change so quickly without appearing insincere, I needed to save face, after all my talk of never having sex again, so I thought if it happened on a holiday you would get the credit and your mother would not be surprised and be proud of you. Elle, of course, guessed, we had a that talk in Polish. I told her that I was going to give in to you on the second night, to let you seduce me, we laughed about it. We were talking in Polish but James guessed what we were saying. Later when we were alone, he took me in his arms, that was when he told me he would give us the holiday and for me to get on with it, to give all my love to you, you deserved it for waiting so patiently, he always knew that I wanted sex and would soon love again but needed a kick up the backside, he was never going to be the one to do it, that I promise you, John."

"Okay, I get all that, Ava, but you have not answered the question."

"I know, John, but I wanted to make it quite clear that James has never given me any encouragement. It is not fair to a man that has done so much for me and that I love, not to make that point clear to you. Elle took me back to his house when I had nowhere to go except council care. He tried to welcome me, but Elle sent him away as I was not in the mood for middle aged men. So, typical of James, he went out and bought me a whole basket of continental treats. Over time I saw the way he was loved by his ex-wife Joan, all his daughters and Lucy, and the way he loves my friend Elle; it is impossible for a girl not to love him. Just as I wanted a mother, I saw him as a father. He hugged me when I cried and gradually my love turned into so much more. Let me think for a while, John, this is complicated and does not reflect well on me."

After an hour lying in silence in John's arms Ava continued. "I began to be obsessed by the sex side of the rape and Elle's explanation of how she rationalised it. Please do not repeat this but she went on to have fun sex in the brothel with respectable married men and others. As I thought about her explanation, I began to want to experience sex again. I wanted rough sex with a strong man, one that I loved and trusted, in fact with, frankly, I admit, James. I talk to Elle and know just what he could do to me if I pushed him into it. The simple fact is, John, I have a fantasy that I am being raped by James, not the men that did it to me. It is hard to explain but I think that if I block out the rapists, substitute James, then the experience becomes an extreme erotic pleasure, one that I want to repeat. There, now you know my secret, why I cried out his name when you started to play with my breast while I was aroused in bed with you, but asleep. Had I decided to give in to you on the first night rather than the second, none of this would have happened. I am so sorry, John. I asked your mother how I could love two men. She said that I am confused. That is a simple truth, because you are so gentle and loving, a perfect husband. But James is capable of being wicked in a way that excites women, me because of my abuse, it makes me want to rationalise the experience like Elle did to get over it. It is not normal, but we all have to come to terms with trauma in our own way. Do you understand, John, none of this is your fault, you are kind and loving, I have to get over the past before I can move on and marry."

"Stand up, Ava, come here, you will obey me now, forget James. I will give you my answer. Stand in front of me and strip naked. Good and now those silly briefs, take them off. Stand up straight, girl, put your hands on your head and turn round slowly. Good, you are super sexy, Ava. You have not talked to Leona and her sisters about me, have you, Ava? You think I am not man enough to give you rough sex to drive away your trauma. I want you, Ava, I love you, I intend to marry you; it seems I have to prove that I am man enough for you. That is exactly what I am about to do. I have a simple choice for you, Ava. Would you prefer rough sex now and the spanking in the morning or the other way around? Yes, James told us in the pub about being attacked by Elle and how he struggled to subdue her."

"John, it's a nice idea and I enjoyed stripping for you, it is the least I could under the circumstances. But I am bigger and stronger than Elle. If you can force me to have sex while I struggle to stop you, then give me a good spanking in the morning, which I will not let you. If you can do both then I will marry you any time you want, and you can do what you like with me. I will fight to stop you so be warned, I am no pushover, nor will I give in as Elle always will. This could be fun, John, but watch out, I am nearly as big as you and pretty strong."

Before Ava could move John was holding one of her arms behind her back and had his knee between her legs. He threw her on the bed and followed on top of her, forced her legs apart and pushed his hard cock into her. He had her arms pinned above her head with one hand. Ava was quite helpless, it all happened so quickly she had no idea how he did it.

He said, "Now, my girl, what shall I do, stop, or give you a good shagging?"

"You are the boss, John, do what you like to me."

John started a vigorous motion but came almost immediately and went limp on top of her.

"Sorry, Ava, that was not very rough, but I was too worked up to make it last."

"John, that was amazing how did you suddenly become a rapist? No man would have lasted longer than that after what you have been through these last few weeks of denial and arousal. One minute I was standing up next I was on my back with my legs open. Come here, big man, let me hold you. That will do for part one. You have seduced me, John, there will be no more play acting. In future you do what you want to me."

"Ava, go to the table and write on the hotel stationary that you will marry me when I complete the test tomorrow morning, sign it, and date it."

They lay in silence in each other's arms thinking about all that had happened, eventually falling asleep.

In the morning John held Ava in his arms kissed her and said, "I too had a plan. I was going to give you until our last night then if you had not given in and had sex, I was going to get a bit forceful, not rough but demanding. I felt sure that you were ready, as you have admitted you wanted it then I was correct, I could see that, but was not sure you realised it yourself. I am in charge now, Ava so, never again will we have secrets from each other. I do have one remaining myself that I will admit to you later after breakfast. Now, I do not intend to jump you as I did last night, so when shall I spank you?"

"Let us have a cup of coffee John, then we can see what you can do. You were lucky last night, I was not ready. It must be across your knee or it does not count."

Later they faced each other by the bed.

"Why are you grinning like that, John? I am not going to let you spank my bottom. I am not little Elle and you are not James."

By way of reply, John stared into her face to disorient her. She did not realise that he was already moving quickly until he took hold of her arm, turning her around to face the bed. John again threw her on to the bed, this time face down. He had both her arms pinned behind her back and his leg over hers as he simultaneously pulled her up over his other leg. This, as the night before, all happened so fast she had no time to wriggle or fight. She was trapped across his leg with the other over hers and both hands pinned in one of his, her face in the bed. He had great satisfaction spanking her bottom hard until she cried enough.

"John, I give in."

As Ava sat up and looked at John in amazement, he said, "About the last secret that I have, remember I said you had not talked to the girls about me. Well, if you had they might have told you that I was under eighteens' Judo champion, for the south of England." Ava started to laugh, and John joined in before telling her, "I am now going to take charge of you, Ava. You are confused and need someone to guide you. I will do that, you will obey me now that you know that I can enforce my will on you. Your bottom is super sexy over my knee, so watch out. We will marry in one year on this day, our anniversary of engagement as per this contract that you signed last night."

Ava started to get emotional. "That is what I need, John. I now have a new mother, a father, but most of all I need a lover to help me forget the past. I do not mean the recent past. I will tell you how I came to lose my virginity at fifteen and go off the rails. No one else knows, not even Elle, it will be our secret. I could not get up courage to tell your mother, but it is my original problem."

"Will you tell me now, Ava?"

"No, John, I am just letting you know there is more for you to know about me. For now you have done enough, you have more or less eliminated the James fantasy, thank you, you are now my strong man, as he is Elle's. I want to enjoy the rest of the holiday with you in charge. I will relax and maybe for the first time since I was a teenager, I will be genuinely happy. Enjoy yourself with me, do anything you want with me, John, you deserve it so give me plenty of love and sex, maybe try something you lust for but cannot get from your past partners who no doubt were inexperienced young girls."

That night, after another luxury dinner and plenty of drink, they went to bed early. This time they showered together, taking their time, soaping and exploring each other. John held out a towelling dressing gown to Ava, then he put one on himself. He poured two miniature brandies and patted the sofa for Ava to sit down beside him.

"Now, my pretty Polish darling, I am the boss. From now on everything is going to change for you, whatever has happened to you in the past, and you can tell me about it another time, it appears to have caused you to become rather obsessed with sex of an advanced nature. You want me to join you and have fun doing what I like with you, as you put it. Ava, I do not believe this is the real you, it certainly is not me. Now and again perhaps, this morning was fun for example, for me at least, but I am going to wean you off this type of sex, for the sake of our future relationship. We cannot get married if you are wanting rough sex, it may be fun now and again, but long-term relationships must be based on gentle love and understanding. Talk to Elle, Ava, she knows how to get the best out of their relationship, including attacking James to let him give vent to his caveman needs once in a while. Starting tonight, I want you to be gentle and loving and that is what I shall be. I think that I have proved myself enough, you know that I can be rough if I have to be, now I will be gentle John again. You are a beautiful young girl, Ava, why should I be rough with you? It is up to you now to prove to me that you no longer need rough handling, except in occasional playacting. I will respect and treat you accordingly, so forget the bedroom gymnastics. I want you soft and feminine please, while we sort ourselves out, please be submissive and let me look after you as you say you want me to.

"John, you are right, I do not know what the real me is any more, that is my problem. Sex is like a drug before I came to England I had been associating with older more experienced men, well never mind now, I thought it was normal. Now I realise they were using me. I do want to be loved and spoiled by you, John. I have loved you since we first met. I want to start again; I will do whatever you say. I want eventually to have a normal married life, for now I want an education, while I have the opportunity, so help me to readjust, please, John."

"We are agreed then, Ava, here is to our future, you and me together. Come on, my love, we will go to sleep in each other's arms, you will feel safe and loved, but be warned, if you call out any name tonight, make sure it is mine or tomorrow morning will start as today did."

Their relationship had matured overnight. They began a friendship that was to grow as they made plans for university and found that they had many interests in common. Sex was not an issue or mentioned again until the final night.

So, John was my James all the time, it is so deceptive, because of his youthful and gentle ways I completely misunderstood his true character, which is odd as he has been so strong these last few weeks. Now I am fully in his care, which is what I needed all along, I will just relax and do as he tells me until I feel strong enough to be at least an equal partner for him. I do love him completely. If we can somehow manage to live together, then in a month or two, I will know if he is the one for me.

They lingered over the dinner, savoured the wine and liqueurs, the coffee in the lounge, then went up to the bedroom. The lovers shared a bath before finally climbing into bed. John whispered loving words in Ava's ears as he slowly explored her with his hands and mouth. Ava knew what he expected of her and relaxed to enjoy the rare experience of being aroused by a lover who wanted to give her pleasure. With a supreme effort, John controlled his own overwhelming urge to end weeks of restraint and give full vent to his lust and passion. He embraced Ava as he moved up between her open legs. She guided him in and together they experienced their first normal sex as an engaged couple, something neither had thought possible two weeks before. Again, John came prematurely, and Ava again consoled him, fully understanding the effort he was making, and had been for weeks for her sake. They both knew it really was not the time for holding back and gentle loving sex, there had been much too much tension built up between them, but he was bound by his own new rules.

In the morning Ava said, "Now you relax, John, while I give you a treat." She gently worked him up and lying on top, she took the lead and slowly brought him to an explosive climax, finally releasing all his remaining tension, and dispelling the notion that Ava could never have a normal relationship again.

They were ready to return home and face Elle, James and John's mother and explain the sudden change. To announce their engagement and ask James if he would let them live together in his old house, while they went to university.

***

Elle and James entered Cedar Hall through the main entrance and were met by Miss Terode, who escorted them to the headmistress's study. Mrs. Judy Palmer welcomed them with a warm smile.

"I am pleased to meet you both. Lucy is a personable and intelligent young lady. She has told us all about how you two met and married, it is quite a story. She is a credit to you both, she fully understands the circumstances, as do we all, with the publicity and public sympathy you received at the time of your wedding. You have our sympathy and support as well."

James replied, "Thank you, Mrs. Palmer. I can confirm that Lucy knows what she wants. As you say, I too have found since I have known her that she is mature beyond her years. My wife has always put her daughter first and will do whatever she can to give her the best education available so that she can make full use of her talents later in life. I fully support my her in this."

"Good, then let us talk about Lucy. With time and the extra testing we have been able to give her, we have concluded that in some areas Lucy is as talented as any pupil of her age we have had here at Cedar Hall. In others she is of a normal ability, then in certain areas no amount of effort on our part will persuade her to take it seriously, or I regret to say in some cases take part at all, mainly sport and recreation."

James smiled to himself. *That is our Lucy,* he thought.

"I see you smile, Mr. Jefferies, you recognise our diagnosis, I think."

"Yes, Mrs. Palmer, that is my conclusion since I have known her, just like her mother, I might add."

Elle intervened. "James, do you mind, I am here; I can speak for myself and my daughter. My Lucy is, I hope, always polite and willing. She just has had to cope with some unpleasant times in the past and her method is to see the bigger picture and dedicate herself to what she believes matters. She is advanced for her age. I regret this may be as a result of a recent marital situation and an abusive father. We have discussed this together, we talk about all these things, she understands more than she should have to. I am proud of my daughter. No one will prevent her achieving her goals in life when she decides what they are, that in my opinion is the role the education should concentrate on. She cannot be easily driven, but can be led. She has a thirst for information. Nature is near the top of her list at the moment, although her talent is for maths. She loves animals, the dolphins, for example, and butterflies."

"I agree," said Jane Terode, who had been listening with interest to the exchanges. "Lucy is a lovely girl. We have had long conversations; it like talking to an equal. She is very loyal to both of you and appreciates her current situation, including being sent to our school. As you said, she understands much more than one might expect for a girl of her age. Sit her in the library and give her relevant information and she will work all day."

"Thank you, Jane," said Mrs. Palmer. "Are we agreed that we will concentrate on her priorities for now and see how Lucy develops? She will stay in the appropriate year, which for her is with eight and nine-year-olds."

The teachers noted the look of love exchanged between the newlywed couple. *These are the parents we appreciate*, they thought with satisfaction, *a talented pupil fully backed by generous parents, this may be good for the school in many ways, they have powerful friends and a daughter that may be good enough to make a name for herself and enhance our reputation.*

Later that evening, as Elle was in the bathroom preparing to go to bed, she suddenly shouted out loud. "James, come here now."

When he arrived, Elle was in a highly emotional state. She flung herself into James's arms.

"Elle, whatever is the matter?"

"James, my darling man, what would you want most of all?"

"You, baby, you, what else do I want?"

"How about being a father again, darling? I am pregnant."

"Elle, that is amazing, we are going to have our baby, what can I say. I know this means so much to you, to have a second child, but also it means a great deal to me, it makes our marriage complete, you me, Lucy and baby. Let's go and tell Lucy she is going to have a brother or sister."

Lucy was still awake, so they gave her the news. Elle said to her. "Lucy, this is our family, we three, but soon we will be four with a baby, what do you think of that?"

"A baby, Mummy, I have always wanted a brother, so make it a boy, please."

"We will have to wait and see, my love, so far James has only made girls and so have I."

"I will spoil you now, Elle, you must take it easy. No more jumping on me, no rough housing, no heavy work." He held her in an embrace, kissing her, overwhelmed by the news. He had never expected to do the baby bit again; he was retired and fancy free until a few short months ago, having three grown up daughters. Now the woman he loved more than anything in the world was about to carry and deliver his baby, turning the clock back nearly twenty years.

"James," Elle said, "I do believe there are tears in your eyes. I have never seen you like this before, so emotional, you will set me off again. I am so happy that you want our baby as much as I do. In the morning we must tell everyone."

They went to bed naked, with Elle fitting into James as they faced the same way. Contented, they both reflected on the changes this new life they were incubating would bring.

I cannot believe that this is happening to me, on top of everything else I am pregnant, I know we were trying but somehow I never actually took the possibility seriously. James was so emotional, there were tears in his eyes. That means so much to me, the only tears he has come near to having since we met are for our baby, my strong man reduced to tears by the thought of me having his baby. I can see them now, big strong James holding a tiny baby, what more could any woman want. What more could any baby want. This changes everything, our life will now be rooted in domestic affairs, not pleasure seeking.

The girls were due to arrive back that morning. Elle wanted to tell everyone the news together so James thought a supper at Dunwood House would be a way to show off the completed renovations and use the kitchen living room for the first time. They invited Joan and Simon and Ava invited John. Lucy managed to keep the secret but was bubbling over with excitement.

The new kitchen had been fitted out by the specialists and the interior designer with a full range of pots, pans and electrical aids such as processors and mixers, everyday cutlery and most of the essential things needed. However, there were many tools and gadgets yet to be obtained, some of which James wanted to bring with him from his existing kitchen in Landford Cottage. The same would apply to the rest of the house, ornaments pictures and many personal items and some furniture would come to Dunwood House to make it a home and these would be replaced with new at the old home. For today, they would go to the supermarket and stock the store cupboard, the refrigerator, and the freezer. It will be an ideal exercise to start with a buffet supper for the family and friends. A second load came from Landford Cottage, mainly of wine, two bottles of champagne, glasses, a corkscrew, also plates and dishes and many more odds and ends.

"That's it," said Elle. "Enough. Whatever is missing we will have to do without and sort things out before we move in next week."

James, Elle, and Lucy went early to Dunwood and laid out the buffet, preparing the salad, cooking new potatoes, party sausages and plating a range of cold meat and seafood. The other guests arrived together; they all went to explore the house, taking their drinks with them. When they gathered back in the kitchen, James handed out champagne.

Now he announced, "Elle and I welcome you all to Dunwood House, our new family home. We will drink a toast to this and to our news. We do have bedrooms for any of you that want to stay with us rather than at Landford at any time, all the extended family are welcome, also friends," he said, looking at John. "However we will have one less bedroom than we planned for. Elle tells me that she wants to use one of the bedrooms for a nursery." He paused then continued. "For the latest member of the Jefferies family due to join us in seven or so months' time."

After a pause to let it sink in, he raised his glass and said, "Here is to Elle and our baby."

There was a stunned silence while they continued to absorb the unexpected news, none of the guests or family had ever thought of them, particularly James, having a baby. The girls were the first to react, grabbing Lucy and all four dancing a jig together with the familiar cry of, "Oh Daddy, what have you done," Lucy this time fully one of the gang, still beside herself with excitement.

Ava hugged Elle, then kissed James. Joan and Simon were full of congratulations, Joan making a private comment to her ex-husband that made him smile, before embracing Elle and saying that it was exactly what they needed and wishing her every happiness.

James shook hands with John and said, "There you are, John, that is how it is done, get on with it and they can grow up together."

Ava piped in and said, "I heard that, you boys, I will have some say in that."

Elle

I am having one of my moments. As I look around the kitchen of our new house, that I own jointly with James, as we celebrate our news with his family and others, and as I watch my Lucy dance around with her grown up step-sisters, I once again have the feeling that I am dreaming and taking part in a film, that I will wake up and find that I am in back with George. How can this be me, standing here, pregnant, being congratulated by this excited and happy gathering? James my husband and father of our baby, is looking at me with love and concern, he knows me so well he can guess how I am feeling, he can see my doubts and insecurity. Thank you, James, he is coming to take care of me, he will hold me, reassure me, and tell me again that our baby is everything he could wish for. He loves me, he has done so ever since he first saw me, that is why we are here today. I love him back and have done since that fateful day, I know all this, but I need him to hold me, to reassure me once more, and make me feel safe, to make it all real again for me. Dreams do come true, I have to believe that. Do I want a boy that all the girls can spoil rotten or another girl for James to spoil? I must not have a favourite myself; a son would be my choice if I made one, but I would love to give my lover one more girl to add to his collection. One more to smother him with love as she grows up and later in his old age. He deserves anything that I can give him, it is just as well we cannot decide our baby's sex, I don't think that I want to know before the birth.

James

Elle is standing there in a trance, the emotion has got to her, poor girl she is unable to absorb all the things that have happened to her. After all we have been through these last few months, or perhaps because of it all, she still has these times of mental, emotional overload. It is just too much in a relatively short time. A new house, me her new husband, happy friends. Her beloved Lucy happy and developing at an unbelievable rate. Now on top of everything else she has the one thing she has secretly longed for, another baby, she hopes that it is truly what I want as well but cannot be sure. I will go and comfort her, she looks so adorable and lost, just as she did when we first met. I will only have to give her a cuddle, whisper a few reassuring words, convince her that I really do want another baby with her, then she will fire up and go again. This baby, when it arrives, with all the drama, the feeding, I hope naturally, and lack of sleep, will finally dispel all her insecurities. She will be doing what she does best, being a mother. My Elle will feel needed by the helpless little mite, this will drive away her doubts of self-worth, it will be her sole responsibility, for once I will be able to take a back seat. She is a wonderful mother; I cannot wait to see her holding our baby, with Lucy that makes a family of four, perfect.

***

James's daughters followed their father to congratulate them both. Leona put her arms around Elle and whispered, "Thank you, Elle, I think that you have saved my father from wasting the rest of his life. He is a family man and has been lost since we daughters left home. I cannot wait to see him hold another baby, my half brother or sister. Mother is also delighted. She was worried about the old fool, now we can all sit back and watch the fun. He will be busy for the next few years doing what he is really good at, being a family man again." She then said, "Come on, Lucy, we will go and hand round some food."

Both Elle and James were happy that the youngest daughter was coming under the supervision of her eldest sister; the whole family was knitting together without any friction or jealousy.

John and Ava came to add their good wishes, and to ask how they felt about them living together. John said it was important that he was able to build on their relationship to help his fiancée over her difficult period of adjustment. James gave his permission and his approval, he kissed Ava and again advised them both to take it slowly, and let their love grow at its own pace.

Later that night as James kissed her stomach, then went on to slowly kiss the rest of her, Elle lay relaxed with her hands behind her head watching him, enjoying his gentle arousal that she knew was going to end in slow, loving, satisfying sex. Much later, it ended up with her lying on top of her lover with her arms around his neck, kissing his handsome face and thanking him for coming to her rescue at Dunwood House.

"James, let's book the removal men for Wednesday. That will give us two days to pack up all your personal things, office desk and all your books. I want to be there now and get ready for Lulu, to make our baby a nursery."

"You are not serious are you, my love, Lulu?"

"No, darling, I am not, but if it is a girl we will have to find a name beginning with L. and not Lolita either. Maybe Laura."

CHAPTER FIFTEEN

Despite only taking some of the furniture with most of the ornaments and pictures, the next week was the usual moving upheaval and stress. Much of what was taken from Landford Cottage would have to be replaced. What was neither taken and nor provided by the developers had to be bought new for Dunwood. It would take time to sort both houses out. Finally, they called it a day and had supper, the family Jefferies together in their new house. Lucy had already occupied the desk in the library corner and set up her computer, much to the amusement and satisfaction of her parents. They were busy sorting out the bedrooms. "What we need now," said James, "is a housekeeper, someone that is more than a daily help, someone who can organise and take charge of the housework, not just follow instructions."

"No, James, I will not have a housekeeper. That is my responsibility. I will look after our house, our garden and family, especially you, my love. Have no fear, you will not be forgotten, you will get special treatment. We will employ as many cleaners and even a young au pair come nanny as we need, but I will supervise them all. I am your housekeeper. That is why you married me, because I am young, fit and healthy enough to look after you and your house, and it appears also to be your gardener, is it not?"

"Yes, darling, it is, but I did not realise you sussed that, I mean what else could I have wanted you for?"

"What indeed, my love, you are much too old to appreciate any of my other assets." Elle was locked in the downstairs cloakroom long before James caught up. When she thought the coast was clear she came out and made it to the stairs before he picked her up and carried her giggling to the bedroom.

"Too old, am I, we will see about that, my fit young asset and housekeeper."

Back at Landford Cottage, the lucky young occupants were having a kitchen meeting to organise themselves. James had designated Leona as the head of the house and threatened to sell up if they did not behave or failed to keep the house in a satisfactory condition. They settled the bedroom allocation, with Ava having the master bedroom as James had stipulated. Leona took the guest bedroom and the other two tossed for the remaining options. They agreed that a schedule would be produced weekly setting out who did the cooking or the cleaning. Their first task was to make a list of all the things that needed to be replaced after the move. Next they agreed that there would be no parties or guests except by a vote with majority agreement. They sent John for a takeaway and settled down for the evening.

***

"Good morning, Jonathan."

"Good morning Mrs. Jefferies."

"Elle, please, Jonathan."

"You have moved in, I see, Elle."

"Yes, I am pleased to say that at last we are here to stay. Now I can take more interest in our garden, but I have not been idle. I have been weeding and dead heading. I also spent time looking up as many of the plants as I could. For example, I see we have quite a variety of fruit in that enclosure. I identified raspberries, gooseberries, and I think blackcurrants."

"That is correct and there is plenty of fruit on the bushes. In the orchard we also have apples, pears and plums with one pear tree that does not appear to have any fruit this year."

"That is all new and exciting. I will learn how to make jam like an old fashioned W.I. cook. There is nothing in the vegetable garden Jonathan, is it too late?"

"No, Elle, it is not too late for some things, but it would be best to buy plants rather than sow seeds. We could also buy bedding plants to fill in the flower beds and make a splash for this year. The problem is time. I am pushed as it is to keep the garden up to an acceptable of standard."

"I quite understand, I do not want to overload you, there will be other things we will want to do as well, so have you any more time you can give us, or shall we look for an assistant for you?"

"As a matter of fact, Elle, I can make another day for you if you would like me to. I have been working for several years for one of your neighbours, that was until she recently sold and moved away. I do not like the new owners, they are not proper gardeners; they are not really interested in the garden at all. They want everything done on the cheap, so I am happy to give my notice and do another day for you. This is the garden that I love best and have worked in for many years. It deserves to be kept to a high standard, which I admit that I struggle to do at the moment. It has great scope for big improvements as well, given time and money and with help from contractors to do some basic landscaping, so it will be satisfying for me to be able to spend more of my time here helping you with that. I will give then a week's notice, and in the meantime I will squeeze in extra hours here during the week."

"Jonathan, that is really good of you, I appreciate it and so will James. We are happy to hire you for as long it takes to make these alterations over the next few months and to spend the necessary money to get the garden up to the standard that you want, then to maintain it. Are you happy with the arrangements that James came too with you? Please say if you are not, I want you to have top rates to make up for the extra hassle of teaching me."

"Elle, I could not be more happy with the arrangement your husband made with me, or if I might say, teaching you. It brightens up my day having you as my assistant, your daughter is also good to have around, she asks sensible questions and is interested, especially in the wildlife. Did you know we have badgers that cross the property at night? They are nocturnal creatures of habit and always follow the same tracks into the field next door. We also have hedgehogs that Lucy is looking for."

"Thank you, Jonathan, it is good of you to encourage her. Do you have children?

"Yes, I have two, David is eight and Jane is ten."

"Let's arrange the date for you bring them to tea with us one afternoon soon with your wife, so they can see where you spend so much of your time."

"Thank you, Elle, Elisabeth is quite keen to meet you and your family."

"I am not surprised, Jonathan, and what about your friends in the pub, do they tease you?" Elle asked with a mischievous smile.

"Frankly, yes, and I have had plenty of pints, thank you, before I agree to tell all, then I explain that this is a normal family household with keen gardeners as my employers. If it helps, Elle, I can tell you that everyone that speaks to me is sympathetic and deeply sorry to hear of the trouble that you and others experienced. We all hope the perpetrators get their just desserts, and by all accounts you are partly responsible for bringing them to justice. I can assure you that I do not gossip, but when my friends hear who I work for they are curious to hear more."

"Thank you, Jonathan, I appreciate that and yes, I will do what I can to lock them up for many years. Not all the women involved have been as lucky as I am, married to a loving husband. I am doing it for them as well as for myself. Shall we meet at Skiptons garden centre on the main road tomorrow morning, Jonathan, to see what we can buy?"

"Good idea, Elle, I have van to bring the plants back, it would be a pity to get your new car dirty. Shall we say nine o'clock inside the garden centre?"

"Yes, that is fine with me. You can start if I am late. I will drop Lucy at school on the way, sometimes we are held up. Now, I will let you get on with your work while I cut the lawn edges."

They met as arranged the following morning and spent an hour loading plants onto two trolleys. They bought compost and pots for the terrace and a set of new tools for Elle to have as her own. Well pleased, they took their purchases home and after Jonathan had explained the various plants, they began to fill the flower beds, Jonathan arranged them in their place and taught Elle how to plant them, a job she enjoyed and would continue after Jonathan went home. It was a great boost to Elle's experience of gardening, and she felt that at last she was being useful doing real work.

James came to watch and was both impressed and proud of Elle. *This is what she needs*, he thought, *a new interest and skill, one that none of the rest of the family possess, a creative way of getting exercise, while improving and maintaining the garden that she clearly loves.* He reflected on what a good choice Dunwood House was with its large garden. He went to prepare the lunch and when Elle appeared, he could not resist giving her a hug and kissing her soil smeared face. "You are so gorgeous and sexy, Elle, all sweaty with your face covered in soil, so earthy and prima., I want you now, baby, just like you are and unwashed, please come upstairs with me, Elle."

"No, James, I am the gardener today, with more work to do. Later when I have finished you can vent your lust on my sweaty body before I shower and collect Lucy, if that's what turns you on, that is provided you are a good boy and promise me a supper at the local tonight. Ava can sit with Lucy."

"It does, my love, turn me on. I think you know that perfectly well, your hot sweaty, cuddly body sends shivers down me just as it does in the mornings after a good night, but now with a dirty face to look at, you are the very ultimate in sex appeal for me. You know how I just deplore artificial, perfumed women. You are always the very opposite and today even more so. I need you naked, baby, so do not be too long."

Elle laughed at her husband but secretly loved his need for her. She wagged her finger at him and went back to work, happy to keep him stewing for another hour, assuming she could wait that long herself. James out of control was an experience not to be missed, winding him up was both easy and fun.

I am really for it this time, she thought, with eager anticipation as she planted marigolds. *I do love this lust in men, especially when it is for me, but I quite see why Joan could not take it. He is bad enough now, as a young man James must have been even more rampant and demanding, not Joan's thing at all. There will be no gentle arousal for me this time, I'd better be well prepared for his manhood before I get near the bed. He will not make sure that I am, or give me time enjoy the sex. I wonder when he will start worrying about our baby, clearly it has not entered his head today, but I bet it will come and add the normal remorse for his boorish behaviour when he is spent. What fun, I might just stir him up a little more, then afterwards mention no rough housing was it, James, just to see him plead for my forgiveness.*

Not wanting to have James pull off her clothes Elle went into the bathroom and undressed. James was naked by the bed when she approached. She put her arms around his neck and pulled herself up, locking her legs around his waist. "Now, my handsome Romeo, what was it you wanted sweaty little me for?"

James did not bother to answer. Elle was already sitting on his erection and, as one of his favourite expressions from way back had it, he pulled her on like an old boot, then he fell on top of her onto the bed. A few hard thrusts and he came in an uncontrolled rush, much too soon, in fact almost at once to the surprise of neither of them. Elle, still holding on around his neck, said with a giggle, "Serves you right, you are so easy to wind up, James, you must learn to relax and slow down, my love, ignore my little tricks and you will have more fun, so will I come to that. By the way, what happened to the no rough housing rule." Elle relented as he started to speak. She put her hand over his mouth and kissed him, "It is okay, darling. I am teasing you, I love it when you get hyped up like you were today. It makes me feel really loved and wanted, so there's no need to apologise. You are a real man, my lover, what more could a girl want. Now that you have me all worked up, James, you are not going to sleep tonight until you have treated me to a decent orgasm, so, my love, let us have some supper at home with Lucy. Then later we will have another session, this time with a little more consideration if you please."

James found his voice. "You little minx, you caused me to get so worked up and overexcited deliberately, keeping me waiting, laughing at me then jumping me. I would not be surprised if you smeared your face on purpose knowing that it would excite me. If you were not carrying my baby, you little tease, I would spank your bottom. As it is, I will do as you order later this evening. I love you, you wicked little madam, your mischievous smile when I am hyped up drives me crazy, but I can see that you are right. I have to be a lot smarter to cope with you and your little tricks. I am not having you making fun of me like you did today and have done before. When I get the urge to ravish you, I become so easy for you to manipulate."

"I know, my darling man, it is mean of me. I just cannot help it; you are so wonderfully predictable. I promise that next time you are filled with lust for me I will help you calm down and make the best of it for both of us, not stir you up as I did today."

Later that night they had gentle loving sex to their mutual satisfaction.

Meanwhile, at Landford Cottage, the four girls and John were retiring to their rooms after an evening in the local pub. The girls were both pleased and jealous to have Ava in the master bedroom with John, who they all liked very much. They agreed with James's decision to let them live in his house and occupy the main bedroom, recognising the special circumstances. Now the two lovers were almost like a married couple, comfortable and fully aware of each other's needs and habits. During the day you might have thought that Ava was the dominant one, but in the bedroom John took charge and controlled everything they did. He was strict and refused to engage in any sexual activity that he considered more advanced than a young couple should experience. His aim was a sex version of cold turkey. Ava wanted more, but appreciated that he was doing it for her. They both know that it would take time for her to adjust and lose the desire for rougher treatment. Ava still thought of James in moments of frustration, but at the same time increasingly appreciated the slow gentle, loving arousal then satisfaction that she was getting from John. John was equally frustrated at times, but knew any aggressive action from him would be a slippery slope to sex perversions that he genuinely did not want them to engage in ever. Ava had been given a place at the university with full scholarship and that, John believed, must be their focus for the future.

As they lay together soaking up the warmth of their bodies, Ava said that she was ready to tell her story, to explain how she got involved with a man who practiced rough sex and bondage. "It started when I was fifteen," she began. "I have always been attracted to older men, hence the James complex. My father was strict and was in constant dispute with my mother. It was unpleasant at our house, neither of my parents gave me the love that I needed while growing up, as a result I spent as much time as I could with my best friend at her house. My friend's father was the opposite of mine. He was a young looking man in his late thirties, he was fun, he took an interest in us and loved his daughter and gave me the attention I did not get at home. As I matured, it became clear that he was attracted to me. When I was fully grown at fifteen going on sixteen-years-old, he began to get handy with me. I regret to say that I did nothing to discourage him. In my innocence I thought it was a harmless game we played. I was totally oblivious to the danger and to what might happen. I was both ignorant and innocent for a girl of my age; at the same time that I was fully mature in physical development for my age.

"One day we found ourselves alone in his house. He took me in his arms and kissed me. I loved his attention. I let him explore me with his hands. He took off my bra and I admit I loved it. I let him undress me and again I thought it very grown up, showing off for him. My behaviour is hard to understand today, as I look back with hindsight. Before I came to my senses, he had me on the sofa and I was no longer a virgin. I was shocked and surprised but did not blame him then and I do not blame him now. I could have stopped him at any time, he gave me plenty of time. But I loved it and him. I felt grown up. He was very considerate and loving, sex was fun, and yes, I went back for more. My friend soon found out what was going on, told her mother and all hell then let loose.

"I still have some love for him so I will not name him but call him Tom. His wife, not surprisingly, threw him out. She started divorce proceedings and took the house and most of what they owned. He simply could not contest the case. He was lucky she did not call the police and have him locked up. Perhaps it would have been better for me if she had.. My parents were so shocked, disgusted and unforgiving that I was forced to leave home. So we went off together to live in a rented flat at the other end of Poland. I had turned seventeen by the time this happened. I went to evening classes to finish my basic education and we were happy for a short time, a few months in fact. But the same drive that led to him seducing me led to the sort of sex practices that we are now trying to make me forget. I left him after he nearly choked me one night; he had gone too far. I at last saw the danger that I was in. I no longer enjoyed what he was doing to me, the pain became greater than the pleasure, I escaped. I went to work in the hotel, I was good at my job and became a receptionist. I finished my schooling and passed the exams. I met many businessmen staying at the hotel and enjoyed being wined and dined at expensive restaurants. My life was normal for someone in their twenties, at seventeen and eighteen I was still young for the company that I was keeping and the sex these mostly married men wanted from me, I still did not have boyfriends of my own age, they did not satisfy me as I had become used to so much more from my experienced lovers.

"To finally break away from my past and start a new life, also to advance my career, I took the job in London. The rest you know. I am sorry that I was not the sort of girl you would approve of, but when it started I was an innocent, groomed and seduced by a man I had come to love over several years. After that, one thing led to another, I could have stopped it all at any time, but I loved Tom. I am sorry, John, but you had to know about my past. I could not marry you without telling you. It is not something I can forget and live with as a secret from my husband. Please keep your promise and tell no one, I am a different person now and want a normal life with you. I love you, John, and hope you will still love me after what I have told you."

"Ava, what a story. I am glad that you have told me. I agree it is not something you could keep inside you for the rest of your life. What an exciting life for a young girl; following all that you were raped in England. No wonder you were traumatised and confused. Come here, darling, it's over now. We must put it behind you, we will move on together, I will look after you. You also have my mother, James, and Elle; we all want the best for you. Of course, I will keep your secret and no, what you did in the past makes no difference to me now. It is not your fault that your friend's father took advantage of you, a vulnerable girl not loved by her own father. Typical grooming, he was a paedophile, so well done for getting educated and escaping. How terribly sad that you then fell foul of the criminal gang here in England. Ava, we have not changed, we are the same two people who fell in love. Now that I know your full story, I love you all the more. I can help you recover but you will not be surprised to hear that in future I shall have to be even stricter with you. I will not risk letting you go back to the sex that Tom gave you. The roughest you will ever get from me is normal rough and tumble fun sex and another smacked bottom. That, if you do not obey me and provoke me beyond a certain point. I enjoyed the fight and rough house with you, but it was only in fun, not to hurt you, which is clearly what you had with Tom. No wonder you fantasised about James and not me, it had to be an older man, I see that now. It's all over now, my love, try to forget it, but talk to me if you ever want to, otherwise I will not ever remind you of the past. We have a bright future together."

***

Elle received a call from Anne inviting her to coffee and a gossip. When they were seated comfortably in the living room, Anne congratulated Elle on her pregnancy. Was James pleased, she asked.

"Yes, I can honestly say he is over the moon, there were actual tears in his eyes when I told him. It was extraordinary, James so emotional, I have never seen that in him before. I do know that he loves his daughters and any more he can collect, like Ava and Lucy, now the possibility of another arriving in a few months' time has really got to him, maybe because it ensures we will be rooted in domesticity for the next twenty years, his life completely changed from the one he expected to live only a few months ago."

"Actually, the issue that I wanted to talk about, Elle, is Ava and John. He feels that he should be paying rent for living in your house. It is so good of you to let them have your old bedroom, but John feels he should contribute to the costs."

"No, Anne, there is no way we would accept rent from John. He is the one that is going to restore the Ava that we all love back to living a normal life and getting over her trauma. James thoroughly approves of their relationship and was the one that encouraged Ava to give all her love to John when they went on holiday. He fully expected that she would give in to John, as he advised her to. That, Anne, is the sort of closeness he has with Ava, that he could advise her to sleep with John, to know that she was ready to do so, and would not take offence at him suggesting it to her. He then insisted on paying, despite giving her a generous allowance. He wanted to ensure that the accommodation was top quality with gourmet food. James wanted to give Ava luxury surroundings, better that they would choose for themselves. Nothing is too much for Ava where James is concerned. It is the same with me, Anne. James understands what we have both been through, he will do whatever he can to help us recover. We Polish girls are truly spoiled by James and we

177

both love him for it. Where would we be had he not come to our rescue, it does not bear thinking about."

"Yes, I see that, but I am surprised that he does all that for a stranger like Ava. You are married to him, so that is not a surprise."

"You need to live with James to know the answer to that, . He just loves all his girls, five of them now, and I am also really one myself, with possibly one more on the way. In truth he loves many women but it is a fact that his relationship and love for Ava goes very deep and is special. As it is for me, but he does not love Ava in the way he loves me. He loved me on first sight, he loves Ava as he loves his daughters. Were any one of them abused, he would do the same for her as he does now for Ava. Anne, I trust James completely, many wives would worry about them. I know that Ava is not herself sure exactly what her love for him means, in her emotional state she would be easy for him to seduce, as I think you know, Anne, but I can promise you that will never happen. James deplores all violence but especially when women or children are involved. But James also knows that he can only do so much, only a true and suitable lover can restore Ava, as he has done for me. That is not James, we both believe that John is the one for her, he is her age and they have a future, if they love each other enough and that only time will tell us that.

"There is no need to worry about the money, Anne. To put your mind at rest and his generosity in perspective, I can tell you that James is well off, the money is not an issue for him. It is not exactly charity but he likes to use his success to help others. He does not need to sell or rent out Landford Cottage now or at any time in the future."

"Good, I agree with what you have told me. I too am sure that James's intentions are honourable, John has told me how much his daughters love him, they would not if they did not trust him with Ava. But I am pleased that we had this talk and offered to contribute. John will be relived."

"I too am pleased, Anne, that you both thought to ask, but be assured as long as John is taking care of Ava, he can expect any amount of support from us. You can tell him not to hesitate to ask for anything they need. I am going to have a dinner for all the family on Sunday, Anne, would you and Ian care to join us? Joan and the judge will be there."

"Yes, Elle, thank you we would love that."

"Six o'clock then."

***

"James, we are putting together a plan for alterations to the garden. Will you ask Tom to come and draw up some rough plans for the builders' work, mainly walls and reconfiguring the paving. Then Jonathan and I will show you what we have in mind, to get your approval before we go ahead."

"That sounds interesting, Elle."

"Yes, I am sure you will be pleased with what we have in mind. We want to enclose part of the vegetable garden in walls, to protect it from the north and east winds and to provide wall space for fruit and roses, halfway to having a traditional walled garden. Then to make more paving space and a sunken area for entertaining, there are other landscaping works needed, mainly to compartmentalise the garden so that you do not see it all in one flat space but have to walk from one area to another. But this does not require plans or any outside permission. We need to get a move on as all this work should be completed before the winter so that it can be planted up with trees and shrubs before next spring."

"Goodness me, Elle, you are quite the expert already."

"Not really, darling, Jonathan is the expert. He is loving the work here now that I am encouraging him and I am keen to give him all the help I can to improve the garden. It has been frustrating for someone like him to slave away all year round, knowing how much better it could be if someone really cared. By the way, James, have you noticed that Lucy has gone with John and Ava again, I think to have lunch with Anne this time. She spends more time with them than she does with us, I sometimes think."

"Yes, Elle, I had noticed. I believe that it is good news all round, John and Ava are becoming very domesticated as a couple which is exactly what Ava needs to anchor herself in the present and forget the past. Ava is also teaching Lucy in several subjects as well as the computer and Polish, again good for both of them. Your little girl is growing up fast and becoming quite independent. How is the next one coming on, darling, can you feel anything yet?"

"No, James, it is a bit too soon for that, but I am beginning to feel a little queasy in the morning. Hopefully it will pass, I did not suffer too much with Lucy."

"Bad luck, love. I am always amazed at what you girls have to go through to produce another person into this world. My part was rather easy, fun actually, when I think about it. Joan was also surprisingly maternal with our three. She became a different person when she was pregnant; it lasted for the duration and until they were about six months old. She then reverted to being a professional in her office mode again, but Joan has always been a good mother to our girls, and she still is a role model for a modern woman. You, my love, are another type of perfect role model, strong, intelligent but family orientated, a little old fashioned for these times, perhaps, but under our circumstances where money is not an issue, exactly what is required. You will control everything on the domestic front, anything that concerns our family and the home we are creating here at Dunwood. You will do everything necessary to preserve our interests, no one will push you around ever again, will they, my love."

"No, James, they will not, I have truly learnt my lesson. I now know who I am, and it is thanks to you that I have property, a husband and a family to care for. I know my responsibility and what I can do for you all. I also know what I want from my life, thanks to you, James, I will as you say take charge for you all. So, you relax, my superhero, tell me what you want and need, I will see to it for you, my satisfaction will come from making a happy, well run home for you and our family and our friends."

"Elle, you know very well what I want, baby. It is you and Lucy and now junior, our family in this house, you have already given them to me."

"Yes, James, you describe an old fashioned family that is us, and that is exactly what we both want. Then in time I will be an old fashioned grandmother, hopefully with lots of grandchildren. So, hello, Grandpa, because you will get there sooner than me with your first family, and you will be exceptionally good at it, as you were a good father. Maybe with Lucy we can even help you and Joan with grandchildren babysitting."

"Come here, you cheeky little minx, let me have a cuddle, old grandfather, am I? There are still some lessons you need to learn from this old man, my insubordinate little housewife. Now is as good a time as any to teach you, while Lucy is out."

"James, you are so manly, what is this time? A new position perhaps that requires less energy from you while I do all the work, or a smacked bottom, I do love your surprises."

"Maybe both when I get those tight jeans off you, wait until I get you upstairs and you will find out what I have in mind, you sexy little madam."

***

This is to be the first family meal with friends that Elle had ever hosted, twelve family and friends all sitting down at her table. It was a daunting first test of her new role as the wife of James Jefferies. Luckily for her, James had plenty of experience entertaining, but unfortunately not much of it as a cook. They sat down and planned the meal together. They decided to make it as simple as possible, relying on the quality of the food and trimmings to carry the day. To start with they went for smoked salmon with prawns and avocado, brown bread rolls and butter. This was all cold and could be prepared in advance. The main course, on the advice of the local butcher, would be a five rib beef joint. They were going to rely on their new oven to cook this large beef joint for them. It was fitted with a Wi Fi probe that worked with the programme set to control the cooking automatically, then keep it warm and rested until they were ready to carve. Elle could then concentrate on the vegetables, which she was fully capable of doing. Various shop bought puddings and cheese would follow.

Happy with this plan, and trusting that the new oven worked as advertised, Elle and James went shopping together on Saturday afternoon. This shopping trip gave Elle the deep inner gratification that only someone with her experience of life in the past, would understand. Selecting food and treats without worrying about the cost, putting them in a trolley being pushed by her adoring husband, was not just fun, but deeply satisfying. She smiled at her husband. James, who was fully understanding of how she was feeling, watched the look of pleasure on her face as she saw an expensive luxury item and popped in into his trolley. He got his pleasure from watching his Elle as she lost her inhibitions and day by day grew into being the mistress of Dunwood House. James resolved to find new ways to boost her self-esteem and confidence before the new baby arrived and she got into her full maternal mode.

Elle

I see James looking at me, by the grin on his face he is fully aware how much I am enjoying this shopping trip. He gives me a look of encouragement, half smiling, half laughing at my obvious pleasure at such a mundane venture as shopping. Little does he realise the stress and sometimes pain of shopping for George, every item questioned, even things I knew that he wanted. If the bill was too high he would hit me. It is even now difficult for me to pick up some of the things I am buying and put them in the trolley, I would not buy many of these fairly normal goods if my James were not here smiling his encouragement at me. How can two men be so different? How lucky to now have a man like James to look after and spoil. I have a strong urge to go and kiss him but better wait until we get home.

James

My darling Elle is looking at me for reassurance. Her anxious face tells me all I need to know about that bastard, George Wheeler, and his abuse of such an innocent and adorable girl. Despite knowing how much money we have, she still needs to know that I will not be cross with her for buying all these items, almost none for her own use, they are for our guests. I smile at her and she almost jumps for joy, as she puts more and more in the trolley. She keeps looking at me to be sure. I smile at her and eventually laugh at the look of sheer pleasure that has now transformed her face. She is almost dancing down the aisles, she is so happy, finding things to buy to serve at our party. I will never be the one to tell my Elle what she can or cannot do yet, after all we have achieved together, she still will not fully accept that she does not need my permission to go on a shopping spree and buy whatever she wants. I love her more every day and wish we were not in a public carpark right now. I will just hug and kiss her and wait until we get home.

***

James watched Elle return the trolley to the park with a deep feeling of love. *Maybe I am the only one that can fully understand how my Elle feels, I am so pleased that she is pregnant, a baby to care for will surely boost her confidence and make her forget that sadistic Wheeler.* They drove home and together they unloaded the car and put the shopping away.

James then led Elle up the stairs to the bedroom and pulled her onto the bed beside him. He lay on top, holding her face in his hands, pushing her black hair aside. James kissed her on the nose, then all over her face. Elle responded and kissed him back.

"James, what are you going to do to me? Do you want me to undress or are just going to kiss me?"

"Neither, my angel, I am going to try and convince you that I am not your boss, but your equal partner and that you do not need my permission to buy whatever you want with your housekeeping money, to which there is no upper limit. I am your husband, your partner and your lover. I do not tell you what you can or cannot do. All I want is for you to be happy and if that means buying a van load of shopping, then good on you. Just be sure to always buy the best, I want us all to have the highest quality of everything, never the cheapest; good value yes, but we can afford to give our family quality food and whatever else it is that they need. You are the wife and mother, you can decide what to shop for. I will help you but you are in charge not me, do you understand, darling?"

"Oh James, I am not sure about that. I of course fully understand about the quality of our food, you have worked hard and become well off, we live in a big house, of course we should live well, it would be an insult to you not to appreciate that. You must come shopping with me and choose what you think we should have until I get it up to your standard. There is a balance to be struck with not spoiling our children and giving them the best and most healthy food. But, James, that has nothing to do with our relationship. I may be the mother and housewife for the family, but you are the head of the household, the man that provides for us and keeps us safe. You are the husband that I married insisting on the old service where I agreed to love honour and obey, the father to care for both my children. I want to know that you will help me get things right while we settle in together. But seriously, James, with my history and your generosity and love, I will always want to be the wife and woman that you want. I put that well before my own interests, so please be my master and guide me always, that is what I truly want, that is my security."

Elle rolled on top, intertwined her legs with his and held her lover's head in her hands. "You, my gorgeous man, are everything to me. I need to believe that you are strong enough to take charge of me as well as the children. I do not ever want to win any fight with you, physical or verbal. When I jump you and start a fight, or when I am deliberately naughty, I want to finish up being manhandled then helpless on your arms at your mercy, wondering what you are going to do to me. I love it when you pull my knickers off and give me that lump that I am rubbing up with my knee. I also love it when I finish up face down over your knee and you have your fun spanking my bum. Do not try to fool me, James, you like to be the boss. You love your naughty little minx as much as I like arousing your lust, you want to teach her a lesson, you want to master me when I play you up, we both know where it will end, go on, admit it."

"Yes, of course I do, you naughty girl, but you start it, you can drive me mad with lust at times, like no other woman I have ever met. How can I not pick you up to stop you making a fool out of me, you are only small, then of course I have to teach you a lesson, especially, yes, I want to get my hands on your sexy little bottom. But that is in the bedroom, in our playground. This is not what I am talking about, you know that perfectly well, Elle. You are starting to work on me now, you bad girl, keep that leg still, you wanton hussy. No, I am not going to let you get your way just now, I know that I am often putty in your hands, but not this time, Elle. Stop what you are doing immediately and talk about the real issue. Oh, Elle, no, please…"

It was too late, his trousers were open and his manhood was already in her mouth. Elle took control. James lay back to enjoy what he knew was coming. She sat on his erection and slowly rode him all the way to a blissful orgasm. A satisfied, happy James looked up at his triumphant tormentor, looking down at him with a grin on her face. He was filled with love for his naughty minx who clearly did not need his instructions in the bedroom, where he was supposedly in charge.

Elle fell down on top again and whispered in his ear. "So, you are in charge in the bedroom are you, big man? That is odd, as I seem to be able to make you do whatever I want, including taking charge of me when I want a fight and am in the mood for some rough handling. You must realise by now that this is the one place where I know exactly what you really want and even most of the time what you are thinking. Men can be so simple; I love you for this weakness that you have. You may be the alpha male, but you need me to play the submissive female well to fully enjoy the games we play. As you admit, Joan would not play; she was too serious to be dominated by any man. I, on the other hand, love it, but who is really the boss here, James? For example, I knew perfectly well what you wanted earlier when I was hot from gardening, I know you do not want me to use perfume or make up, so I never use any when we're at home together, I shower and rinse and smell like nature intended me to. I know exactly what turns you on, my love. I went back into the garden and got up a sweat just for you. Yes, I rubbed a little more dirt on my face and kept you stewing for an hour. That way we both got what we wanted. I loved that look on your face as you watched me lay back on the bed and raise my arms and open my legs. I knew exactly what I was in for and you did not disappoint me, did you, James. I was worth waiting for, was I not, my cave man lover?"

"Yes, darling, you certainly were worth waiting for, as always. I loved looking at your dirty face and the rest of your naked body, you are incredibly sexy. You are also such a complex baby, Elle, my love, there cannot be any other woman quite like you, from the girl that needed my reassurance in the supermarket buying groceries, to the woman that can make me do whatever she wants in our bedroom, to the capable housewife and gardener. I must be the luckiest man alive to have such a wife."

"And I, James, must be the luckiest girl ever to have you, my darling man, for a husband."

They lay together content, knowing full well that they were in fact lovers with equal if different roles to play."

After a while Elle asked James to listen as she had something more serious to say. "James, you need not worry about me. I completely understand the point that you are making and in time we will adjust and have everything exactly as we both want it. Please always remember that I need you to be there to support me when I have doubts, that may be for some time to come. To me that is not you being bossy, it is you being the being the perfect husband for me, that you always are. But, James, there is something else that I would like you to do for me. It concerns Lucy. James, have you noticed how she has shot up recently? I have had to buy her a complete new set of clothes as well as the school uniform. As we both know, she is happy, independent and self-reliant, but my worry is that our baby will change everything for her so soon after she has settled into her new life here with us. I worry that it will bring home to her that she not only does not have her real father, but that he is a bad man in prison, that our new baby has you as father and she has to share me with the baby."

"We must make her believe that we are just one normal united family and that she is an important member. One day I want you to become her legal guardian, that is if you are not able to adopt her completely. That, however, will all take time, maybe years. For now, I would like you to assume the role of her father before junior arrives. At the moment, you are more a super friend and adviser, an uncle maybe, all good fun but nor really responsible for her. I have been happy with your friendship together, especially in the early days when you must forgive me, but I had to be sure it was safe for her. Everything has now changed with the baby on the way. I would like it if Lucy looked upon you as her daddy before the baby is born. I want her to forget George altogether and think only of you as her father. What do you think, darling?"

"Elle, there is nothing in the world that I would like better than to be the father of your super little girl, a carbon copy of you, but we all, including Lucy know that I am not in fact her father. I do see your point though, it would be a shame if Lucy ever thought that I, or indeed we, loved our baby more than her. So of course, with your permission I will slowly, over the next few months, move in closer to her, change our relationship from, as you say, uncle to father. I will assume some authority, not just be her friend. Up to now, all her instructions come from you. Having had three daughters before, I should be able to do that without annoying her unduly, so let's pick a few things, that you might tell her she can or cannot do and I will do so instead. If she later comes to you to complain and says you are in charge not me, that I am not her father, then you will explain that I am acting in her interests and love her very much, how does that sound? Frankly, Elle, I think you worry too much. Lucy is well adjusted and knows full well how much we both love her."

"Yes, James, that will do if we go carefully, otherwise it might have the opposite effect to the one we want. Be more touchy feely and loving as well, to balance out the new bossy side, to become a real substitute father. Do it slowly, for example take her out without me, do the school run, shopping, or sightseeing, perhaps a farm visit to see animals while I am too busy or not feeling well. If we get it right acting as one, then in a year or so she should forget George, accept you are now her father and no doubt play you up, as all your girls do to get what they want. I will make it clear that you are head of our household, which of course she already knows. Thank you, James, for doing this for us. I have worried about this ever since I became pregnant. Lucy is so important to me, I cannot let her down now."

"As she is to me, Elle, as I think you both know. Do not ever think that I might love our child more than I love Lucy. In all respects in the future and in my will, she will have everything that my children by you and by Joan have. She has a special place in my life, I have big expectations of her and cannot wait to see her grow up. You can assure her of that when she is old enough to understand."

"I know that, James, and we need to convince Lucy long before she gets to the stroppy teenage stage."

"Elle, I repeat that I really think that maybe you worry too much. Your daughter is so smart that I think she will work all it out for herself, in fact I expect that she has already. She can see that I have her best interests at heart in everything that I do for her, whatever I am called, uncle or father. When you are busy with the baby nursing for example, I will make sure I am there to hold her hand and explain things, as we watch together. I will give her my full attention. Lucy and I will share you and the baby between us. I will spoil her and never ignore her needs, in many ways because of her history and the way she has responded she mean more to me than my own daughters."

"Thank you, James, we both love you back very much, but this is a new beginning for us all. Up to now it was only the two of us, then you saved us both. Now you relax, my love, I will shower and go and get some supper ready for when she comes home."

***

The supper party was in full swing and proving a great success. The oven delivered the joint in perfect condition for James to carve. He enlisted Lucy as his assistant to carry the plates and ask each person how they would like their meat, rare or well done, and how much. The rest of the meal was as well prepared and served as anyone could expect. The seating plan devised by Elle and James had Elle at one end and Joan at the other. James and Ian sat on one side and Simon and John the other. Anne was placed next to Simon and opposite James. The girls were left to fit in around the men where they pleased. James was quietly delighted when Lucy sat on one side of him and Ava the other, his two special daughters by unofficial adoption or marriage, both sat down before his own daughters had a chance to choose. When they were all finally seated there was much mirth and bawdy comments from the girls, finally joined by everyone else when they saw the humour of the situation. It was the sight of James with his two wives at either end of the table that revived the sultan and his women image. James responded by proposing a toast, "To my wives," who both stood up and curtseyed.

John was delegated as wine waiter. His mother looked on, happy and content that he had become so much at home as part of this extraordinary family. It was becoming obvious to her that James was not only very much loved by all the females that he collected, she was herself not immune to his charm, but it was now abundantly clear to her that he was a wealthy and generous man. She knew her son having fallen in love with Ava, who was accepted as a full family member, would benefit from his influence in their future life, that is if they married, which seemed likely. She could also now see clearly for herself Ava's special relationship with James. Their obvious, openly displayed love for each other here at the table would have worried her had she been Elle, but common sense told her that Ava had told the truth when she recounted James's insistence that he was her father not a lover, and also the superior ability of Elle to judge men reassured her further. She considered the marriage of Elle and James to be a perfect match. She realised that there was a lot more to Elle than the petite beauty with a shady past. She was both tough and a fighter; she would never tolerate her James misbehaving with Ava, and she would know, beside which, not even James needed more than Elle to cope with at this early stage of their marriage.

Simon was very good value at a dinner table. Being a lawyer he might be accused of loving the sound of his own voice, and he displayed a legal sense of humour. Many of his tales, like the burglar that got drunk and fell asleep on sofa for the police to wake up, or some of the almost unrepeatable reasons given in the divorce court to justify dissolving the marriage, were clearly embellished. They caused much laughter and helped the party to go with a swing, encouraging the others to tell their stories and jokes. The wine flowed, followed by liqueurs, port or brandy.

After a satisfying, leisurely meal, they cleared the table and moved around to form new groups to have coffee. Cheese was on offer but by common consent they decided to have it later, if at all. Simon then proposed a vote of thanks to their host and in particular their hostess. He got carried away with the atmosphere and the drink and began to sing Elle's praises; he was clearly an admirer. It would have been better, however, had he not alluded to her recent past and the way she had overcome the troubles and become the perfect wife to their friend, James, and how much they all loved and admired her.

Elle

I am sitting at the head of my dinner table surrounded by my new family, some friends and important guests. I am pregnant with James's child, something that I thought would never happen to me again. This is indeed a new milestone in my life's up and down adventure. Who would have ever thought a year ago that I would be here today, hosting such a party. I just do not recognise myself any longer as the girl that ran away from her sham marriage to a criminal. The man who stopped and came to my rescue at the roadside is responsible for all the good things that have happened to me since that day, he is now my husband sitting beside my Lucy, paying her special attention as I have asked him to do, in order to become accepted by her, as her father in the place of that bastard, George Wheeler, my so first so called husband, hopefully about to be locked up out of her way for the rest of her school and university years.

This house with its three-acre garden is in my name jointly with James, he is effectively giving me ownership of one half of our family home that he has bought for us to live in. Financial security will not be an issue for me or for my Lucy ever again. It is a fairy tale, a dream come true. I am so happy sitting here looking around at all my new friends. I think perhaps that I must have had too much to drink. The room is beginning to spin, I must pull myself together, I am the hostess after all. I will listen to Simon who is thanking James and me for the party, he is being very complimentary and generous with his praise, he is obviously an admirer of mine. Oh no, Simon, why did you have to bring up my past here and now, in front of all our family and guests. Reality has swept over me, I am suddenly sober, and Elle Debronski again. Why does this have to happen to me, why am I still so fragile, so emotional? I cannot help it. How long will it be before I can fully leave my past behind and enjoy this new life in peace? Time will no doubt heal all my trauma, but how much time, maybe the baby will do it for me. I need my James, where is he? Anne is here instead, she is such a good mother figure to me and Ava, she really does understand us both. Joan too, they are all so kind, now James has come, he has brought Lucy to me and hugged us both together, telling us how much he loves us, what a special man he is, what a fine father he makes for Lucy, she must see it that way too, how can she not, I will talk to her later. I feel better, everyone is so kind, we are all getting on with the party again. Simon gave me a hug and said sorry, but reminded me that none of it was my fault and that I am the one fighting back, that is why they all admire and support me.

***

Anne was already on her way to Elle when she became overcome with emotion. It was obvious to her and everyone else that Simon had struck a raw nerve alluding to her abuse. *A judge, how stupid can he be, the poor girl is now in tears*. James watched as Anne comforted his beloved wife and as Simon tried to make amends. He, rather than rushing to Elle's aid, went to Lucy instead and led her to her mother. He explained to her as they went that Mummy was not sad, but tired and happy that everyone had enjoyed her party so much. He lifted Lucy on to the stool, took Elle from Anne and hugged them both together, wiping away Elle's tears with his kisses, telling them how much he loved them, Elle as his wife and Lucy as his new daughter. He then left them to talk with Anne and Joan, who had by now also come to Elle's assistance and to apologise for her husband's lack of tact. Elle was soon smiling again, and after a pause the party resumed.

The men were left at the table as all the women and girls went to support Elle. They made fresh coffee and called for John to supply more drink as they went to sit and gossip in the comfort of the conservatory. Ava and Lucy then managed the final course of cheese and biscuits on their own, mainly for the men, as the women preferred the many chocolates and other treats that the guests had brought to the party. The daughters came under close questioning about their love lives, and who and where their boyfriends were. This was because it was leaked by Ava that boys were known to stay overnight at Landford Cottage without it being declared and sanctioned by the others, as their rules of the house required

Elle

Time for Lucy to go to bed, in fact long past her usual time. I help her to get ready as we talk about the party and how this was the first time we had ever had a dinner party, or even been to one. I ask her what she thinks of our new life in this house with all our new friends. Does she think of the girls as sisters, and then does she think of James as a father—he has just called her his daughter—or just as a friend? Lucy has clearly thought about this because she replied that she does think of Leona and her sisters as her new big sisters, because that is what they told her they were when they were living together while we were on honeymoon. She explained that Ava looked after her, but Leona was in charge of the house and told her that since her father had married me, that made them sisters, and Leona had said that they all loved her and would give her any help I wanted.

What about James, I asked. This was obviously not so easy for her to answer. "James is not my father, is he, Mummy," she answered, "but he is so nice to me I wish that he could be. I know that my father is not here any more, so can I have James as my father?"

I explain that James cannot be her real father, but that he would like to act as a father for her and look after her exactly as her did his own daughters as they were growing up. She would then have two fathers, but only James was here to look after her, he would be called her stepfather.

She asked, "Can I tell people that he is my father? My school friends all have nice fathers."

"Yes, Lucy," I replied. "You can call him your father because that is agreed by us all. He is married to your mother and takes responsibility for you. He does all the things for you that a father does. He would love you to call him your daddy. James wants us to be one family, a mother and father with two children; the second one will be the new baby soon to join us. The baby will be your brother or sister."

Lucy looked pleased; it was obviously something she had already though about. She must feel the odd one out at school with no father to call her own, just as James predicted that she would.

***

That she clearly had no hesitation in replacing George, who she could see never loved her as James did, was a massive satisfaction to her mother, who wanted George Wheeler out of their lives forever. She kissed her daughter goodnight, well pleased with the way her daughter and her new husband had bonded.

Elle returned to the kitchen to find that everything was cleared away, the dishwasher was working, and the girls had finished washing the pots and pans. James had carved some of the beef for their lunch tomorrow and given all the leftovers Ava to be taken to Landford, John was designated driver, having lost the toss with Leona, so James handed him a case of six bottles of wine as a consolation. The younger generation left, no doubt to continue the party at Landford with John's wine.

More coffee was made, brandy and liqueurs were produced, and the six adults sat around the table for a chat.

Anne told them how pleased she was with the developing relationship between John and Ava. She told them how much Ava had blossomed since their holiday. She had matured and was now very focused on her education. She looked James in the eye and said, "I think you had something to do with the holiday, didn't you? Ava told me that you gave her good advice, as well as paying for a luxury hotel for them."

"I did indeed," he replied, "but I think it was already too late, as Elle can confirm. Ava went on holiday with a clear plan as to how it was going to go between her and your John on their holiday."

Elle said, "I can confirm nothing. What Ava and I talk about is confidential."

Anne returned to James, and no doubt emboldened by the drink, asked, "You are incredibly generous to a girl that until recently was a stranger to you. May I ask you why, what motivates you?"

James held the eye contact and said, with a straight face, "I fell in love with Elle the moment I met her. When I learnt about all that she had been through I resolved to do what I could to rescue her, and make amends if I could, and I think that I have. Then when I met Ava who was in the exactly the same situation, both due to our countrymen's abuse, I decided to do the same for her as well. I felt strongly that someone had to make things better for these girls from overseas. It was Elle that had befriended Ava after acting as her interpreter because she did not speak much English at that time. Yes, Anne, it is true that by then I had I fallen in love with Ava as well, but as I already had one pretty Polish girl that I was going to marry, I made Ava my daughter. Then, when we moved, I installed her in my second bedroom." He continued to look Anne in the eye until she blushed.

Elle was already laughing by the time James had stopped speaking, then she said, "He isn't joking, Anne. My James cannot help falling in love with pretty girls, I am delighted to say, otherwise I might not be here myself."

By now they were all laughing and wondering how much was really true. James leant over and gave Anne a kiss, just to confuse her further.

Joan spoke up. "James, you do not improve with age. I feel really sorry for poor Elle. How can such a delicate little wife put up with your boorish behaviour? I was much more robust, but I had the good sense to leave you as soon as you had given me my three girls."

"You're quite right, Joan," Elle said. "James can be very masterful and demanding, hard to put up with for some women, I'm sure, but I do have my own little ways to tame a man who thinks that he is god's gift to poor little women like us. Tell them what happened the other day, James, my alpha caveman, when I came in from the garden all hot and bothered. It was not your finest hour, was it, my love?"

James looked pained. "Don't remind me, you little minx. Yes, you can look smug, my delicate little angel, you managed to make a complete fool of me, I admit it and it was not for the first time, was it? Delicate little wife you certainly are not."

"Do tell," said Anne and Joan together.

James groaned before replying, "Let's just say that the antics of madam, including soil on her face, got me rather overexcited, then she laughed at me when things did not go quite as I had intended. However, later things got back to normal, after which that timid little girl that you are so sorry for, actually lectured me on how to do better next time she plays her tricks on me. Cheeky madam, she got off rather lightly, as I was too tired to assert myself as I should have done."

"Girl power!" Joan shouted like her daughters. "Wait until all the girls hear this."

"No, Joan, please, that was confidential between us as adults to show I am not a bully as you suggested."

Elle went to her lover and put her arms around him from behind. She kissed him and told the others, "This man who I love to pieces is no bully. Trust me, I know what a bully looks like and what he does to girls like Ava and me. This man is the kindest, most generous, loving husband any girl could wish for. I think that I am the luckiest girl alive. James is all mine, Anne." She gave him another kiss. "So you can stop worrying about Ava. John is everything that Ava wants. They are very much in love with each other, I am sure they will marry when they are good and ready. They had one or two issues at the start of their relationship that they have now sorted out. They are very much planning their future, starting with university. James will always be a father to Ava. It is true that they do genuinely love each other, call that what you like, people do love each other, and I am sure you will agree that it is better out in the open. I am pleased to see them so close because I love Ava as well. Together James and I will see that she has what she needs to make it in this welcoming country of yours."

They all looked at Elle, sticking up for her man, with new respect. Joan said, "I knew you were a tough cookie and good with men, Elle, but now I am beginning to feel sorry for James instead. I can see that you must run him ragged at times, poor dear, I do believe that he has finally met his match."

James closed the discussion by saying, "It is quite simple, Joan. Elle and I are actually equal partners in marriage, love and in our life together. Neither of us is the boss; we do, however, both have our moments. That incident I have described is typical of one of hers, cheeky madam that she is. Life is never boring with if you have an Elle around. I never know quite what she is going to do next, but whatever it is she does, she does it to surprise and to please me. I love her for that. Why should I not love Ava as well? She is a lovable girl and will go far, I can assure you all of that. She will make John—who by the way, I thoroughly approve of—a perfect wife. Now, let's talk about something else, our golf for example."

As she was leaving, James embraced Anne. He apologised for teasing her earlier, and she told him that on the contrary she should not have questioned him as she did. She fully understood how well he had behaved, and as Ava's potential mother-in-law she appreciated all that he had done for her. James pointed out that they were Ava's adopted parents and should get together to discuss her needs over a cup of tea. He assured her that if there was anything she wanted, or that she as mother wanted to give her, she was to ask as he would be happy to pay. He told her that giving all his girls what they wanted to make them happy was how he got his satisfaction. He gave her a final hug and let her go.

Elle and Joan watched this exchange with barely concealed mirth. Joan said, "Our husband is quite incorrigible. Look how he is chatting Anne up again, he cannot help himself, can he?"

"Yes, Joan, he is a naughty boy, that's why we love him so much. I will warn him not to come on too strongly with Anne. I'm afraid her marriage is not all it should be, it would not be kind, she might be a little vulnerable." As she was leaving, Joan arranged to meet and discuss the forthcoming trial of her tormentors.

When they finally got to bed, tired but happy, they lay in each other's arms, content that the evening had been a great success.

"Well done, my love," James congratulated Elle. "That was a wonderful evening and you were the perfect hostess. All the food was as special as anyone could have wanted, everyone got on well, it brought us all together, family and those that will in future become part of our extended family if all goes to plan. I think we should entertain like this on a regular basis. We will become the home for all those here tonight to come back to. Then next time we can have more of our friends, without family. Another time perhaps a barbecue or buffet party for all comers."

"I would love that, James, it was so satisfying having a nice big house and all the family around us. It is all new to me but after today it is what I want to do for the rest of my life. As you say, I want to make Dunwood House the happy friendly place for them all to come to when any of them is in trouble and need help, or just somewhere to chill out. Others will come home to show off their boyfriends and, in the future, their children."

"We will do just that, my darling. Now I am going to make love to you gently and without getting overexcited as you instructed me to."

Elle just giggled and hugged her lover tight around his neck as he entered her and began to carry out his promise. Slowly, and with all his insight into her emotions and erotic zones, he used his considerable skill as a lover to bring her to the edge of her orgasm. Then he paused and looked at her as if waiting for instructions.

Elle cried, "Please, James, don't stop, I am nearly there."

James put his face close to hers and said, "I thought I had better check that I am doing it right. Which of us is in charge here? If it is you, please tell me what to do next, I do not want to make a fool of myself again."

"Oh, James, my love, please, you know that I did not mean it. I am so sorry, I will never tease you again, you are always in charge in the bedroom. Don't be mean to me, darling, please go on, finish me off. It was so good and I was so close."

"Oh, Elle, baby, you look so cute when you are all hyped up and annoyed at the same time. Relax now, baby, and keep your eyes open. I want to see deep into your soul as I make love to you."

When he'd brought her back to the edge again, James put her arms above her head and held them on the bed in one hand; with the other he played with her nipple. By now Elle was breathing hard and writhing helplessly under him. With a few hard thrusts and a good pinch, James launched his lover into a series of noisy orgasms, adding to it by exploding himself and collapsing on top of her.

"James, my darling, you are such an amazing lover. That was fabulous, maybe my best ever. You get better and better, you are so special, it is uncanny the way you know exactly how to do that to me, you know me so well now."

"I enjoyed that as much as you did, Elle. I love it when you come like that. You were so noisy, but you are wrong about me knowing you better now. Actually, Elle, my love that is not what has happened at all, I have known everything about you since our eyes first met and I fell in love with you. I understand you completely and I always have, but you are such a complicated if totally adorable little girl. The change that has happened between us over time is in you yourself, my love, not my understanding of you. At the start of our relationship, your doubts and insecurities were so overwhelming they prevented you from connecting with me as you are able to do now. Remember, you did not think that you were good enough, despite all the efforts that Joan and I made to reassure you. Slowly, step by step, you have grown into your new life and begun to believe that you really do belong here.

"Tonight, the party was another major step forward for you, and the results were here in bed for us both to enjoy. You were fully switched on and receptive to my efforts; indeed so much so that you became really stroppy when I paused to get my own back. Elle, you were so cute, all worked up, about to cum and seriously annoyed with me at the same time. You would not have reacted that way to me a few months ago. You would have waited for me to continue then possibly faked it. We are nearly there, Elle, my love, but not quite yet, a little way to go still. The tears tonight show that you are still ultra-sensitive to what people say. You need to be able to take crass remarks like Simon made in your stride. There will always be malicious people making unkind comments. You must accept in your subconscious self that past events were not your fault and ignore such remarks.

"I believe that when you bring our baby home and put him or her to bed in the Dunwood nursery, you will finally know deep inside you that you truly do belong here. You will know that you're the mother of the children that are living and growing up here, and that you are mistress of the house and all of us in it, You will then realise the simple fact that none of us can manage without you, that you are the focal point of all our lives. The whole extended family will come to your house for holidays, especially Christmas. My daughters and Ava will spend much of their time here simply because this will be a happy family home with fun and games, children, and plenty of good food. None of this will happen without you, Mummy. So, believe, please, darling, believe in yourself, for all our sakes, we need you."

"James darling, Daddy, I do believe. I will be what you all want, just as long as I have you beside me. It takes two to do all the things you say. I will never be able to do it without your support. We will be the base for the family to come to as married partners, not me alone. We all love and look up to you, James, we will do it together."

"Yes, darling, that is the point that I am making. We will do it as husband and wife, but only you can be Mummy."

They cuddled up, content and happy. The future was looking bright.

CHAPTER SIXTEEN

Elle could see Joan's car entering the driveway and put the coffee machine on. She was putting the cups on the table when Joan walked into the kitchen. They embraced, before sitting down.

"Elle, thank you once again for the most enjoyable dinner party last Saturday. I am so pleased that you and James have renovated this house to cater for entertaining. It is a perfect set up for a party. I regret that entertaining was never my strong point and James does like to be sociable. You, Elle, are the perfect hostess for him. I can see that you will be like a mother hen with all the family gathered around. It is what my girls need to keep them on the straight and narrow. They were beginning to lose touch with their father before you married him, and they do need him. Leona is with me and thinks as I do, she will concentrate on her law career, but the other two are a little wild, I am afraid. You can help by giving them advice."

"Thank you, Joan, it's nice of you to say so, that it is exactly what James has been telling me. It is also what I have always dreamt off, being a mother with a big family to care for. I promise you that I will devote my life to the family, especially to making James happy, then all the children including your girls, if they need me. Although I am not that much older than them, I have a lifetime of experience and will watch over them to help or advise if necessary. James will always be my first priority, Joan. I do have bad moments and it is not as simple as James thinks; it sometimes hits me that without him I might be in complete poverty and back in a brothel with my Lucy. He thinks the baby will finally drive away my last demons. I hope so but I need him close by and in my bed at night or I am afraid that I will not cope.

"James is shopping on his way back from school, so Joan, come with me to see the alterations we are making to the garden and meet Jonathan, our super gardener and landscaper, my patient instructor on all things gardening. I absolutely love the garden. I have never had one before but with the house as well I can be inside in bad weather and outside when the sun shines. Jonathan is also helping Lucy with her passion for wildlife and bugs. We will have some fun with the wives' bit, shall we? Good morning, Jonathan. I'm sorry that I'm not here working this morning, but I was taking advice from the first Mrs Jefferies. Joan, this is Jonathan."

"Hello, sorry, but I did not understand what you said, Elle."

"Jonathan, this is James's first wife; she advises me on our husband's foibles."

Jonathan looked bemused and did not know how to reply. Then he saw Elle giggling and realised it was a joke. "Very funny, Elle, you had me there for a moment."

"Actually, it's all true," said Joan. "I am James's first wife and we do talk about him behind his back, but we only say nice things, as we both think the world of him."

"Now, Jonathan, let's have a tour of the estate and then you can explain your plans for the redesign and landscaping."

"Right, well, as you can see, starting here we have redeveloped and extended the paved area to be more useful for a family. The last owners were an elderly couple. That brick structure is a barbecue. The whole area is no longer just rectangular, it is now freeform. We wanted to avoid straight lines. As you can see, the edge on that side bordering the rose bed is half gravel. The idea is that the paving becomes separated and random, crazy paving style, with gravel in between, that will be planted with drought resistant plants. From the rose bed to the orchard, we will plant ornamental trees, a golden rain tree, walnut, laburnum and crab apples amongst others. None of these are too tall. Underneath these and on this side will be a dense shrubbery; together they will break up the garden and block out the vegetable garden without dominating the skyline. From this side of the terrace an oak pergola will stretch all the way to the orchard. It will snake both ways rather than form a straight line. This will leave an area in between to be a high quality putting and croquet lawn."

"The pergola will be covered with roses and clematis mixed up together, that is until the last third, which will have a rambling rose with honeysuckle over it. They will explode and envelop everything and not be pruned. On the outside of the pergola will be a wide perennial border.

All the rest round to the driveway will be lawn, a playing field in fact, but surrounded by shrubs and flower beds. Now this is the vegetable garden. As you can see, we have some new walls to protect the crops from the cold north and east winds and provide space for fruit cordons. We have ordered new tool and potting sheds. But the most exciting thing of all, something I cannot believe that I am going to work in, is a new, large Victorian greenhouse, almost an orangery, with the usual cold frames. This greenhouse comes equipped with everything including its own heating and ventilation system. It has heated benches and LED growth lights. Very few private gardens have such a greenhouse. We will grow all sorts of exotic things and all our own bedding plants. To go with all this, may I tell my own news?"

"Shall I tell Joan for you, Jonathan? Starting next month, Joan, Jonathan will be working for us full time as a salaried employee. The garden will be his responsibility, but he will also help wherever he can with maintenance and he will have responsibility for keeping Landford House and garden in shape, with authority to see that the youngsters do the chores. I am keen that it does not become a worry for James, he will sell it if it does. Thank you, Jonathan. That is all very exciting, Joan, isn't it?"

"Yes, thank you, Jonathan, I am impressed with your plans and look forward to seeing the finished garden."

"I think James is back so we will go inside to meet him. See you later, Jonathan."

"Yes, goodbye, Elle, nice to meet you, Joan."

"Good morning, James."

"Hello, Joan, you have been inspecting Elle's garden development with Jonathan. What did you think of the plans? I'm impressed and delighted that Elle is so keen."

"Yes, I'm impressed too. I see that you are going all out to make this a show garden. I agree it is good to see that you, Elle, are so interested and involved. I cannot think of anything more therapeutic for you than to become an expert, green fingered gardener. You are also lucky with Jonathan; he seems to a very sound man to have working on your property."

"Yes, Joan, that was pure luck, but we have taken advantage of it to have him around full time on both properties. There is a lot to do here and I am determined to make Elle's life as easy as possible. I don't want her running between both houses to make sure they are up to scratch. Her life will be comfortable and fun if I have any say in the matter."

"You will have a say, darling, and I love you for it. Jonathan will be so helpful and good company. We're going to meet his family next week, he has children Lucy's age. Of course, his wife is anxious to meet me and make sure he is safe here."

"Now, now, darling less of that talk."

"Okay, you two, enough of that, but I agree with James, Elle, you were a victim; you are now a respectable wife and mother. Now, next week the trial begins. You have made your victim impact statement, Elle, this forms part of the court documents. You now have to decide if you are going to leave it at that and it will be included for consideration, or if you want to introduce it verbally, assuming that they are convicted or, as is more likely, plead guilty. Either way, it will be considered by the judge when determining the sentence. I will not try to influence you, except to say that you can have it read out for you. Obviously this has less impact. However, if you do decide to make it yourself you must be coherent and honest. Any loss of control or serious deviation from the written statement, or insults and abuse directed at the accused, will have the opposite effect to the one you are trying to create, which I will remind you is of an honest girl, in your case a virgin, horribly abused and suffering damage. You are also speaking for Ava and all the other girls. You will be well respected for this by all who hear it, and for your bravery in standing up to them, that is provided you can hold it all together. If not, remember they might be the winners."

"Joan, I have lived for the day that I can face my tormentors in court and tell the world what they have done to us. Now, however, in my position as a wife, the family's interests must come first, so I will ask James to make the decision in all our best interests. I will be content to do the right thing for the future of us all. Were I single, I would look them in the eye and make sure they know who put them there and is going to maximise their sentence. They can rot in jail thinking of me lying on a deck chair in my garden raising two fingers at them."

"That, Elle, is exactly what I am afraid of, you sticking up two fingers and gloating at them."

James laughed and said, "We will just have to make sure it is a metaphorical two fingers then, won't we."

Joan looked at him quizzically and said, "What are you inferring, James?"

"It's a no brainer, the family is right behind Elle. We will support her one hundred per cent. Who cares what other people think? I will speak to Lucy and the girls. If Elle gets some closure by facing the bastards in the dock, then as far as I am concerned that is all that matters."

Elle was close to tears as James gave her his support. She had expected him to say that her interests were in ensuring her family's happiness, so not to create a drama or scandal.

James kissed her, and instead said, "The family will not be happy unless you are, darling. I don't ever want to think that we have not done everything that we can to stand with you. You suffered; we will all support you one hundred percent as you face your abusers in court, if that is what you truly want. "

"What about Lucy, James, what will you say to her?"

"Your Lucy is a brave and sensible girl, Elle. She already knows much more than you realise, the school bullies have seen to that. She has spoken about it more than once with me. She does not want you to know that she is bullied in this way, so keep that to yourself. Lucy can handle it well enough, she is a chip of your block. She knows you have had a rough time and she will do what she can to help you. She fully appreciates what you have done for her despite the way her father treated you. She told me she saw your bruises and heard you crying. She does not, however, know, or at least understand, the sex part and of course I will not go into that, but again, it will not be long before she has sex education, either from the school or her friends with porn. Better she gets the outline of events from me now, and later, when she fully realises what they did to you she will know that we were honest with her to the extent that we reasonably could be. Some of her less able classmates resent her top marks in every subject; their parents will gossip, so they will know all about the court case. Sooner or later Lucy will understand all that you have been through, Elle, and Ava as well. There is no way that we can prevent that. No, honesty with her as far as we can be is the best long term strategy. She will not let it affect her for long, then as she grows up she will love you all the more for shielding her and being such a good mother, despite all that you were suffering. Especially that will be true when she learns the full extent that her father has played in your abuse. I will not mention that at this stage, that will be the biggest shock of all to her when she eventually finds that out; her own father was the gang leader and how innocent you were on your way to a new job in London."

CHAPTER SEVENTEEN

Ten days later, the crown court met to sentence the defendants. It was Elle's chance to make a victim impact statement and she intended to do just that. The judge invited her to speak from the witness box. Ava stood at the solicitors' table to be counted in the statement. The lawyers for the prosecution and defence and their team of mainly female pupils looked on with interest; having read her statement, they marvelled at her courage in coming to speak in public about such a personnel matter.

Elle stood up straight and faced the four defendants in the dock. She did not blink or look away; she gave them a constant withering stare as she made her statement without notes. She spoke calmly and clearly. She began describing the offer of a job in London and how she came to this country to better herself. She then spoke for nearly an hour, giving an account of her kidnap, her imprisonment, then all that took place in the brothel, in such detail, giving names and such graphic descriptions of what they did to her, a young virgin, that many of the younger women in the various legal teams were close to tears. Elle continued in a measured voice to dispassionately lay bare the feeling of pain and helplessness she felt while on the receiving end of the sex and abuse that not only she, but all the women—here she turned and pointed to Ava—that she was representing suffered.

There was complete silence in the court as all those present, including reporters and visitors in the balcony, came to understand the strength and bravery that it must take to stand there and give such an account, as if it had happened to someone else. As with the police earlier, it was later described by lawyers as the most detailed and comprehensive account from a victim ever likely to be heard in open court and utterly believable. The defendants looked shocked; they could see the damage that she was doing to them.

Elle paused to let her story sink in, then went on to explain why she agreed to marry the main abuser, intending to use the opportunity as a way to make her escape. Her plan became impossible when she found that, despite precautions, she was pregnant. This happened before she had worked out her escape route. She decided that her only remaining option was to stay put for the sake of her unborn child, using the medical facilities available to her as Wheeler's wife. She described her marriage and her acceptance of it as loveless and abusive but tolerable compared to her alternatives. All the women trapped in the brothel believed that they would be deported as illegal immigrants if they ran away and were caught by the police. The criminals had convinced them all that they had no passports or right to stay in England. They believed that they would be sent back home and that the gang in Poland would intercept them and traffic them to another country, or even to the Middle East. They were all brainwashed and unable to resist. Elle told the court that after she was married, she believed any attempt to escape would result in her daughter being taken away from her by her husband, or into care by the authorities, as Lucy was English born. She explained that none of the women had homes or families in Poland to support them. She presumed that this was why they were chosen for jobs in London. They had no idea that Polish people were free to live here as EU citizens.

Elle went on to give an unemotional commentary of the events of the day when she finally ran away. She explained that although she was regularly abused and beaten, it was the first assault by George Wheeler on their daughter, who he had treated well enough up to this point. It became all too clear to her that once started this would be the normal pattern of behaviour in future, that they would both be illtreated. Elle said that she had to protect her daughter at all costs, and to her that now meant that the lesser of two dangers was running away as far as possible, finding lodgings and trying to earn money in a way that did not need identity papers. Elle detailed her unsuccessful attempt to get the housekeeping money, then how she collapsed in despair beside the road, suffering with concussion, unable to move any further or return home, as a result of a punch she had received to the side of her head.

Elle could not help a change of tone as she went on to tell the court how things changed for them both after they were rescued from the roadside by the most wonderful man, who took them home, gave them shelter and had done everything possible to make up for the abuse that they had suffered. Elle told them how he had called on his ex-wife, a solicitor, for help. Together they dealt with her residency issues, found out that she had never been married and took her to her embassy to get a passport. Elle explained to the court that the marriage to George Wheeler was a sham all the time and how he had tricked her. She concluded by thanking her husband and Joan, her solicitor, and all the authorities that had helped her, and the other girls, in particular Ava, who was standing up beside her to be counted. The hushed silence continued as the packed court absorbed the full horror of the wretched life that an innocent girl had been forced to live in their own town.

Elle was about to step down from the witness box when George Wheeler mouthed obscenities at her as the other three co-defendants grinned. In that instant all Elle's calm and determination to be above petty revenge evaporated, to be replaced by cold hatred of them all. That her four tormentors appeared to mock and belittle her drove her beyond the edge of reason. The memory of her years of torment and utter despair flooded over her conscious self, blanking out any other thoughts or emotions but fury and revenge. Elle, now oblivious to her surroundings, jumped to the floor and ran towards the dock that was eight feet above the ground. In front of the dock was a handrail. Elle leapt on to this. She stretched up and grabbed the metal rail of the dock then, driven on by hatred and fuelled by adrenalin, she hauled herself up onto her extended arms like an Olympic gymnast on the parallel bars. As she came face to face with her sham husband, Elle issued a torrent of profanities, all the swear words that she had learnt with her English lessons from the men in the brothel; they were many, colourful, and quite unreportable. She ended with the hope that they would all rot in prison, then she spat in George Wheeler's face.

George Wheeler watched Elle run towards the dock, curious to find out what she intended to do. There was no way she could reach them, so he thought she might have something to throw at him. He was astonished when her face appeared above the rail of the dock and she extended herself up on her arms. He leant forward to face her and responded to the tirade of abuse with a malicious sneer. He was amused and felt quite safe as his personal sex toy of the last few years balanced precariously on her hands in front of him. That was until she spat a globule in his eye. As had happened so many times before, his quick temper flared up, and his automatic reaction was to strike out at her annoyingly pretty face.

The punch caught Elle squarely in the face, breaking her nose and a bone in her cheek. Her eye was struck hard by the blow but turned out not to be too severely damaged. Her reaction, together with the force of the punch, caused her to lose her grip on the handrail. Elle was launched backward into space with her arms outstretched. She landed on the courtroom floor, with a heavy thud, dislocating her shoulder, followed milliseconds later by a crack—heard around the room—as her head made contact, causing damage internally and to her skull. She lay unconscious on the courtroom floor.

James, who had started after her when she ran across the room, was soon beside his wife guarding her as pandemonium reigned all around them. People were moving in all directions; some were shouting, a woman was screaming, many were in tears. Others were just staring at the scene in shock, unable to believe what they had just witnessed. The judge was ignored as he banged his gavel and shouted, "Clear the court."

The prison warders led the prisoners towards the stairs to the cells below. One gave George Wheeler a vicious shove in the back, sending him tumbling down the stairs, breaking his wrist. Despite his many complaints later, he was ignored as the warders both swore that he had tripped.

James was about to lift Elle into a cuddle to comfort her when a court usher with first aid training arrived and stopped him. He was joined by a colleague and together they started the routine checks on airways, breathing, circulation and other priorities.

Paramedics from an ambulance already parked nearby arrived soon afterwards and took over. The medics were extremely concerned with the condition of their unconscious patient and called for back up. While waiting, they gave Elle oxygen and continued with the preparation to move her on to a stretcher. It would be a delicate job as they could not know what injuries she had sustained to her back and neck, as she was unable to help them. A roving paramedic doctor with extensive trauma experience arrived next, followed later by the crew of an air ambulance that had put down in the car park. Under the doctor's supervision, they put Elle's shoulder back, then with infinite care and the help of the first aiders, they lifted Elle—now in a neck brace—on to the stretcher and strapped her on. Their progress through the building was watched by participants from the court and many more from throughout the building who were, by now, filling the hall and landings, curious to see what all the fuss was about. The short walk across the carpark to the helicopter was supervised by the police, also through a crowd that had gathered outside. The helicopter was a draw, as was an account of the courtroom drama rapidly circulating by word of mouth and on social media.

The helicopter rose into the sky and soon covered the thirty miles to the regional A and E hospital where most serious casualties with life threatening injuries were either taken direct, or finished up after stabilisation at one of the other hospitals' casualty departments. James and the doctor accompanied Elle and followed her as she was rushed into the building. They were met by a team that had already been briefed by the doctor. After connecting her up to a multitube of tubes and cables, they did running repairs to Elle's face and put her into an induced coma. Their major concern was her head injury, so she was taken straight to the radiography wing. The roving doctor assured James that his wife was in the best possible hands and left to be reunited with his ambulance car.

James sat alone in the waiting room, inconsolable despite the attention of some nurses who had by now all heard the story of their casualty's attack on the dock. James blamed himself for allowing Elle to make the statement herself; he should have guessed something like this might happen, but even he had underestimated her blind hatred for Wheeler in particular; he had been sure that she would hold it together to achieve her main objective.

Elle reappeared an hour later, having had multiple scans. She was rushed past and disappeared into a lift. One of the medics stopped to give him the news. They found that she had no injuries to her body beyond the ones they were already aware of, but that she had a cracked skull and severe bruising inside with an increasing build-up of pressure. She was now on her way to have an operation to relieve that pressure. James asked if they had a private room that he could book for Elle. He was told that she would have a single room so there was no need to worry; it was not just her medical necessity, but they were expecting intrusion from the press and others as often happened in newsworthy accidents.

Joan arrived to find James in a highly emotional state as he gave her the latest news. "Well, James, it's good news that Elle had no spinal damage. It's all down to the head injury. The doctors are very much on top of problem, scanned and straight into surgery. She's in the best of hands, please believe that and try to stop worrying. I had a word with the sister on my way up and she says to go home and come back in the morning, Elle will be in a coma for at last twenty-four hours and possibly longer. I will take you home now, James, Lucy needs you. Ava and John have moved into the spare room to look after her, but you should go and comfort her."

"Yes, Joan, I must be there for Lucy, you're right about that It's what Elle would want me to do."

Lucy ran to James in tears. He picked her up and carried her to the sofa to comfort her. "I saw Mummy lying on the floor, she was crying."

"How did you see her, baby?"

"On my computer, there are lots of pictures and a video of her falling."

"Mummy is going to be fine, Lucy. She's asleep in hospital, they have given her some medicine to make her sleep. You can visit when she wakes up, maybe tomorrow. Now, stop crying. I will take care of you with Ava. You must be a brave girl. Mummy will need you when she comes home. You will not go to school for the next few days, I will telephone Miss Terode and explain that we have to look after Mummy."

Ava came to take Lucy to bed and John came to talk to James.

"Someone in the court must have pulled out their phone and filmed the incident, James, it's on all the news programmes and social media. Both film of Elle at the dock, then falling down and lying unconscious on the floor. There will be photographs and reports in all the papers tomorrow. What's more, it has gone worldwide, on news channels and social media. Elle is famous around the globe for attacking her abusers in court. Before long there will not be a single person around here that will not have seen film or photos. We can expect reporters and film crews outside any time now. We may need some security, James. I think we should call the police for a start. Mother is coming over in the morning to help with Lucy and run any errands that we need."

"Thank you, John. We must keep Lucy away from the television and her computer until it blows over. Joan is upstairs. I'll ask her to ask for some police help, at least to keep an eye on anyone trying to get up to the house. Would you go and look around and shut the gates, please?"

Leona arrived and volunteered to answer the phone and text messages. Her mother joined her and telephoned the police to ask for help outside the gate if there was a crowd gathered.

James waited for Lucy to finish her bath and get into bed before he pulled up a chair beside her and started to explain what had happened. "Mummy was giving evidence against your father, Lucy, when she lost her temper and tried to hit him. Your father then punched Mummy in the face, and she fell down and banged her head, which is why she is now in hospital."

"But why, Daddy? Why was my father there and Mummy giving evidence?"

James was taken aback by being called daddy and wondered if it was Lucy's way of disowning her father for hurting her mother again. "Lucy, darling, I don't want to tell you about the bad things your father has done to be in court. You know how he hurt Mummy. That was why she was there, to tell the truth about him. He did some other bad things as well to other people like Ava, but I am not going to talk about that. I want you to forget the problems Mummy had. I don't want you to think about it. It is all in the past now, Lucy. You and Mummy live here with me, so please, it's best if you try to forget your father. When you're older you may see him if you want to, but for now that is not possible. He is in prison, do you understand? Mummy will never want to see him again, so please try not to talk to her about what has happened, it will only upset her. I will answer all your questions. I will always be here to look after you and mummy Lucy. If you need me tonight, come to my room, or can go to Ava. Try not to worry. Lucy, Mummy will soon be home, and you can help me look after her, we are her special people. We all have to prepare for our baby. If it is a girl then I will have five daughters and Ava. How many of your school friends have four sisters? It will be fun, and you will not be the youngest any more. Try to sleep now. I will leave the hall lights on and come back later. Good night, Lucy, daughter number four." James gave her a kiss and Ava came to tuck her in and say good night.

After leaving the bedroom, Ava could see that James was upset and emotional. She put her arms around him. James responded by holding her tight and telling her that it was all his fault, he should never have let Elle make a statement.

Ava answered. She told him that it was not his fault, that Elle would have never been happy if he had stopped her, and that she made a good statement then for some reason lost her temper. "When this is all over she will have no regrets, James. It was all a bit too dramatic but, provided she has no lasting ill effects, she will have achieved her long held ambition to get her own back. George Wheeler and his mates will come out of this the losers and will know who put them in prison." Ava kissed him and led him down to the kitchen where the others were gathered.

They had a sombre meal, discussed the situation, and watched the news on the television. Filming from outside the court, the reporter detailed the case and the events in court, complete with a short video. It all made a compelling story with Elle portrayed as the brave hero who finished up in hospital. Despite regretting the publicity, they were all pleased with the story about Elle's part in downfall of the gang. It might have been so different had she not spoken out, but had later been identified as one of the sex workers in the local press, where the story was always going to be front page news. Now, as they had planned before the wedding, the local press featured Elle at her wedding reception, quoting from the speeches and showing the happy photos with the important guests there in support.

When everyone had retired to bed or returned to their homes, James sat alone with a brandy and his thoughts. He decided that as soon as Elle was well enough to travel, he would take her, with Lucy, away somewhere quiet for a complete break. Eventually he too went upstairs to bed, looking in on Lucy on the way.

CHAPTER EIGHTEEN

James rose early in the morning and laid the breakfast table for Lucy, John and Ava. He then telephoned the hospital and was able to speak to the night sister in charge of the intensive care wards. She gave him the news that Elle was stable and out of danger, that the swelling had nearly gone, and the specialist did not think that there would be any permanent damage, but time and rest would tell. She advised him not to come until lunch time as Elle would not wake up until the afternoon. Hearing movement from upstairs, James made tea, coffee and toast. When Lucy appeared, he gathered her up and sat down with her to give her the good news. "

I will go to the hospital at lunch time and if you can visit later today, I will phone, but I expect we will all go tomorrow."

James followed the instructions that he was given and found the reception desk for Elle's ward. The nurse led him into the single room where Elle lay still connected to many pieces of medical equipment. She was asleep with her head heavily bandaged; she looked tiny and helpless, bringing tears to James eyes.

The young nurse looked at him sympathetically. "Try not to worry, Mr Jefferies, we are taking good care of your wife. You can be quite sure that everyone in this hospital is on her side and will do all that they can for her. Sit here I will bring you a cup of tea. She should wake up in an hour or two."

James went to Elle every ten minutes and kissed her, whispering in her ear, telling her that he was there and that it was safe to wake up. After an hour and a half, Elle opened her eyes and gave a smile. James kissed her once more as the nurse who was monitoring her condition entered the room. She was soon followed by a doctor who examined her and asked questions. Satisfied, he stood back as James said, "Welcome back, Elle, darling." The doctor left the room as the nurse hovered in the background. After a while, as Elle appeared to go back to sleep, the nurse asked him to move back and let her patient sleep again.

The nurse showed James into a small waiting room and brought him more tea and biscuits. "That was the top neurologist, Mr. Jefferies. He was well satisfied so you can relax now."

"Call me James, please, and thank you for your care."

"James, I'm not the only one here that is in awe of your wife, so small and brave. We've all seen the film and read the reports. Elle has done more for abused women than anyone could imagine possible. It's headline news; the authorities must take it more seriously in future. Those men will suffer in prison; just like paedophiles they will be loathed by other prisoners. How could anyone hurt someone as beautiful as Elle or the other girls?"

"Write your name down for me, nurse, you must come to visit us so we can repay your kindness when all is back to normal, if it ever is."

An hour late Elle full regained consciousness. She looked at James and asked, "What happened to me, James, why am I here.?"

"You had an accident, my love. Don't think about it, just rest and get better. Lucy and Ava send their love."

Elle drifted in and out of consciousness until the doctor came to conduct a more thorough examination. "Your wife is doing fine, Mr Jefferies. There are no obvious, lasting effects, but we have to continue the close monitoring for another twenty-four hours to be sure. I have given your wife a sedative so you can safely go home until tomorrow."

James drove home and again went through the posse of press and photographers gathered at his gate, which was opened this time by a security guard hired by Joan. He stopped and got out of his car to make a statement.

"Thank you all for your interest. I have just come from the hospital and am pleased to tell you that my wife has woken up and is in a stable condition. The doctors do not think there is any lasting damage, but they will keep her in intensive care for another twenty-four hours to be sure. There will be no further statements from any of us so please pack up and go home. My wife has suffered enough. I will not tolerate any harassment or intrusion in the future as we try to get or lives back to normal. Please leave us alone, thank you all."

James had kept the family fully informed during the day and was not surprised to be greeted by a much more cheerful group than the one he had left in the morning. He picked Lucy up for a cuddle and told that her mummy sent her love and a kiss, which he gave to her. "You are a good girl, Lucy, thank you for being so sensible. Tomorrow I will take you with me. You are my special daughter, Lucy."

Ava watched this bonding session with satisfaction. She loved Lucy and was herself concerned about the effect the new baby might have on her relationship with James. It was now obvious to her that James was making every effort to head the problem off before the baby arrived.

***

The following morning James drove Ava and Lucy to the hospital, arriving at ten o'clock. They were taken into Elle's room by the same nurse, who held Lucy's hand. James was delighted to see that the situation had changed very much for the better, Elle was sitting up with most of the medical paraphernalia removed. She still had a bandage around her head and was very pale, but she had a smile for her visitors. The nurse held Lucy back as James went to exchange a loving greeting with his wife, then he gave her a kiss as he held her hand and beckoned to Lucy who ran over and hugged her mother until James gently pulled her away, then it was Ava's turn to say hello. They sat around the bed as Elle closed her eyes and drifted in and out of sleep. The ward sister who had been watching the visit on her monitor appeared and led Ava and Lucy away, suggesting they go to the café while their father sat with his wife giving her comfort, holding her hand, and speaking to her when she was awake. An hour later, James came out and said that Elle was fast asleep so he would take them home and return later in the afternoon to sit at the bedside to be there when she woke up.

On returning to the ward in mid-afternoon, James found Elle fully awake and waiting for him. They had a long, gentle, silent hug as they bonded back together after the hiatus of the accident and Elle's coma. Then Elle started to tearfully apologise for what she had done after she had promised to keep her temper and act sensibly. She had remembered everything that happened and was sorry for the trouble it had caused everybody.

James stopped her in mid flow with a kiss. "Elle, my love, you did what you did. You were provoked, but the important thing is that you had already managed to make an incredibly good statement. It is over now, darling. There is no point in looking back. You must rest and concentrate on getting better. We all need you at home, especially Lucy. I cannot live without you beside me, Elle. The house is so empty, the love has gone, all that matters is getting you back to Dunwood House where you belong with your family. We will not speak about the court again until you are fully recovered and I have taken you on holiday with Lucy and possibly Ava."

James sat beside Elle's bed while she dozed off again and stayed there until the nurses came to prepare her for the night.

***

Lucy went back to school next day, after Miss Terode had spoken to James on the phone promising to look after her. She explained that the whole staff and all the parents that she had spoken to wanted to send a message to Elle and wish her a speedy recovery. James was assured that the pupils in Lucy's year had been told not to speak about the accident to her. Miss Terode and the other teachers would make sure that there was always someone watching during break and activity time.

"She has to come back some time, Mr. Jefferies, so better that it is straight away. We will keep a close eye on her. I can tell you Lucy, even without her mother's brave exploits, has caused quite a bit of interest among the staff here, not just for her intelligence; it is her work ethic and maturity well beyond her years that we admire. We have high hopes for her; we will take every care now."

So back she went, not in the least concerned, anxious to get on with her studies.

Much later, Jane Terode who was, by then, on Christian name terms with James, admitted with a laugh that some of Lucy's enemies had tried to goad her, only to be asked if any of their mothers had ever had the guts to attack their enemies and become famous, or were they just housewives and thick like their children. "That made her even more popular with most of her class and friends, and with me when I heard about it, and she never had any more trouble. Your Lucy is a tough cookie like her mother. Trust me, she understands much more than you might realise. She has confided to me that her father often hurt her mother and made her cry. She will defend her mother against all comers."

Three days later, Anne visited the hospital and discovered that the doctor in charge of Elle's rehabilitation was an old colleague of hers from the local hospital. She volunteered to look after Elle at home and change her dressing. This was agreed by the hospital, with a visit from the doctor after the weekend to check on Elle's progress.

The following day Elle was duly discharged from the hospital and driven home by James, with Anne, and installed in the Dunwood guest room. Ava and John were there to greet her; Joan came later to add her welcome, and Lucy would do so when she came home from school. Anne laid down strict instructions for Elle and James. Elle was allowed out of bed for short supervised periods but was not to get excited or do any exercise for the next few days; definitely no fun and games at night, no television, or social media; this last because her release from hospital had stirred up the interest in the case again and brought reporters to the gate once more, much of which was still unknown to Elle..

All went according to plan during the next week. Elle spent an increasing amount of time in the kitchen-living room. Her bandage became a small dressing; she still sported a blackeye. The doctor came to supper with his wife and signed Elle off. At least on the surface, everything was back to normal. Lucy reported that everyone was being nice to her at school and that she was getting on well with her lessons. Elle made it to the garden where Jonathan fussed over her and could not resist giving her a hug, then apologising, much to Elle's surprise and pleasure.

"Thank you, Jonathan ,that was kind, there is no need to apologise. I am better now, thank you and will soon be back to work with you in the garden."

The following week Joan came with all the latest news from the police and the reconvened court hearing. "George wheeler has been charged with Elle's assault and with contempt of court. He pleaded guilty to both and was given a sentence of two years in prison. The court then resumed its original sentencing hearing and the judge sent them all to prison for twelve years, the maximum possible. George's two sentences are to run consecutively, making a total of fourteen years for him, which under the new guidance means at least ten years in prison. Does that make you happy, Elle, despite not being there to see it and raise your two fingers?"

Elle hugged James. She was in tears of joy at the realisation that it was now case closed, that they could all draw a line over the past. Her enemies were all in prison where they belong. Finally, she whispered, "I am free, Lucy is free with her father out of her life, at least until she is grown up, Ava is free and can also draw a line on her abuse and concentrate on her education. It's over for us all. "

"Well done, Elle," Joan said. "You played a big part in their downfall, and they all know it. But I have to tell you that you had a lucky escape yourself. The judge wanted you charged with contempt of court as well, but neither the police nor the Crown Prosecution Service thought that it was in the public interest and declined to pursue the charge against you. It is possible that you may still get a caution, but not if the police have any say in the matter, they are so much on your side."

Simon later reported that the judge, a friend of his, was only going through the legal necessity. "He had no choice after what you did to the smooth running of his court, but he was content to let it drop when the official prosecuting authority refused to take it up. Moreover, he was delighted to be able to add two years to the maximum possible sentence that he had already decided to awarded George Wheeler and his gang, sentences that he considered inadequate for the crime."

With Lucy happily back at school, it was decided that Ava would look after her while James and Elle went for a holiday together. They chose a luxury castle hotel on Dartmoor that had a golf course of its own. James booked a suite to give them maximum flexibility; if Elle became tired James intended to stay in the apartment rather than mix with the other guests. There was also always the possibility that she would be recognised and again James would want to keep to themselves. A quiet week with good food and relaxing fresh air was what Anne prescribed. He did not intend for Elle to mix; she still did not realise the publicity she had received and that was how it was to remain, as long as James was able to keep it that way. Anne had advised James that stress and exercise was to be avoided at all costs; he understood what she meant and promised to behave himself.

***

They were shown to their room by a porter that appeared to be dressed as a gamekeeper, which turned out to be a dress code for some of the staff of the five-star hotel. The balcony in their room looked over the golf course that ran along a valley with a stream winding through it; it all looked perfect from above. They were about to go down for tea when the receptionist rang to ask if they would receive a visit from the manager. Intrigued, they waited for the knock on the door. The manager came with a waiter pushing a trolley with a large bunch of flowers, and a bottle of champagne and a range of treats on it.

Jim Farquhar, the manager, explained that Elle had been recognised and checking their address confirmed it. The management and staff wished to welcome them, and they all hoped that Elle had a relaxing convalescence in their hotel. They were not to hesitate if there was anything that they needed to enhance their stay. There was a private lounge next to the dining room for VIP guests which they were free to use. Their table would be secluded in a bay window and quite private.

James thanked the manager for their kind thoughts and said they wanted as little fuss as possible.

When the door was closed, Elle asked how it was possible that she was recognised.

"Let me order tea from room service, my love, and then I have something to tell you."

Later over the tea, James explained. "You, Elle, are famous, not just at home or even just in the UK, but pretty well worldwide. Someone in the court filmed your performance—I will show it to you on my iPhone— and it went viral on news programs and social media, together with a full report..

Elle was shocked and initially speechless. Eventually she said, "What are we to do, James? That makes our normal lives impossible."

219

"Nothing we can do, darling. There is not a thing we can do that will help. The good news is that, like Mr Farquhar, they all appear to be on your side. Our foresight and plan at the wedding has worked even better than we could have ever hoped. You are the innocent victim. Just like the hospital staff, everyone wants to help you."

"I see, that's why Jonathan was so pleased to see me, with a hug."

"A lot of people would like to hug you, Elle. You'd better make the most of it, we have thousands of get well cards in bags at home."

Elle wrapped up in a coat and hat before they went for a short walk before supper.

As they got out of the lift a gamekeeper came and escorted them to the private lounge where they had one glass of champagne and ordered a light meal for Elle and a ribeye steak for James. The head waiter and a female assistant escorted them to the secluded table. James noticed a few heads turning to look at them, but decided that he was being too self-conscious The service was exceptional. They could not be sure that they were getting the same as everyone else, and the waitresses were especially attentive to Elle. The food was as good as any they had eaten on the holidays or honeymoon; the chef even appeared to ask if everything was to their liking. Elle could not help giggling when the restaurant manageress did the same. They clearly all wanted to take a closer look at Elle. They were led back to the lounge where they had coffee before being escorted up to their suite; time for a last brandy for James and a weak brandy and ginger ale for Elle; despite her protests, James was being strict.

Finally, after all that had happened since the fateful day that Elle had gone to court to make her statement, they were in bed together. "

It seems forever, my love, since we were last in bed with each other. I have missed you so much, you cuddly little baby angel."

"Yes, James, I have missed you just as much, so what are you going to do to me tonight to make up for it? I see you are well prepared. I have never seen you so frighteningly monstrous. Were I a younger girl I might get up run away from that thing."

"Nothing, darling, is the answer to your question, nothing at all, except kiss and hold you close to feel your sexy body against mine."

"Why not? I want you, James, now. I have wanted you every night when I was awake. I need some serious loving from you. I have missed the feel of your strong body on top of mine. Don't be mean to me now, please, you are as hard as a tent pole. Give it to me nicely."

"Sorry, darling, it simply is not allowed. Sister Anne forbade me to do anything at all to you. She was quite crude in her language so that I would be in no doubt what she meant."

"But why, darling? I'm better now."

"I'm not a medical man, my love, but it is to do with not banging or shaking your head and causing the swelling to come back. There is also the baby to worry about; it has had a bit of a shake up. Don't be surprised if its first words are a complaint about your rough treatment."

Elle laughed. "It's much too soon to worry about the baby, James. Did Joan kick you out of bed this early in her pregnancy?"

"Maybe not, but we were not that bothered at any time."

"You poor boy, you're desperate and leaking. You will never sleep like that. I can wait, but you can't, so lie back and relax, try to practise making this last. Let's see if you can go longer that ten seconds." Elle disappeared.

"No, no, Elle, not like that, come back up here now." James gently pulled her back up level with his face and kissed her. "That is certainly not allowed. What are you thinking? Take this seriously, Elle, or we will have to have separate beds. With me like this that would shake your head more than any other way. Just use your hands, you naughty girl."

"Wow, how did you last this long, my poor neglected lover? That was about what I expected in timing, but you were so fully charged, you really can't last long without a woman, can you? I just love you to pieces when you are that desperate for me, but what a mess, I have never seen so much. Look at my nighty, I'll have to go and rinse it out. I was not prepared for this or I would have had a towel. I can't put it in the laundry like this."

"Take it off, baby, and stay here, I want to feel you close to me. I love you, Elle, you are so good at knowing how to look after me. I can't last long, as you say, but I do not need to with you. You will always see that I get what I need, one way or another. You are one in a million, Elle, my angel. I will take better care of you in future, I promise." James got serious. "Elle, I am so sorry about what happened to you. It was all my fault; you gave me the decision to make and I made the wrong one. You were doing so well then lost it. I should have seen the danger and insisted that Joan read your statement. I promise to look after you much better in future. Don't worry about the public reaction, we will keep within our family and friends until it blows over. Jonathan is taking charge of everything outside and I have asked him to hire an assistant with security experience, but also an interest in gardening or at least building maintenance. Joan has recommended a woman to work inside the two houses; she's an ex-policewoman and will act as your assistant. You will take her with you when shopping and she will act as chauffeur to us all, taking Lucy to school for example. These are simple precautions for the next few months."

"James, it's not your fault. I am fully responsible for my actions and I'm not sorry that I gave that bastard an extra two years. I will put up with what happens to me, but I regret what I have done to the rest of you. I will meet the woman, we will need more support, but it's over now so I will try not to look back. But what about Lucy, James? Does she know any of this?"

"Oh, Elle, your amazing little daughter is a real chip off the block. She has known much more than you realise for some time. She talks to me about it and did not want you to know what she had to put up with at school. She saw you on social media, as has everyone else. I kept her back from school until Jane Terode persuaded me to send her back, saying it was better now than later, so that she could look after her. So back she went without a care in the world. Jane later told me that she was goaded by her very few enemies and quickly shut them up, much to the delight of all her friends and Jane herself. Lucy asked me why you were there with her father. I explained that you were giving evidence about the way he hurt you, then you lost your temper and George punched you, which is why you were in hospital. Lucy thought about it, knowing it was true, then she started asking more questions. She also called me Daddy, quite deliberately. I took it as a sign that she was disowning her father for what he has done to you. You will have to spend time alone with her, Elle. She needs to tell you all she knows, and you need to explain as much as possible so that you are both on the same page and can talk about everything as mother and daughter should. She loves you so much, that's why she has not talked to you before—she didn't want to upset you—but now you must help her to come to terms with the facts which cannot be swept under the carpet any longer, especially about her father.

"I do not think she will understand or hopefully have even heard about the sex angle, but you have to be ready as it will not be long now before the older girls tease her about this. Everything is now in the public domain and her school friends' and enemies' parents will talk. When that happens, she must feel able to come to you, not to me. I will help, but you and Lucy must both face the facts together. Be honest with her as much as you can be to fit in with her knowledge of the subject. She will love you all the more as she grows up and comes to fully understand how you were abused and have suffered. I will join in and explain things that you do not want to talk about so that we stay as a family against the world."

"I am so sorry, darling."

James comforted a sobbing Elle as she realised the full implications of her actions. "Think about it, this may well be all for the best in the long run, because it had to come out sooner or later. Lucy could not grow up with friends that all know about the case without understanding your full history. She needs to hear it from us, a little at a time, as her understanding increases. My opinion is that she will worry about you much more than she will care what others think. Your daughter knows full well how you have protected her over the years as you were abused by her father. She will never forget that, or forgive him."

The rest of their short holiday went without incident. Elle drove the buggy as James played golf with another guest and his wife. James invited them to drinks and dinner because it was obvious from the way that Jill helped Elle out the buggy, asking her if she was not too tired, that she was clearly concerned about her. Showing that she was recognised, tactfully, it was never actually mentioned. This incident and the manager's comments ensured that they drove home in relaxed mood and ready to face the chaos that they both expected to come their way in the immediate future.

Lucy ran to her mother as soon as they walked into the kitchen. Elle sat on the sofa and pulled her daughter on to her knee. "Here I am, Lucy darling. I am all better now. We have had a nice little holiday in Devon. How are you getting on at school? I didn't get a chance to talk to you before we went away."

"I love my school, Mummy. Everyone is kind to me, especially Miss Terode. I am top of the class in most things."

"Tonight, Lucy, when you go to bed, we will have a talk and I will explain what happened to me. Now I must speak to Ava and John and thank them for looking after you."

That night, mother and daughter had a long conversation about the sins of George Wheeler, how he had hurt her and other women like Ava and tricked her into thinking she was married.

Lucy said she now had a new father and never wanted to see the old one ever again, "Because of what he did to you, Mummy. With our baby and James, we will be like all my friends, a real family. Our new daddy loves you, Mummy, and would never hurt anyone, would he?"

"No, Lucy, he would not. He will take care of us all, as he has done ever since he took us home. No one will ever hurt us again with James to protect us. You concentrate on school, Lucy, that is your future, then you can look after us when we are old."

Elle thanked Jonathan for his support and invited his family to tea so that they could get to know each other. They came the following afternoon and were soon made welcome, with Lucy taking her new friends on a tour of the house. Elisabeth was a few years older than Elle, a typical country, motherly woman who immediately embraced Elle and told her how worried she had been and how she would like to be friends and help in any way she could, to give support. She explained that Jonathan had been so worried since the accident and spoke of little else. He loved his new job of taking charge of everything outside their two houses; he was no longer a jobbing gardener but a proper head gardener, in charge of two properties.

"He has been so concerned about you, Elle. He watched the video and was nearly in tears."

"I am so sorry, Elisabeth. I have caused so much trouble and worry to all my friends and family." To everyone's astonishment Elle burst into tears and cried on Elisabeth's shoulder. Elle later explained that she did not have any women friends her age other than family and Anne, who was much older, and the sudden sympathy released the tension that had been building up ever since James told her about the publicity she had generated. James was coming to the rescue, but Elisabeth pointed to the door, so he went to find Lucy and her new friends to take them outside and show the children the garden.

Elisabeth continued to hold Elle and soothe her with comforting words, telling her to cry and let it all come out. Eventually the tears stopped, and Elisabeth made them coffee, which they drank sitting at the table. "Is that better, Elle?."

"Yes, thank you, I'm sorry, Elisabeth, I don't know what happened to me."

"It's perfectly normal, Elle. I expect that was the first time since the accident that you have let it all come out, it had to happen sooner or later. I have heard so much about you, Elle, from the news but mostly from Jonathan, as I said, and I would like to be friends with you if you want one. Our children are the same age. Actually, I know all about Lucy. she is very highly regarded by everyone at school."

"How do you know that, Elisabeth?"

"Well, I have not yet had any dealings with her myself, but I am a teacher at her school."

"You are? Jonathan has never mentioned that, how strange."

"I think he's too busy talking about his beloved garden, his new full time job and his famous boss to think of much else. You must know he is one of your biggest fans, Elle."

"Yes, please, Elisabeth, I need friends with children Lucy's age. I do understand what you mean about Jonathan, but everything will settle down as we get to grips with all the renovations in the garden, I will make sure of that. Your husband, like mine, is a special person and James and I both know we are fortunate to have him in charge of the properties. It has all been a bit exciting for him, which is no fault of his. My reputation follows me around, again no fault of mine, but it is inevitable that he would be teased by his friends about me. I am used to all that now and will make sure it all works out for the best. Men, I have come to understand over the years, both good ones and I am afraid bad, like the one I attacked in court. Our husbands are two of the absolute best.

Everything will work out, I promise you, as we settle down and I bring a new baby home."

"I'm sure it will, Elle. Congratulations, I didn't know that you were pregnant. That might help to explain your tears. I am sure it will work out as you say. Anyone that can climb up to the dock and spit in the eye of her enemy is capable of anything. I for one could not have done that. I imagine there are countless men that would like to meet you now, you must know that you are an exciting and very sexy woman, Elle. Your action-packed courtroom drama would excite the pope, let alone mere mortal men."

"Yes, for my sins I have always looked like every man's wet dream, but I was in fact a virgin when I came to England to be abused. Many men have wanted me ever since I was fifteen and I ignore them, or in one important case kicked him in the balls, but look where it got me, locked in a brothel. Now my darling James has rescued me, and my Lucy, I am pregnant with his child, so I will be forever more devoting my life to our family, but most of all to that man that I love above everything else, so please do not worry about Jonathan, Elisabeth. He is clearly concerned about me. I appreciate that, any man worth knowing would be wanting to look out for my interests, but Jonathan behaves correctly at all times, I can assure you of that. Let's see more of each other as families. How is your cooking, Elisabeth?"

"Good, actually, I am responsible for that part of the senior girls' education."

"That's good. How about we have bake off type lessons here with the children during the holidays? I would also like to learn how to bake and make jam from the fruit we grow. Then we can bring the men in for lunch or tea to eat what we cook, and all be friends together. The children would love that, I think."

"Excellent idea, Elle, I see what you are thinking, that this will water down the one to one relationship you have with working with Jonathan in the garden."

"Partly, but not that I think it is necessary, Elisabeth, but it will be fun for me and for the children as well. Gardening and cooking go together as we will grow a lot of our food in the years to come."

Elle went to find the children and bring them in for tea. Elisabeth found James and told him of her concern. "I have not met Elle before, but I think she is more upset than she might appear, not too far from a breakdown if you are not careful."

"I think you're right, Elisabeth; she has been extraordinarily strong up to now, but a combination of the bang on her head putting her in intensive care, and the publicity, has hit her hard. What can we do? We went on holiday and I think that helped."

"How about getting all your friends and family together, James, so that Elle can see that they all still support her."

"Good idea, a repeat of the wedding reception for a buffet supper, would that do the trick?"

"Perfect, but make it a surprise and we will all dress up to show Elle off at her best and to give her a lift, knowing that they still love her despite what they heard and saw on the television. Make sure all the men you know come, that should boost her self- confidence, to have them all slobbering over her, as I am sure my Jonathan will, given the chance."

"Elisabeth, I can assure you, it's not just him. You should have seen the staff at the hotel we stayed in with Lucy; I was completely ignored as they fawned over Elle and escorted her to the table."

"I'm sure you loved it, James."

"Of course I did. I love that girl more than I can put into words, and will do anything for her. She is the exact opposite of what people expect: she is gentle, most of the time, faithful and feminine, very much a one man girl, and a perfect mother, as you can tell by talking to Lucy."

CHAPTER NINETEEN

The supper was arranged for the following Saturday. Elle was enjoying a long relaxing bath with soap suds, James sitting on the stool and occasionally unable to resist running his hands over her curves and massaging her breasts. This Elle loved. She shut her eyes as she followed his hands' gentle progress around her body. "Where are you taking me tonight, James, why the mystery?"

"We are dressing up and going out to dinner, my love, so that I can spoil you and show you off, maybe candlelight for two, just wait and see."

"James, how romantic."

James ordered a taxi and not for the first time regretted that Elle had refused to employ Joan's policewoman. As they drove out of the village she said, "James, this is the way to the hotel where we got married."

"Yes, darling, but they do a very upmarket dinner evening."

The head waiter led them to the banqueting room and opened the double doors wide. There was a complete silence as those on both sides took in the scene that had opened up before them. Elle, expecting a dining room, could not assimilate in her brain the room full of people; it was like a flash back to the wedding. The spell was broken when Lucy ran up and put her arms around her mother.

For their part, the waiting friends and family were stunned by the sudden image of Elle dressed up in her gypsy frock with her long hair in ringlets shining around the emerald necklace. Standing in the doorway of the candle lit room with the lights of the hallway behind her, Elle was the very image of the film star that James wanted to show off to his friends.

James's three daughters looked at the expressions of those not used to seeing Elle dressed up in her expensive London finery. They smiled at each other and said girl power. Ava joined them and whispered, "I wish I had that effect on men. Look at my John's expression, he's mesmerised, but then who would not be? She is stunningly beautiful, not just sexy." They giggled as they watched the women watching their men, especially Elisabeth and Anne.

Joan came up and said,"Girls, whatever is your father up to? We all look so plain with Elle dressed up like a Hollywood movie star, but looking like a rabbit caught in the headlights and as if she wants to run away, poor girl. Whose idea was this?"

Elle turned to James and asked, "What is going on? Why am I dressed like this and why are they all here staring at me? I want to go home."

James embrace his frightened wife. "It's okay, darling, they are all here because they love you and want to see that you have recovered. It was Elisabeth, your new friend's idea, to make you look at your best so that we can all see that you are back to full health and looking beautiful once more. Come on, let's join them. Relax, enjoy yourself, my love, everyone is here just for you."

They were soon swallowed up in a melee of well-wishers, all keen to show that they were still on her side, most well aware that Elle, already fragile from past experiences, had suffered a severe knock to her self-confidence following her exploits in court and the associated publicity.

A full buffet was served, and Champagne and other drinks were freely available to make the party go with a swing. Elisabeth, as her new true friend, made it her role to accompany Elle and make sure she spoke to everyone in the room and had plenty of refreshment. After a while, even she could relax as Elle sat down with her stepdaughters, Ava, and Lucy, to have a girls' gossip. They were soon giggling as Lisa, who had a wicked sense of humour, was describing the men's stunned expressions at the sight of Elle in the doorway.

"I looked at your John, Ava, I swear he had a full hard on to go with his open-mouthed ogle."

"I would not be surprised, Lisa," Ava replied. "He is a full blooded man, after all. I would be disappointed if he did not fancy you dolled up, Elle, dear." She followed this with a rather explicit sentence in Polish that made Elle laugh out loud, then too late Ava realised that Lucy might also understand. She obviously did as she too burst out laughing. She was clearly not totally innocent and unaware of sex, as James had presumed.

Later Simon took Elle to one side. "You know how much Joan and I love you, Elle, don't you, so may I give you a hug and a kiss?"

"Yes, Simon, I do. You have both been so kind and helpful, especially Joan earlier on when I most needed help."

Simon gave her a kiss. "Elle, never tell anyone, not even James, but that was from another admirer of yours, his honour the judge. Clearly he cannot let it be known that he sent you a kiss, but he's a fan of yours in a big way, not just the incident at the dock which he described as outrageous, but the way you made your statement. He told me that was quite exceptional. He hopes that you are fully recovered."

"Thank him very much, Simon. I really appreciate that message more than any other. I was truly sorry that I disrupted his court. Tell him that, please, and pass on this kiss."

"Later in the year, Elle, would you come and be my guest at the chambers' end of year party? You are the toast of the inns of court, chambers and the watering holes around them. It was the main topic of conversation for days. Nothing like that has happened before as far as anyone can remember. The juniors have a picture of you, taken at your wedding, on their common room wall. They are pestering me to bring you up to London for a visit. His honour has been teased about losing control of the proceedings. He went for his usual drink in our local and was met by a chant of, "Clear the court, clear the court, knock, knock, knock, clear the court." He took in in good part then sent you his kiss."

James came to claim his wife. "Well, my love, are you happy now that you have spoken to all our friends?"

"Oh yes, James, thank you. Everyone has been so kind and supportive. I feel better than I have done at any time since before the accident. We have so many friends here, James, even some from the golf club. Maybe I can now put it all behind me and get back to domestic life, but I will never forget today and all this love. By the way, James, you will have to rethink Lucy and what she knows. We were having a proper girls' gossip when Lisa, who is very funny and a mimic, teased Ava about John and his expression when he saw me dressed up. She said he was mesmerised with a hard on. Then Ava spoke to me in Polish. It was crude and gave a different insight into gentle young John and his ability in bed with rough sex. I laughed, but so did Lucy. Ava had forgotten that she might understand."

"I am not really surprised, Elle. Now, let's say goodbye and take Lucy home."

Later when Elle was helping Lucy to bed, she asked her what she thought of the party.

Lucy was enthusiastic. "I loved it, Mummy. We have so many friends now. My new sisters and Ava treat me as one of the family and are such fun. They all said such nice things about you, they called you stunning and beautiful, but were funny when talking about the men and rude about John. Lisa said something I did not understand about how hard he was looking at you and then Ava spoke to you in Polish. It was funny but I did not quite understand all of it, but what she said was rude wasn't it, Mummy?"

"Don't worry, darling, it is just girl gossip, teasing Ava. They did not mean it. Now hop into bed and tomorrow we will do some gardening."

Elle found James in the kitchen with coffee and brandy. "Lucy knew that what was said was rude, but she claims not to understand it all. My guess is she knew it was about his cock but not the rough sex Ava talked about. Either way it is part of her growing up and inevitable with her sisters that she will be educated sooner rather than later. James, I am going to give you a special treat when I get you in bed, for what you have done for me tonight."

"No, Elle, my love, not tonight. I have already had my reward: it was watching you happy with all our friends. You have had an exciting time and I am still told to make you take it slowly. Anne spoke to me earlier and forbade me having my wicked way with you tonight, cheeky madam, but perhaps in the morning we can have some gentle loving. Tonight, I shall cuddle your sexy body, kiss you and hold you tight as we go to sleep. Tomorrow let's do something with Lucy, perhaps a trip the coast and a paddle."

True to his word, they cuddled up naked and giggled as they swapped erotic ideas of what they would like to be doing to each other. Then Elle lay on top of her lover, intertwined their legs, held his head in her hands and said, "James, my beloved husband, I feel as if I have been travelling through a dark tunnel and have suddenly come out the other side into the light. I feel free and ready to live the rest of my life as mother of Dunwood House. Thank you for everything." She put her hand over his mouth to stop him replying. Then kissed her man.

Elle

I cannot believe what has happened to me in the last two weeks, but they are almost certainly among the most momentous in my life. Life changing, in fact, as it draws a line under the whole chapter of my humiliation and abuse. A dramatic end and now I hope a new beginning. I had such good intentions when I stood up to be counted at the committal hearing, it was going so well until that bastard Wheeler mouthed off at me, then I lost it completely. I got face to face with the man responsible for my torment, delivered a tirade of abuse and spat in his eye, so far so satisfying. I don't know what I expected, but the inevitable punch he gave me sent me into space. I do not remember anything more until I woke up in hospital. When I realised what I had done and all the publicity it created, I was afraid my new life was at an end, that everyone would despise me and say what do you expect from a common foreign sex worker. Tonight has changed all that, thanks to Elisabeth and my adorable saviour, lover and champion, James. Almost everyone I know was there to wish me well, they were all so kind. If I ever had doubts, which of course I did, I now know for certain who I have become and where I belong. I will strive to be worthy and never to look back. I am now wife, mother and the glue that will hold the extended family together as we all go forward and make Dunwood our home, now and into the future down the generations.

CHAPTER TWENTY

The following morning at breakfast, Elle suggested that as she wanted to have a day at home and in the garden. Perhaps Lucy would like to go to Bassett Farm where they had a visitor centre with attractions and a café with farm shop, in addition to the animals that they could stroke. "Maybe they also do horse riding, what do you think?"

"Yes please." Lucy paused, then said, "Daddy will you take me please?"

James, delighted to be called Daddy, agreed at once, so later they changed and went out together. Schools being on holiday, Elle phoned Elisabeth and had a long conversation during which they agreed the plan to have a regular cooking school at Dunwood. Elle then went into the garden and spent the next few hours working with Jonathan and planning the winter planting.

Later, Lucy came running in glowing and excited. "I held a little piglet, Mummy and it squealed so I had to let it go. There were llamas and cows and lots of sheep."

James came in grinning. "We had a lot of fun, Elle. They do have a riding stable, but you have to book, so we are both going riding next Wednesday."

"You too, James?"

"Yes, darling, why not? I would not want to miss it if Lucy is going."

"Wow, James, wait till I tell the girls that their father is going horse riding. They will burst their sides with laughing at the thought of you sitting on a horse. I must have a photo please."

"Maybe, you little stirrer, but if perhaps Lucy wants to do some serious horse riding in the future, as many girls do, then I want to understand all about it."

"Well, you two, I also have news. We are going to have regular cooking sessions here. During the day it will be a bake off type lesson like you see on television, perhaps ending with a competition making something different each time—for a start, cupcakes would be simple. This will be for me and all the children and anyone that wants to learn to bake pastry, cakes and pies.”

“What about bread?” James asked. “I have always wanted to bake bread.”

“Yes, why not. Then, in the evening, it will be serious cooking, mainly for the adults. We will cook a full meal and invite everyone to supper to eat it. Elisabeth is a cooking instructor, so why not educate the whole family and have fun at the same time.”

“Brilliant, darling, gourmet cooks for all Jefferies’ households and future husbands to enjoy.”

Elle went to do a small shop for supper, so James made tea and crumpets for himself and Lucy. Deciding to take the risk of serious conversation with his new daughter, he sat beside her and began by asking her what she knew about the court case involving her father.

“I know that my father was a bad man and hurt Mummy and that was why she was there, to say what he did to her.”

“Lucy, I am going to be honest with you because it may be important, that is if you know more about this than you admit, but do not have anyone to talk to. I can help you if you have any worries but do not want to talk about them to your mother. I want to help you if you need it, but also to protect your mother who, as you know, has had a hard time. Your father was given fifteen years in prison. That is a very long time, Lucy, that was not just for hurting your mother at home was it?”

“No, it was because of what they did to Mummy before she had me.”

“Yes, Lucy, it was, but how do you know that?”

“Because two of the big girls took me into a room and told me about how Mummy was made to do bad things with men.”

“Lucy, my love, that is just what I suspected, and you have kept it to yourself.”

Lucy was close to tears. “Yes, I cannot talk to Mummy, she would hate it if she realised what I know.”

“You are such a good and clever girl, Lucy. I am astonished how well you have behaved, protecting your mother. But now you can talk to me about anything that you know, I will help you. Your mother came to England and was kidnapped and made to do these bad things, that is why they went to prison for so long. Your mother was very young. She is a special person, everyone loves her and are sorry for what happened. We all want to make it better for her. That is why we had the party, so that everyone could let her know that they love her, but please, never talk to her about any of this, at least until you are grown up, unless of course your mother brings it up herself with you. I will not tell her about our conversations, then she can forget the past. But we will talk about everything, Lucy, because I am here to help you as well as your mother. I am your father now but also still your friend. Now tell me, Lucy, when you were all joking, what you understood when Ava spoke Polish to Mummy, and you laughed."

"I cannot tell you that, Daddy, it was about what John did to Ava in bed, it was rude."

"Lucy, you darling, you know so much more than a girl of your age should, but it is good for you. You have grown up fast, you are top of the class and can do anything you like when you grow up. I am proud to be your new father, Lucy, but talk to me. I will explain anything to you, we will be friends, not just father and daughter."

"Yes, please, I often hear things that I do not understand."

"Come here, my clever daughter, let me give you a cuddle. It was my lucky day, Lucy, when you and your mother came into my life. I love you both so much. So please talk to me if something worries you, do not let bullies hurt you. I will stop them with Miss Terode, who I am friendly with. You concentrate on having fun with your new friends and work hard at school. I promise you that I will take care of your mummy."

Later, when Lucy was in bed and they relaxing with a night cap before retiring themselves, James said how well he as getting on with Lucy now. "You do not need to worry about the new baby spoiling things, Elle. Lucy talks to me more than my own daughters ever did. I think it is because she knew me before I became her new father. We are good friends. She tells me all sorts of secrets. I asked her what she understood about the Polish conversation. She clearly knew what was said. She told me she could not repeat it as it was rude about John in bed. Elle, you and Lucy have made me a new man. My sole interest now is the next year for you, our baby and Lucy. You need stress free time to get over the past and I am going to ensure that you both have just that.

Any distraction like more reporters at the gate and Jonathan and I will see them off with his new assistant. I will spend much more time with Lucy and I think that we should ask Elisabeth to talk to her as well in case she needs help with anything that she does not want to tell us. We will spend days together as a family, both here and short trips away. What do you think?"

"Oh, James, thank you for all you have done for Lucy. I know how you have changed. Joan is amazed and tells me about it. So do the girls, they love the new you, so I agree with everything you say. We will focus on getting Dunwood exactly as we want it and spend time together while we wait for the baby, then I will be busy. Lucy will be big sister, not junior any more and you, darling, will wish it had never happened."

"Rubbish, Elle, I love little babies."

"So, you will do the night shift and change nappies will you, James?"

"If I do it will be the first time, but I would not rule it out. What are you laughing at? Do you think I am not an expert in that department with three children already?"

"Yes, darling, three children and a nanny."

***

The long summer holidays were a happy time at Dunwood House. Elle, fully recovered, worked tirelessly to put her mark on every aspect of their life. She took the cooking very seriously, developing her own everyday family recipes, ones that she hoped one day would be loved by grandchildren and called a Polish granny's recipe. With Lucy she went shopping for pictures, ornaments cushions and other feminine touches, as all the furniture and James's effects were male oriented, having not had a woman's hand for many years. She was using her own money until James insisted that they were housekeeping. He also bought her a set of pretty glass animals and promised to add to the collection on special occasions. In the garden Elle also made her mark, helping to design the perennial borders with plants that she chose. Elisabeth helped and gave Elle additional support and encouragement. The children all got together with other friends and played in the garden, or on wet days on their computers or did cooking.

Lucy, noting her mother's happiness and comforted by her close relationship with her father, was experiencing another burst of growth, both mentally and physically. She was just as pretty as her mother but rapidly catching her up in height; she was clearly going to be much taller. Like so many gifted children, she also excelled at games and any other activity that she tried. She loved the riding lessons and spending time at the farm. James was fully resigned to one day buying her a horse when she brought the subject up.

Lucy

I am so pleased that Mummy has finally put her past behind her. She is loving her role as housewife and gardener, looking after us all, but always paying special attention to James who she loves as much as she hated my father. I can stop worrying now. I have always felt guilty, thinking that I was the cause of him hurting her. I know now why she hated him, and I also know what it was all about, thanks to the nasty girls that showed me pictures and made me hear what they did to some girls like Mummy. Of course, I know about sex, how can we not with free access to the internet and big bullies making us watch porn on their phones. I laughed at Ava because up to then I thought John was being rather soft and she was mean to him.

I love everything about our new house and life and my school, but most of all I love James, my new father. It made me so happy when he asked me to call him daddy. I have loved him since the day he picked us up. He treated me as an adult and he was so kind to Mummy. He carried her to the car, then he made her better. He loved her then and has spoiled her ever since. Me too, he has spoiled me and is never cross. I get goose bumps when he hugs me. It is nice to have someone to talk to, but I will never say how much I understand. Why spoil my little girl image? I will work hard and one day pay them both back for everything they have done for me. I work on my new super laptop studying science in agriculture, that may be what I will study at university, especially plant or animal breeding with genetic modification.

***

John and Ava bought camping gear and went on a month's tour to show Ava her adopted country before starting university together. Leona was working full time, gaining experience during the holidays. The other two were having fun and were regular visitors to the new family base, to show off boyfriends and eat home cooked food. They enjoyed playing with their little sister but were never sure if they understood her; although having fun, it seemed sometimes as if she was humouring them and was more interested in hearing about medical school and university.

Over the holiday, Elle became rather large and the baby was becoming very active. She had to slow down and rest in the afternoon. So, not surprisingly, they were looking forward to the next scan. Elle was reclining on the bed as the sonographers moved the probe up and down. James was sitting looking on anxiously. The kind young woman who introduced herself as Mary had a reassuring smile on her face as she moved the probe around Elle's tummy; it gradually turned into a broad grin. She looked up and asked, "Well, you two, do you want a boy or a girl?"

Elle looked up at James and said, "Shall we ask, or shall we keep it as a surprise?"

Mary, with a broad smile, interrupted their discussion and said, "I think you should ask."

Elle looked at James who said, "Why should we ask?"

"Because," Mary replied, "if you want a boy you will be pleased and if you want a girl you will be equally pleased."

They looked at her for an explanation, then Elle put her hand to her mouth and squealed, "You don't mean twins, do you?"

"I do indeed. Both, I am pleased to say, are a good size and healthy. I hope Mr Jefferies is a modern man. Two babies are much more than double the work of one."

All James could manage to say was, "Elle, my beautiful wife, what have you done to me."

The two women laughed at his mock distress. Mary, still with the smile, said, "Typical man, serves you right, you must have had something to do with this."

Elle, still laughing excitedly, hugged her husband. "James, isn't this the most wonderful news? I will three children, you will have five. Of all the things that you have given me since we met, this tops them all and I know it is perfect for you as well, so stop pretending. Another daughter for your collection and a bonus son and heir. You had better hide when your girls hear about it, the thought of you with two babies will have them in hysterics for a week."

James smiled indulgently. "It is perfect, darling, and exactly what you deserve. You are mummy to my daddy and Lucy will no longer be little sister, but now big sister. It will all be such fun. Dunwood will be a mad house when we all gather at Christmas, when we will all rely on you, my baby angel."